D0455756

THE DANDELION ON THE IMJIN RIVER

THE DANDELION ON THE IMJIN RIVER

A Novel by
Kang Shin-jae
Translated by
Sol Soon-bong

Dong-suh-Munhak-sa, Inc.

First printing 1990

Published simultaneously by DongsuhMunhaksa, Inc.
683-116, Hannam-Dong, Yongsan-Gu
Seoul 100-392, Korea

Printed in Korea

Price : 7,000 won

The weather was sultry for days on end with the clouds hanging low and grey over the capital. But once in a while, there was a spell of rain after which the sky looked quite blue and shone in a romantic hue. Then some citizens would notice that tall white clouds were lining up behind Mt. Samgak forming additional peaks of vapour above the mountain ridge.

The summer of 1950 was approaching. The sight of straw hats stacked on the pedlars' carts at street corners reminded the dwellers of the city that another summer was stepping over their threshold. But this did not make any real impact on most of them because, as if blindfolded—just as it was their fate to be so—they were merely preoccupied with looking after their daily affairs, oblivious to anything else.

Quietly the dawn crept across the elegant and massive Korean—tile roof of Ihwa's house with its ornately—designed eaves that were pointed and tilted at the four corners.

Mr. Wu Taegap, who was Ihwa's father, went out into the courtyard as soon as the paper screen door of his bed chamber turned greyish light. Coughing up the sputum noisily and spitting it out in any direction, he walked around the corner toward the backyard. After throwing an inspecting glance across the backyard, he continued with his morning stroll around his premises, touring the other side of the house this time, with his hands folded palms outward behind his back as was his custom.

Mr. Wu Taegap was in his fifties. He had a dark-complexioned broad face which had a touch of crude vulgarity unbecoming of the yangban background he might be alleged to have. He seldom spoke, nor was he quick in showing his feelings outwardly so that it was not easy for anyone to guess his mind. Although he was quite severely pock-marked, people felt hardly disconcerted by it because his face was always so solemn and unperturbed. Unlike in most of these cases, nobody ever made fun of his looks even indirectly. He looked, in fact, so natural and dignified with his pock-marks that one would have thought he might have looked rather unnatual without those marks.

He took several more tours around the house spitting profusely onto the raked-up earth where garden-partulaca were planted, along the edge of the flower bed in the backyard where peonies were coming out, or, in fact, at any other spots he could find along his path. Finally, he moved on toward the sarangchae(outer building used mainly by the master of the house and his guests). Entering this outer section of his house, Mr. Wu Taegap cast a slow appraising eye over it.

In a way, this part of the house was even more elegant than the main building. The roof was more daintily slanted up at the corners and one could see other indications of extra care and effort which had gone into building this outer structure of Mr. Wu Taegap's mansion. Especially, harmony with its physical environment and good ventilation had been given particular attention in the overall plan for its construction, as Mr. Wu Taegap could recall only too well.

Ever since Tonggeun, Mr. Wu Taegap's elder son, had a western-style annex built right next to the original sarangchae, however, the elaborately-built outer house came to lose all its former elegance and harmony. The western-style annex which was a square block of a construction finished with white tiles looked like a huge chunk of laundry soap standing up lengthwise.

The addition of the western-style construction, for one thing, blocked the view of the pine grove on Mt. Nam which Mr. Wu Taegap enjoyed taking an occasional glimpse at despite the intervening house roofs. The ventilation, too, was not half so good as before now that the bulky chunk of a tile building stood there to break the delicate balance of the air circulation provided in the original plan of the outer house. Yet, Mr. Wu Taegap did not complain about it. Even now, there was no expression of anger or remorse in his eyes as he perused the unbecoming adjunct to his formerly elegant and faultless sarangchae. Likewise, he had not uttered any words of reprimand or displeasure when Tonggeun came to him with the idea of building this western-style annex. He had not even reminded his son that the latter had so recently squandered a good deal of money to have his fling at horse-riding.

Not that Tonggeun, on his part, could say that his father's permission for building the annex came readily. He had to work for it for some length of time in order to finally make his father give his consent to his expensive new project.

"Let me do this, father, please" "Gees, father, why can't you let me do it" Tonggeun had begged and nagged his father daily, standing askance on the stone step outside Mr. Wu Taegap's room in the sarangchae, both hands stuck in his trouser pockets.

"I found out that horse-riding is too dangerous a hobby. A man I know broke his ankle riding a horse recently."

"He nearly broke his neck."

On some days, Tonggeun went directly to the sarangchae, his book-bag in hand, upon returning from school. And it was on one of these afternoons that the son got what he had so long awaited.

"Father," Tonggeun called to his father, standing outside

his door as it was his way these few weeks.

Wu Taegap opened his sliding door and looked out at his son. Tonggeun felt that his father was finally going to say or do something. In the next moment, the son saw a white check on the upturned palm which his father held out toward him in silent.

For months after that, Tonggeun made himself very busy alongside a carpenter he employed and the outcome was the block-shaped annex now standing next to the original sarangchae. He then moved the piano that had been standing in some corner of the main building to his new hide-out and started practicing from the Bayer, the invariable primer for all beginners in piano lessons.

His skill on the instrument, however, did not show signs of improving and after a while he began to slacken his practice sessions. Finally he stopped altogether. Maybe he decided that this, too, was not interesting enough to devote so much of his time to. He began to look bored with himself and with the world again.

It was after he entered this now-disfigured sarangchae that Mr. Wu Taegap's day properly started. First of all, he took his usual seat in front of the low desk of red sandalwood and gave a thoughtful look at the framed calligraphy that was hanging across the wall a little below the ceiling. After this, he slowly went over the Bipahaeng(poem by T'ang poet Paek Nak Chon) written lengthwise on a hanging scroll. Aside from the desk and the pieces of calligraphy, there was no other furniture or decorations in the spacious room. In front of the maru(connecting hall between rooms floored with wooden panels) of shiny dark wood, there was an elegant and massive shoe-stone stretching the length of the maru. A bronze wind-bell hung from the eave swinging or turning around in the breeze.

After perusing one particular line in the Chinese poem on the scroll intently, Mr. Wu Taegap drew to himself a large ink-stone of bluish-green, still without casting a glance toward the 'western room'at the other end of the maru. "Will somebody bring the water," he called in the direction of the main building knowing that Ogyop, his second daughter, would be up by now.

It was a wonder how Ogyop could hear him when other members of the house who happened to find themselves closer to him at the time of his call could not. If she did not respond to his second call, it meant that she was not home. This was the reason why Mr. Wu Taegap called with his voice instead of using the calling-bell that had been installed on his wall. Maybe he did not wish to use the mechanical device when calling his favourite daughter. "Yes, father,"answered Ogyop and soon he could see her appearing at the connecting gate between the main building and the sarangchae. She was wearing a white apron with the sleeves of her pink joksam(summer jacket of traditional Korean attire)delicately rolled up above her wrists.

"Good morning, father," she greeted.

"Good morning, daughter. You're up already?" said Wu Taegap affably.

It was not too unusual for Wu Taegap to speak to his second daughter in this way, although to greetings offered by other members of his household, he hardly ever responded.

Ogyop came to his side with the yonjok(container of water for the ink-stone) and, letting a little water drip onto the well of the ink -stone, proceeded to make the liquid ink. After she finished this preparation for her father's calligraphic exercise, Ogyop left the room quietly.

(A strange girl that one is . . . .)Wu Taegap seemed to be saying to himself as he watched his daughter walk out of his sight.

It was, of course, not to make her tend the house that the family had urged Ogyop to drop out of school. There was a kitchen woman and also a servant girl in the house so that all she needed to do was to make herself comfortable and take a good rest so that she could recuperate from her chest disease. Yet, as soon as she was made to stay at home, Ogyop began to help with the house-keeping, making herself busy with the various affairs needed to maintain a house. Soon, she became the chief manager of this fairly large household. People went to her when they could not find things they wanted and when there was a need to purchase new supplies of shirts, underwear, or socks, Ogyop was the one who saw to it. Also when anybody needed a new dress or suit, it was Ogyop, not her mother Madam Shim, that accompanied the person to the dress-maker's or the tailor's and helped with the choice of material and design. When a festival, birthday, or family memorial day was approaching, Ogyop prepared for the event without fail.

The kitchen woman took orders from Ogyop when preparing the family meals or when entertaining and the Old Man who looked after miscellaneous affairs in and out of the house brought bills and notices from the tonghoe(district office) to Ogyop. Not only that, but even about such matters as at what time the hen should be killed for cooking or how the ribs should be cut, Ogyop was consulted.

All her family including her older sister Ihwa, brother Tonggeun, the fastidious last-born Tong-hun and, of course, Madam Shim, who was lazy by nature, thanked her perpetually for her services. And it was not seldom that her father Mr. Wu Taegap, too, felt gratitude toward this daughter. And this was quite understandable considering the fact that this young woman who was barely eighteen years old had the composure and ability to solve any problem anybody brought to her.

"Little Sister!" the boys called her in urgent, nagging, but affectionate voices. Madam Shim's voice when she called her second daughter to ask her a favour was contented and confident while the voice of the servants when calling to their young mistress conveyed their trust in her. As for Inwa, Ogyop's older sister, her attitude toward her younger sister was somewhat peculiar. It was true that she had a smile on her face when asking Ogyop for any favour, but it was a smile that had an element of skepticism about her younger sister's spirit of devotion to the house. Not that she was not thankful to Ogyop for what she did but at the same time she could not understand how a young girl Ogyop could be content to just serve everybody like that.

Of course, Ihwa, too, thought that serving others or sacrificing oneself for others' benefit was a beautiful thing. But what was incomparably more important than that to her was to live for herself. Something in her was telling her incessantly that she was right in thinking this way. This inner voice said :

(Maybe, when you are about fifty, you can start living for others. Or, maybe a few years earlier. But not now. . . .)

Ihwa would smile roguishly to herself, hugging her chest with both arms as if to keep her youthful body from bounding off into the air. That she was becoming very egoistic she was well aware and this realization made her feel a little ashamed. Yet, nothing could be done about it. There seemed to be just too many pleasant and exciting things in store in this world for her to enjoy! It was for this reason that she even felt pity for her younger sister despite the latter's mounting popularity in the house.

Mr. Wu Taegap dipped the Chinese brush into the ink water after spreading out a fine sheet of rice paper on the desk. This meant that he was about to give himself to the only enjoyment he seemed to have in life, dabbling in the calligraphic art. This particular occupation of his which was likely to uplift his cultural status in the eyes of others formed an essential part of his daily life in this secluded part of his house.

This spring, something meaningful happened to Ihwa who had just turned twenty. She fell in love. The young man whose name was Ji-un, appeared to be intelligent and sensitive enough to satisfy her vague but inextinguishable longing for intellectual life. He seemed to stand above and ahead of Ihwa. If Ihwa had not been sufficiently confident of her feminine attraction—that is, if she had not known that Ji-un was madly in love with her—she might not have had the courage to meet him on a steady basis. To her, he seemed to contain something exceedingly superior to her in thinking and feeling.

At the same time, however, she was having difficulty trying to internalize this strange experience called love. To tell the truth, the intellectual girl in her was constantly making her stop and recoil while she was feeling attracted to Ji-un's handsome face, well-built body, powerful hands, and even the way he walked.

Every time they had any intimate contact, she felt somewhat frightened by the maturity of his sexual behaviour. For instance, he would embrace her passionately or kiss her in the way she thought men who were mature in age and experienced in sex would go about such an act, and she found it impossible to endure these actions to the end. She either pushed him off in the middle of the act or right from the beginning resisted his approach under one pretext or another. An inexplicable uneasiness kept making her behave in this way. Because of this tension between them, they quarrelled and broke off their dates earlier than planned now and then.

Ji-un always came back to Ihwa with a tragic look on his face. Instantly Ihwa's restlessness and melancholy would turn to joy and relief. She would give herself more willingly to his caresses and he would be more careful and tender as he embraced her.

There was no question at any event that Ihwa's world opened up far wider thanks to her encounter with Ji-un. Happy and gratified, Ihwa looked around her with a new sight, her large eyes shining like stars. How sweet and wonderful it would be to wade through these rose-hued clouds of my dream with Ji-un, she exclaimed inwardly.

Ji-un, on his part, was something of an idealist. He would say :

"If our lives do not even modestly contribute to humanity —or to our neighbors, if you object to lofty phrases—, they are worthless." Or, he would exclaim :

"I don't exactly believe in the doctrine of man's innate

goodness, but, all the same, I cannot avoid a conclusion pointing in the same direction. None of us can be completely freed from such things as history or society, which means that we are all trained to aspire to goodness in order to be happy. Let's try and grow together so that we will be able to be good and happy."

"You can stop worrying as far as I am concerned because I, too, have a bit of understanding of those things, you know. Otherwise, why would I have taken up medicine as my major? Have you heard it said that medicine is merciful? Well, I have, and I believe it. Medicine is a direct line through which I am going to reach your humanity. Do you see now?"

"Hm... I see. But, you know, Ihwa, the thought that you are studying medicine is so unconvincing to me, begging your permission, of course. I mean you and the fact don't seem to go together."

"I see. Then what do you think would suit me, if I may ask?"

"Well...let me think.... If you were a citizen of some western country, I would say you might be studying to become an actress, or I might say you could be some drop-out from a school of music or some such arty affair."

"What horrible things you say!"

"But, seriously, I admire you for what you are doing, or rather, for what you have dared. It was a courageous thing for a girl like you to decide to take up medicine. Tell me, have the stones by the road begun to look like human bones, yet? I hear it's when that happens that a person can honestly call himself or herself a student of medicine."

"That question does not deserve an answer. Besides, I know no names of bones except the one that came out of Adam's ribs. Right at the moment, I am up to my ears in my study of languages in case you're interested, Mr. Learned."

"Okay, okay, I give up. Study whatever you like. I just urge you not to consider me a mere anatomical specimen, all right, young lady?" Saying this with affection in his voice, Ji-un touched Ihwa's cheek with the tip of his nose.

Ji-un's major was politics. When Ihwa first found this out, she had said,

"You look like a very ambitious young man."

"Do I, really?"

"Yep! And your mouth shows that you are stubborn and your eyes are deep-set which is a sign of" Ihwa could not continue because a laughter broke out of her. But after a while she continued,

"Your ears. . . . but ears are no use here. Your neck is thick and tipped a little forward. They say a person with such a neck is combative, and that is putting it nicely."

Ji-un kept a good-natured smile on his face while Ihwa went over his physiognomy in this way but now he interrupted her,

"People always tell me I am pliant and most gentle-hearted."

"What people? I don't believe you!" Again Ihwa broke into laughter which lasted for some while. And it was true that Ji-un looked more spirited and aggressive than soft-hearted and yielding.

One day, Ji-un arrived at the place of their rendezvous half an hour late. To Ihwa, who did not hide her mild displeasure, Ji-un explained that the delay was owing to a duty he had toward the Student Association. He was a staff member in this rightist student organization. Starting to walk toward the path around the wall of Duksu Palace in the descending dusk of the early evening, Ihwa asked Ji-un,

"Is politics fun?"

"I wouldn't call it fun, but. . . ." Ji-un's voice was unusually melancholy as he responded to Ihwa's question in this indefinite manner. Maybe he did not feel up to giving a full answer because Ihwa had asked in a somewhat jeering tone.

"Isn't what the leftist side claim theoretically more valid, anyway? Don't they also have a better intellectual basis?"

Ji-un looked at her without answering, Ihwa attempted a smile. "The reason I asked those questions was simple enough.

There's a leftist circle in our school, as well, and people in it are trying to persuade me to join them."

Now Ji-un's face became visibly hardened. Pausing abruptly he asked,

"You don't mean you are going to side with such a group?"

"I thought I might go and see what's happening since Sukja naggs me so hard to come to their meeting with her. Don't you think one needs to know what the other side's doing even if the sympathy is all on this side?"

"Is it a great secret what they are talking about? Don't let yourself play the fool. Unless you insist on contradicting me."

"Why are you getting angry? Is it a crime if I think it might be an experience I could use?" Ihwa's voice, too, came out angry. To tell the truth, she had not really decided to go to these meetings. She was not as stupid as to believe that her belief in the peaceful future of the human world and what the radical communist groups among the students were expostulating could coexist. What she had said about her intending to attend their meetings, therefore, was just a casual suggestion. Yet, she was upset by Ji-un's despotic reaction.

"Have you read only historical materialism and no other doctrines? Haven't you read Kant, Hegel, or Husserl? If you have, you will know how well-argued and logical their thoughts are. You could not then say that the leftist theories are the more convincingly presented or give any such facile eulogy for them. The only thing you can say to the credit of Marxism is that it has its own raison d'etre as an economic theory. Even about this, however, I must add that there are other economic thoughts that can counter the Marxist theory point counter point. Like any other system of thought, Marxism, too, needs to be studied objectively and patiently. Nothing can be gained from getting yourself all worked up by it as if it were some heretical religion. I can't understand why you think it necessary to run around with the leftists holding secret meetings with them for the purpose of learning about the thought, as you put it."

Ji-un's face had turned purplish dark showing the extent of his anger and agitation. For some unexplainable reason, the face of Kim Oshik loomed up in his mind. He was a member of the Namnodang (the communist party operating in the southern half of the Korean peninsula) and was generally thought to be bright, fearless, and good-looking, to boot. For no justifiable reason whatsoever, Ji-un felt an acute sense of jealousy for the man for a flitting second. This was absurd, of course, because except for the couple of times that Ihwa had seen him in his company as they ran into him in the streets, she could not even have had a chance to meet him in person.

Ihwa did not say anything and together they continued to walk. The last of the sunset was throwing a greyish pink shadow on the whitish grey pavement.

"Do you think that it is right to sacrifice our one and only life on the altar of the proletarian dictatorship? Do you think we need to go to that extent in order to eliminate the class conflict that does not even exist and to annihilate the state which is not exploitative, even?" Ji-un continued impatiently, making a grimace.

"Of course, it's best if nobody goes hungry or gets exploited. This is a belief that has never died ever since the Greek period. And I am glad that we now live in a time when this thought is shared by everyone in common. Now the motto is building a better world for as many people as possible. This is humanity's historical mission at the present juncture. See for yourself. Is the world really evolving in the way they claim it to be? They say that capitalism is fated to be superseded by proletarian revolution after it reaches its last stage of development. Yet what we witness in such a successfully-developed capitalistic system as that of Great Britain, for instance, is that society is going through a gradual reformistic transformation, from a capitalistic structure to a socialistic variation. And this great change is taking place quietly and almost imperceptibly, I might say. This is what is meant by the spirit of welfare so earnestly promoted by free states. It is ironic that bloody revolution is occurring not in countries where capitalism is most fully developed but in small, poor, underdeveloped countries first. We can easily refute their claim that the present time, with its war between the bourgeoisie and the proletariat, forms the last historical stage beyond which stretches a sheer paradise, as a contradiction and bigotry on no other grounds than their own theory of the dialectic of class conflict. From another angle, can we not say that if, as they say, humanity is forever directed toward further progress and the world needs new constructive improvements continually, a transformation through baptism of blood is a most self-contradictory doctrine on their part? I think it's most apparent and clear that an orderly progress is the best and only way." From the way his voice sounded, Ihwa could see that he had recovered his composure.

"The supposition that the proletariat of the present age should shed blood so that the proletariat of the future will be able to prosper, too, is nonsensical, if you ask me. Because what good can all their sacrifices do for them when they do not even believe in an everlasting life or in the worth of spiritual values?"

With the flicker of a bitter smile at the edge of his mouth, Ji-un continued :

"In short, I hate terrorist dictatorship whether of fascism, or of communism. I abhor the thought of hanging a medal on a chain around my neck at the expense of my liberty."

Then coming to a halt as if remembering something, Ji-un said in a changed tone :

"But let's change the topic, now. I have something more important to talk over with you today."

After saying this, Ji-un stared at Ihwa with pensive eyes, both hands stuck in his trouser pockets. Then, he opened his mouth again,

"Tell me, Ihwa, do you like me at all?"

Ihwa felt as if the pupils of his unusually big eyes were

overflowing with black doubts about her.

Ihwa could not help smiling in the face of this innocent misgiving in such a self-assured man. In any case, politics was not of much concern to her. If Ji-un did not like Soviet Russia, the dislike would be hers, also. If he abhorred the red flag, she, too, would feel her heart fill with hate for it. Then, why are those big eyes, those deep-set, thoughtful eyes brimming with doubts about the sincerity of her love for him? How can he be so foolish? How could she help smiling when Ji-un was acting so much like an innocent and ignorant young boy?

Only when he saw that Ihwa's left cheek made its charming little dimple and her mouth displayed its strings of shiny pearls did Ji-un seem to feel reassured. Not caring that they were in the middle of a public path, Ji-un threw his arms around Ihwa's waist, clasping her. His arms tightened and the pressure of his chest nearly choked her.

"What if somebody sees us!" whispered Ihwa barely escaping his kiss.

"Nobody will see us," said Ji-un smiling contentedly, "but if you are worried, let's go in there and sit down for a while."

There was an old church building by the road and one could see that the narrow side gate overhung with a rose bush was open. The two walked into the church through this side gate and went around to its backyard where there was an abundance of rose bushes. There was darkness in all the windows of the building.

The two sat down on a stone step. A greyish darkness enveloped them and already there was a star shining in the sky which was as clear as fresh water.

"I love you, Ihwa," whispered Ji-un, embracing her again. "You must never break my heart. Unless you watch over me, I can never do anything. Loneliness is a frightening thing. . . ."

Overpowered by the hotness of his breath, the sharp sensation of his shaved beard, and the heavy pressure of his embrace, Ihwa kept completely still, hardly breathing. Yet, she was conscious of a joyful feeling running a desperate race against fear. She did not know what awaited her at the end of this course run by her inexpressible fear. All she was aware of was the fact that it was there on the race course, threatening to trip over her joy at every point.

Ihwa kept still. She was going to stay like that, as always, her eyes closed, until her fear, reaching the point of explosion, would make her push Ji-un off without thinking what she was doing. But today, it was Ji-un who first broke the knot of the embrace. Then suddenly he said,

"Isn't it true, Ihwa, that sometimes—I don't mean always—you find me disgusting? Isn't that true?"

Ihwa's small mouth gaped a little when Ji-un attacked her in this way. Then shaking her head rapidly, she said,

"What a thing to say. . . ."

Yet, in her mind, she was thinking that maybe it was not so untrue as she would have liked to believe. As if to make up for what she felt, or, rather, for what she could not feel, Ihwa brought her shoulder against Ji-un's chest saying,

"If I act clumsy, it's only because I have never met anyone just like you. You must believe me. . . ."

After declaring this in a hurry, Ihwa drew her father's image in her mind's eye. Her father Wu Taegap surely did not have the kind of look that would make his daughter introduce him to people with pride and delight. No, he did not have that kind of a look. Her brother, Tonggeun, too, looked plain and common enough with his dull-featured big face. There was such a contrast between him and Ji-un. Of course, Tong-hun was a different case. He was quite intelligent and had a refined look, too. But he was still a child and so didn't count.

While she went through the catalogue of male specimens with whom she had a closer contact, she realized all over again that the appearance of Ji-un in her life was a truly phenomenal happening. It was almost a miracle. Looking into his eyes with affection, Ihwa put out her hand and stroked him around the neck.

"It is a rare fortune for two people who can make each other happy to be thrown together in this wide lost world. So let us be happy and grow as much as possible in all our good human capacities, shall we?" said Ji-un. The two whispered into each other's ears for a long time, sitting on that stone step. A whiff of a wind carrying the fragrance of grass drifted by.

The front door of the church squeaked open noisily, revealing the figure of an old man holding a lit candle. Maybe he was the warden of that church. He was big and wore black hanbok(traditional Korean attire) matched by a pair of old-style wooden shoes—fantasy-evoking relics looking like miniature log canoes each carved each from a whole block of wood. Making a clattering noise against the stone steps with his wooden shoes, the old man began to descend the stone steps. The two lovers made way for him without getting up. With an expressionless glance at the two young people sitting next to each other, the old man walked in the direction of the rose bushes, to disappear into the dusk beyond them.

"Let's go," said Ihwa, getting up.

"No, let's stay a while longer," said Ji-un, looking up at the night sky which was like black satin now with stars sparkling as if they were myriad fragments of diamond.

While Mr. Wu Taegap was picking up the sheets of rice paper on which he practiced his daily calligraphy with a neutral expression on his face (it was impossible to know from his expression whether he was satisfied or disgusted with his workmanship), most of his household members were still sound asleep. Soon, however, they began to stir and one by one they came out of their sleeping quarters to go to the backyard to wash their faces. The supply of water with which they washed themselves came from a small well dug in a rock into which a thin stream of ice-cold clear stream water from the mountain, tapped by a pipelike wooden contraption, trickled. Because of the peony bush, one could not see this natural fountain from Ihwa's room.

"How can you tell the water tastes sweet when it's so cold

it freezes your tongue?" Ihwa had skeptically doubted the veracity of her mother's appreciative evaluation of this water as the sweetest water in the whole world. Mr. Wu Taegap did not make any comments on this issue but one could see him going to the stone well several times a day to scoop up the water with a gourd dipper and drink it. Green moss covered the entire inside surface of the wooden contraption making it look as if the open wooden pipeline were lined with luscious velvet. Ihwa, who, also, came out here to wash and drink, felt an esthetic satisfaction at this sight. Yet Tonghun, who seemed to be repelled by the moss, had his washing and drinking water brought out to him from the tap.

Ihwa woke up latest among all the members of this house. Naturally she was the last to appear at the well to wash and brush her teeth. Even the notoriously slow-moving Madam Shim had been through her washing for some time by then. In fact she often forced her lazy legs to walk to the room where Ihwa slept and, sliding the paper screen door open a few inches, peeked in to see if her elder daughter was still not budging. If Ihwa should be awake, the older woman would smile an indolent and contented smile and walk away slowly from the door.

Madam Shim looked younger than her mature age and still retained some feminine beauty. She had the peculiar habit of letting her well-ironed skirt of invariably good material hang around her waistline instead of tying it properly around chest like other women. Her excuse was that she felt suffocated if she wore it high up around her chest. The result was that she swept the large expanse of the wooden as well as the ondol floors of the inner quarters with the bottom of her skirt. Her delicate small face, however, was always carefully made up and her hair done with a crimson hair tie and jade pinyo looked clean and luscious at all times.

Having little else to do, Madam Shim took time and care in washing and adorning herself every morning. Yet, she had as yet to learn how to use the lipstick. Her way of putting color on her lips was to leave some sort of a smudge in the middle of her mouth as if she were a little child who had sucked at a red crayon. To tell the truth, her mouth was the one feature in her general configuration-her rather attractive eyes, shapely nose, dainty hands, small but well-contoured body-that was rather ungainly. To begin with, her lips were a little protruding which gave her mouth a stupid look. Then, there were countless tiny perpendicular wrinkles on her lips. Ihwa loved this ignorant, lazy, but good-hearted and childlike woman for a mother well enough. Yet, she could not overcome an aversion for her mother's mouth, especially those ugly wrinkles on her lips. The wrinkles disgusted her as much as did her father's gold teeth when he opened his mouth.

"Wake up, daughter. How can you sleep so much!" Madam Shim exclaimed good-naturedly, standing in her daughter's doorway.

Looking up at her mother with her eyes half open, Ihwa thought she looked beautiful in her jade-green chima(the skirt of a woman's traditional attire, usually long), dainty white chogori (jacket), and her pretty traditional hair-do adorned with the jade pinyo. She could well imagine her mother to have looked like one of those incredibly pretty and fragile women in traditional figure paintings. What would her mother have felt on marrying her father, who had a dark, pock-marked face and a mouthful of gold teeth(supposing that he had those gold teeth as early as that)? Yet, her father was a son of a rich family and, it seemed, was considered trustworthy.

Madam Shim laughed easily. Ihwa's inherently outgoing character which, to the eyes of others, struck an interesting contrast with her outward reserve, seemed to have come from her mother's carefree optimism. Madam Shim's laughter did not desert her even when she was sitting with her humorless husband.

(Yet, how precarious and undependable an image she presents as a woman!) Ihwa could not help feeling that her mother's happiness lay entirely on the contingent basis of luck.

Her sense of well-being was not very different from that of a new-born baby. This applied to Tonggeun, too. He would keep on finding things that interested him but could not keep up his concern for any of them for long. There was no trace of effort in him to really absorb himself in any one thing or to create meaning in his life. He never demonstrated any capacity for appraising things on the basis of his own individual sensibility but merely accepted them mechanically. Then, after a while, he lost all interest in them.

"Stop speaking turnip!" said Madam Shim laughing good-naturedly at her son. This was her way of commenting on some remark Tonggeun made which was comical merely for lack of any adroitness. On Tonggeun's part, whatever comical element there could be found in his utterances was entirely unintended. He said those pointless things only because they were what he normally thought.

(Tonggeun is too much out of tune. . . .) Ihwa would think to herself.

Could she say that her father was all that dependable, then? It was not so. She thought that her father, too, stood on a very precarious balance. That the textile company owned by him had so far kept afloat did not owe much to this man's business ability. The mildly surprising fact that the company had not yet fallen into bankruptcy was rather attributable to the accumulated strength of his family over generations of collective mercantile endeavours. Wealth was something that never flew away as long as the owner sat and watched over it. In the case of Mr. Wu Taegap this maxim applied more forcibly because what he had was on such a scale that it was likely to take at least several decades to completely disappear. And this large house with its stylish pointed roofs, too, was still intact in Mr. Wu Taegap's possession. All the same, there was no denying that the business was slackening rapidly and Mr. Wu Taegap kept on being mostly unconcerned about the state of his financial venture. Instead, he was getting himself involved with some trivial law suit. . . . No, it was not possible for Ihwa to deem her father a strong and reliable character.

Ihwa wished to become strong herself. She felt a need for something tangible to give her confidence in her strength. She desired a power that could be compared with the motive power of a machine that produced a great mass of manufactured goods within a short time, or with the power of a human body that can fight against multitudinous germs. Maybe that was why she had chosen to enter the college of medicine. She had a fire in her heart. But she did not know how she could make this fire flare up as if bursting into a blaze. Nobody in her house seemed to think that her choosing a medical career had any meaning. Nor were any of them interested in knowing her inner motives for wishing to go to medical school. Ihwa was pleased when Ji-un showed understanding of her choice of school and career. If he had merely showed interest in her physical appearance like other men she had met, she might have felt uneasy about Ji-un in the same way that she was uneasy about her brother Tonggeun and her father.

"It's Sunday, today, isn't it? Why must I get up so early if it is?"said Ihwa with a mischievous smile. She did not make any move to get out of her bed.

"What are you saying, Ihwa? Do you know what time it is now?" said Madam Shim exaggeratedly. Having no particular work to attend to and always at leisure, Madam Shim seemed to find this kind of bantering with her children endlessly amusing. She now took a step into her daughter's room saying:

"So, you won't get up, will you? maybe, you need your mother to tickle you out of bed?"

Seeing her mother come closer to the bedside with her hands stretched ready to start her tickling routine, Ihwa, said :

"Don't, mother! I'll get up."

(I wish mother hadn't come to wake me up. I could have thought longer about Ji-un and about our meeting last nigh-t....)

Yet there was no helping it. Madam Shim was all smiles as

if she were overjoyed that she could make her daughter get up and about.

Ihwa went to the backyard and washed herself. Afterwards, she hurriedly returned to her room. She had just remembered that she had promised to go to Seoul Stadium with Ji-un today and that she needed to do some work before going.

Madam Shim was making conversation with Tonggeun in the taechong(the maru of largest size and central position) in her good-humoured joking voice :

"Don't talk turnip, son. Really you mustn't."

"Oh, no, this is no turnip, mother."

They both burst into merry laughter, Madam Shim's good-natured giggles merging comfortably into Tonggeun's loud chuckling.

Through the window of the chankan(floored area adjacent to the kitchen where more elaborate preparation of food takes place), Ihwa could detect the cherry-blossom sleeve ends of Ogyop busy at work. The Old Woman moved in and out of the kitchen letting her apchima(apron, longer and wider than usual western-style aprons) sweep against the high threshold of the kitchen area every time she stepped over it.

Ihwa slid the paper screen door of her room open as wide as she could. Since her room faced the east side of their garden, she could look out at the mountain slope nearby on the other side of their outer wall. She could feel the air fresh with the dew-moistened grass blades and she could smell the fragrance of the late-blooming crimson peonies that was as pleasant as the morning breeze and yet as agonizing, too, as the feverish whispers of a lover. Resting her chin on one cupped hand with the elbow riveted onto the top of her desk, Ihwa sank into her thoughts of Ji-un again.

Ji-un's family home was in Kyongsang Province and it seemed that his father was the chief of staff at the provincial hospital. And his mother had studied in the U. S. in her younger days. Ji-un was an only son.

It was not difficult to imagine Ji-un as having acquired an

intellectual inclination from his early years. It was something Ihwa could not say for herself and her family.

The small gate at the back of the house was pushed open and through it emerged Tong-hun with some electrical apparatus that looked like the inside of a radio. He seemed to have carried the thing out into the grass field that stretched out from their away wall. To toy with some such electrical gadgetry was Tong-hun's favourite pastime. Unlike Tonggeun, he was steady and self-absorbed. Maybe he was finding satisfaction and joy in the mysterious world of machinery.

"Out so early? You found some gold mine with that detector thing?" asked Ihwa in a loud voice. Tong-hun smiled a little and then without any answer walked on toward the corner room which served as his laboratory. Tong-hun's taciturnity seemed to have come from his father Mr. Wu Taegap. Yet, unlike his father, Tong-hun was more responsive in his facial expression. He was neat to a fault and in his room nothing could be found misplaced or thrown about. Among her brothers and sister, Ihwa liked Tong-hun best.

"Bring in my breakfast. I want to go and see Lawyer Kim." Mr. Wu Taegap could be heard hollering as he entered the taechong for his morning meal. His voice was low-pitched and dull. Yet one could hear him from any spot in the house.

"This is Sunday. It won't be easy to see him today, father."

"What day is it?"

"It's the twenty-fifth of June," said Tonggeun in his characteristic lazy voice.

Sprightly dressed in a white skirt and blue blouse, Ihwa left the house for the Seoul Stadium a little past noon so as not to be late for her one o'clock date with Ji-un in front of the Stadium. Despite the hour, however, the atmosphere of the street was desolate and gloomy like that of the end of a day. The sky was leaden all over and hung down low. Altogether, Ihwa felt as if she were looking out at some ominous seascape of an uninhabited northern country. Heavy and sticky air was seeping through the alleyways between the buildings.

Crowds thronged the shopping areas as usual, but only a little distance from these spots of everyday hubbub, the thoroughfares of the city were overhung with a sinister atmosphere of imminent disaster. Maybe it was an effect wrought by army trucks and jeeps speeding by at short intervals.

While waiting for the tram at the transfer stop, Ihwa noticed one army jeep swishing by camouflaged with leafy twigs and branches. It was a strange and interesting sight to Ihwa. The soldiers riding the jeep were wearing helmets and holding their rifles upright. Covered with dust, they were staring straight ahead with bloodshot eyes. Maybe there has been some sort of combat somewhere, thought Ihwa vaguely.

Small-scale commotions were no rare thing near the Thirty-Eighth parallel and newspapers carried brief reports on these happenings now and then. Usually, these newspaper accounts said no more than that a few North Korean soldiers invaded the demilitarized zone, that they were shot down with rifles, or that the disturbance ended within half an hour.

People were indifferent to these reports. As long as the ROK Army didn't care-or gave out the impression of nonchalance, any way—, why should the citizens trouble themselves with these negligible happenings?

The jeeps dashed towards the south as if with vengeance. Where are they going, Ihwa wondered. Maybe they are headed for some sort of headquarters down that way, she thought indecisively.

The people in the street seemed to be experiencing a sense of some imminent fear or some unspeakable anxiety for short spells.

Waking up from their momentary lapses into apprehension, however, they moved on toward whichever destinations they had been hurrying to. As long as the international forces had the power to maintain balance in world politics, occasional irregularities committed by the North Korean soldiery along the demilitarized zone could never develop into a real threat. This was how people felt, anyway.

A soldier who appeared to be on leave stood in front of the bulletin board along the pavement perusing a notice on it thoughtfully. He glanced at his wristwatch and then took a few steps in apparent dismay. Immediately, however, he halted again as if not knowing what to do next.

Standing in front of the entrance to Seoul Stadium, Ihwa waited for Ji-un to appear. Although the time was past the hour when cheering voices and clapping hands ought to be coming out of the stadium where games were scheduled to have begun some time back, no sound could be heard and there seemed to be some foreboding atmosphere of calamity hanging over the inside of the stadium.

Ji-un was on time but he was covered with perspiration and his face was flushed.

"I am sorry I made you wait. It seems that something's happening at the thirty-Eighth Parallel. I must go there immediately," said Ji-un breathlessly, with apology in his voice.

"Go to the Demilitarized Zone? Now?"

"Yes, a truck carrying supplies is likely to take off from our school and. . . . You aren't going to be mad at me, are you?" he asked, already turning away.

Shaking her head in denial and breaking into a trot to keep pace with Ji-un, Ihwa asked suddenly,

"Isn't it dangerous?"

"I think not. Nobody can tell for sure. There hasn't been much communication. The plan seems to be to transport foodstuffs up there, for a start."

Ji-un raised his hand to stop a passing taxicab which, however, went by at an accelerated speed without heeding him.

"I tried to call you at home from near our school. But was told you'd left already. So I had to come although there was hardly any time to spare," said Ji-un, raising his hand to hail another taxicab. This one, too, swished by without stopping.

But this time, the driver made it clear that he had no intention of stopping by moving his head sideways.

"Why aren't they stopping? It's uncanny."

"There's a rumor that all the vehicles are being mobilized. I don't know. . . . But one thing's clear, you must go home right away. I will let you know as soon as I come back."

Then, looking at Ihwa apprehensively for a second, Ji-un went on, "I'm sorry I can't take you home. You will be all right, though, won't you?"

"Of course. Go quickly. And be careful."

"Sure. . . . I think it'll be quicker for me to walk."

"You will come and see me as soon as you're back, won't you?"

"I will. I promise!"

For a moment, Ji-un stood close to Ihwa, facing her, his broad chest blocking her way. Ihwa felt breathless. But the next moment Ji-un had turned with a slight grimace and started running. Once he looked back and waved his hand. Ihwa waved back feeling a lump in her chest. She walked in the direction of the bus stop.

Small groups of people were coming out of the stadium looking discontented. They looked up at the leaden sky, then at the army jeeps that were swishing by along the thoroughfare. Looking dismal, they dispersed in different directions.

The bus took a time to appear and there were no more taxis either. Only the tramcars passed, packed full and without stopping.

Maybe I ought to walk, too, mumbled Ihwa and started to walk. A rowdy popsong was coming out of a radio in a shop by the street. Then suddenly it stopped in the middle so that a special announcement could be made. The content of the announcement was that all soldiers on leave should return to their respective units without delay. This communique was repeated several times, after which the popsong was resumed as if it were some incongruous tail to the body of the radio announcement just made.

Upon returning home, Ihwa told her mother and sister about what happened to her date with Ji-un and the things she observed in the streets....

"So that's where Ji-un said he was going. I think there's a bunch of student association staff members that are going with Ji-un," Ihwa concluded her report.

"Why, why would he do a thing like that? He can get hurt, can't he?" said Madam Shim with genuine worry in her voice. She was fond of Ji- un's rather wild but noble looks.

"He will go anyway. He said he had to go because communications had been cut."

Madam Shim fanned herself slowly with the round taeguk fan, lying flat on her back on the floor and with her other arm placed under her head in place of a pillow.

"If there's such a difficulty in transportation, your father shouldn't be out so long. Why isn't he home yet?" said Madam Shim. But her voice was sleepy.

"It seems the vehicles have been mobilized by the army," said Tonggeun with a knowing tone.

"Is that so? How odd...."

Yet none of them knew what it was like to be in a war which meant that they were unable to feel really afraid.

Mr. Wu Taegap came home in the evening his bowler hat comically aslant on his head. He did not seem concerned with the change in the atmosphere of the streets, however.

"Wonder where Lawyer Kim was all day....Couldn't get in touch with him no matter how hard I tried...." muttered Mr. Wu Taegap to Madam Shim in a dull discontented voice.

Now and then, Mr. Wu Taegap brought up the topic of this law suit in front of his family. Because the issue was dragging on so indemfitely long, much to his chagrine, and, what was more, did not seem to be moving in a direction favourable to him. His face and throat turned red with fury as he sat in his quarters at the sarangchae and one could tell in these moments that his thoughts were occupied with the law suit against his elder brother Wu Taeyong.

Mr. Wu Taegap and his brother grew up together comfortably as offspring of a wealthy yangban house. At their father's death, the brothers inherited their shares of the family property. Since he was the elder son, Wu Taeyong inherited a greater part of what their father left behind while Mr. Wu Taegap took possession of what portion of the entire property his father, or his elder brother thought fit for him.

Since most of what Mr. Wu Taegap inherited was farmland, he came to lose a substantial part of his property at the time of Land Reform. Yet, even after the loss, he had enough to make himself and family comfortable. And by then he had managed to make a number of business investments on his own, too, which helped his financial situation.

In recent years, however, all his businesses declined one after another for no perceivable reason—or, rather, for no reason Mr. Wu Taegap could see—so that there came to remain only one operating business out of all the enterprises he had ventured and even this last one, a textile company, was dwindling. At first Mr. Wu Taegap could not understand this because he had managed to keep his businesses in some sort of a shape even during the last years of the Japanese Occupation and there were some among those involved with the same kinds of business ventures as he was who were even prosperous now that the Occupation was over. Mustering up all his resources, therefore, Mr. Wu Taegap had tried to set at least his last surviving business, the textile one, on its former footing. But it was to no avail. Not that Mr. Wu Taegap was too slow to catch up with the new tactics in business, such as importing raw materials from Macao or installing foreign-made machinery in the plant. He was tolerably proficient in handling the rather complex calculations involving demand and supply or wage levels. Yet, he lackedthe essential ability and flexibility to grasp the bigger trends of the modern economic world and adjust his affairs to them. It was questionable that he had even given a thought to economics as a subject of some import, anyway, for one interested in doing business. No wonder then that Mr. Wu Taegap's textile plant with its typically outdated facilities and operating system should have been declining steadily throughout the recent years. Losing interest in an affair that no longer offered him any satisfaction, either material or psychological, therefore, Mr. Wu Taegap gradually took his hands off the textile plant, finally leaving it altogether to the care of his manager. Now he was occupying himself in rehabilitating a brick factory on the outskirts of Seoul which he had, for over a dozen years, abandoned to ruin.

This brick factory was now not much more than a tall red-brick chimney which one could see from afar and a dilapidated hulk of a factory building which was itself only the remains of a one-time factory building. Anyway, this factory building or what was left of it had belonged to Mr. Wu Taegap as long as he could remember.

One day(it was last year)Mr. Wu Taegap went out to this old factory of his in his usual gray suit with its longish jacket the color faded around the shoulders and trousers that were shorter than they properly should be. Except when he went out in the city, Mr. Wu Taegap never wore a suit and the idea of owning more than one suit was indeed very remotefrom his way of thinking.

As he plodded along the country road in his fading, ill-fitting apparel the figure he cut against the backdrop of the open deserted field was that of a provincial government servant out on some round of his rural jurisdiction. Yet this was no concern of Mr. Wu Taegap. Just as he was at home with his Korean attire from the vest of which hung the platinum chain of his pocket watch, he looked perfectly unselfconscious in his present outfit. He was wearing his customary bowler hat and carried a walking stick.

The soaring red-brick chimney could be seen soon enough.

As Mr. Wu Taegap walked toward it, however, he came to discover a strange scene. A modern factory building of a fairly large scale was on the site of the old building. In utter consternation, Mr. Wu Taegap noticed also that the man who was supervising the work of a band of men was an employee at a company headed by his brother Taeyong.

Wu Taeyong was a man of quick intelligence and diplomacy. It had been quite some time since he launched a trade with Macao, and even aside from this, he was being successful in a number of business projects in a way a man of such limited capacity as Mr. Wu Taegap could not even fathom. He and his family lived so luxuriously that they became a topic of conversation in the city and his property had grown several times bigger than it was at the time of inheritance.

"Our Tangjudong(name of residential section. It used to be customary to use place names in appellations of people, especially relatives or friends) Sister wears only high-heels and western clothes, they say." This was how Madam Shim summarized the situation in her carefree simple way. She went on,

"And they say she wears clothes of red, yellow, and azalea pink so that one can't tell which belongs to her and which to her daughter."

Lying comfortably on her back in the taechong, Madam Shim idly went on in this way without envy or malice.

"I heard from someone that she wears four diamond rings all at one time. . . ." Saying this, Madam Shim brought her small white hand in front of her eyes and spread out her fingers. She was wearing a leaf-green jade ring. Personally she did not care for any precious stones except a few traditional kinds such as jade or agate.

"That house has dance parties going all the time, doesn't it? I heard even the boy who goes to middle school brings in girls to dance with," said Tonggeun.

"Nonsense!"exclaimed Madam Shim pretending to be shocked but still in good humor. "What a horrible boy you are to be imagining such a thing,"added Madam still from her lying position, and continued.

"She travels to Hong Kong as easily as she would go to the

nextdoor neighbor's house. But she is an unusual woman. She even speaks several western languages . No wonder he doesn't concern herself much with the like of us." Tonggeun laughed his pointless hollow laugh.

Mr. Wu Taegap's elder brother might be outstanding in his accomplishments but certainly he was no caring loving brother to Mr. Wu Taegap. He never offered any partnership in business albeit his business enterprises were so numerous and thriving, nor did he extend a helping hand when Mr. Wu Taegap struggled with serious problems in his business. Mr. Wu Taegap himself, however, never manifested any resentment about this. Only on that day when he found construction work in progress on his old factory site, with a red-pepper dragonfly fluttering atop his fading bowler hat, did Mr. Wu Taegap feel, for the first time, anger toward his unkind brother. But once ignited, his anger was so great that he shook under its intensity.

He went straight to see his brother.

Coming out of his brother's office, Mr. Wu Taegap had looked even more infuriated than out in the field, his face flushed with an ominous dark red pigment and his thick-lipped mouth agape with anger too great for utterance. He sought a lawyer that very day and requested a law suit against his brother Wu Taeyong.

Several people tried to ease out the relationship between the brothers but every attempt failed. Rather, these well-meaning interferences had the effect of worsening the conflict by bringing the elder brother's heartlessness more into focus which ended up by intensifying Mr. Wu Taegap's ill-feeling toward his brother even further.

Mr. Wu Taegap was firmly convinced that he would never lose the law suit. That his brother was extremely rich was known to the whole world. If so, the act of appropriating what belonged to his far poorer younger brother was sure to draw a sympathetic judgement in favor of the latter(even if there had been some procedural negligence on the part of Mr. Wu

Taegap). That he would win seemed as clear as day to Mr. Wu Taegap no matter what the lawyer might say.

The main reason why Mr. Wu Taegap wanted so urgently to see Lawyer Kim was that he wanted to report to him about the result of a most recent visit made by a person on Mr. Wu Taegap's side to the elder brother to talk to him about a compromise. The man had been turned away without even being allowed to see the elder brother. Mr Wu Taegap had decided that this needed to be included in the document the lawyer was preparing for the trial. He had felt that the happening was important enough for him to look up his attorney even if it was a Sunday. The telephone was not much help with this man because even on week days he was difficult to catch on the phone.

"I hear there's something the matter in the streets. How did you come home? Did you have to walk, too?"said Madam Shim.

But Mr. Wu Taegap kept his dignified silence as usual and after changing into his customary household attire, went out to the sarangchae.

Ihwa waited late into the night for Ji-un to call. But there was no call.

On Monday, the city was even more restless than on the previous day. Ihwa, who had set out from her house to go to her classes, had not gone to school. Troops of students of varying grades were going back to their houses which they must have left only a short while ago. Ihwa followed their example.

It was around ten thirty that morning that the first din of gunfire could be heard in the city. It was a sound that seemed to fall into a person's insides with a sinister adroitness.

"Goodness! What was that sound?" exclaimed Madam Shim wide-eyed.

"It's gunfire, nothing more, nothing less,"said Tonggeun unhurriedly throwing down his satchel. He, too, had come back home like his sister Ihwa and like all the other students.

"What? Gunfire? Is it true? What if a cannon ball flies over here?"

"Simple, everything will crash down," said Tonggeun without emotion. Then he added,

"Go out in the street and see for yourself. A lot of things are happening out there. There're even hundreds of country people rushing in with their calves and all, you know. It's all quite funny."

"Why? Why would they come in here? What's happening? Is it a war, really?"

"Who knows? There are some people who are bleeding."

"What did they tell you at your school, son?"

"All that the teachers were doing was running about with stupid faces. And all we did was talk our heads off in our rooms."

All this time the radio station were broadcasting military songs which was interrupted every now and then by a report about a battle fought in the Euijongbu area. Mainly it was about how bravely the ROK Army was standing up against the invaders and how confident it was of a quick and complete victory. "It seems many people are taking off to the south," said Ogyop who had been out to catch the general atmosphere. "Shouldn't we pack some things and get ready, also?" she asked, turning to Mr. Wu Taegap.

"There's no call for unnecessary fuss. We'll wait and see," said Mr. Wu Taegap with finality.

"Except that we are quitely likely to be right in the midst of a battle if we stay, you know. I mean we may have street -to-street fighting right here in the city," remarked Tonggeun sagaciously with his back aslant against a pillar.

"Didn't you hear the radio just now? The fighting's almost over, it said."

"But listen to that sound of gunfire, dear," said Madam Shim timidly. But this, too, had no effect on Mr. Wu Taegap who merely said decisively,

"That's our cannons firing."

His wife and children helplessly looked at his dark-red pock-marked face realizing that nothing could change his mind now. Also, just as Mr. Wu Taegap was saying, maybe it was the National Army army shooting the enemy with the cannon, they hopefully thought. Maybe it really was what they call scare shooting. Anyway, the military march flowing out of the radio at the moment was certainly confidence-inspiring. "I wonder if the Communists have a strong army," muttered Ihwa uneasily thinking of Ji-un and his trip to the demilitariz ed zone.

"I don't know, but my guess is they will be defeated and chased out of town even if they come down here and have a street-to-fight. But if they win, father, don't you think a capitalist like yourself will have it tough?" said Tonggeun in almost a joking tone as if it was impossible for one with his kind of disposition to become serious under any circumstances. Throwing an expressionless glance at his son, Mr. Wu Taegap said,

"I have nothing to fear even if the communists take over here. I have nothing. Maybe it's different for those who have money stacked away."

Maybe Mr. Wu Taegap was thinking of his brother Wu Taeyong when he made this remark. Maybe he was picturing in his mind the dismay his brother and his family must be experiencing in their extravagant house in Tangjudong.

(They say the communists confiscate property and harm the people.... The rich cannot come out unscathed in their system, it seems. Then....)

It was with a vestige of satisfaction, to be quite honest, that Mr. Wu Taegap went over this thought, but more than that, he was apprehensive for his brother and his family despite everything. I am only a failure of a businessman, but not he. He won't get by so easily.... Mr. Wu Taegap kept on thinking, a sense of misgiving building up in his mind as time passed. Yet, his relations with his brother had grown so complicated and discordant lately that he could not bring himself to go over to Tangjudong to look up that family.

"Can we have lunch soon?"

"Yes, father," answered Ogyop hurriedly leaving for the kitchen. Soon the sound of the kitchen knife hitting the chopping block was heard.

As if he remembered only then, Mr. Wu Taegap telephoned his company and the house of his manager. Although he himself had not planned on going to the office today and nobody could be expecting him there, he felt an obligation to call and ask if everybody was all right at that end.

Nobody answered the phone at the company. Maybe there wasn't anybody there. The manager's home phone seemed out of order. Mr. Wu Taegap hung up the receiver without having been able to talk with anyone among his employees.

The tension of the outside world did not take long to infiltrate the innermost room of Mr. Wu Taegap's tall-hedged house. The sound of gunfire came from far closer now than in the morning. True, the radio was still making announcements about the successful battle in the Euijongbu area and about how fearlessly our soldiers were attacking the enemy. Yet, it was no mystery, now, that the North Koreans were coming closer to the capital.

The strange thing was that despite their instinctive understanding of the real situation, people listening to the radio announcements reassuring the citizens of safety and of the military prowess of the ROK Army could not help being carried away by the words they heard, so that to the end they kept having hope against all odds. This was especially true of Mr. Wu Taegap who, sitting with his legs knotted crosswise in front of the radio, continued his favourite exercise of moving the upper half of his body from left to right in an even tempo, with a bland but confident look on his face.

The Old Woman who had gone up to the changtoktae(raised platform where kimchi and soy sauce jars are kept) to take a look at the outside world came back saying,

"The people nextdoor are digging holes in the ground and burying large toks(earthenware jars) in them, I mean those that can hold twenty mals of grain. They buried three of those in the ground. It seems they are going to hide their household things and some other things in those jars and leave for the south."

The Old Man who was standing behind her looked at the family gathered at the taechong with an anxious expression on his face. He seemed to be urging with his wordless counsel that Mr. Wu Taegap should follow the example of his nextdoor neighbor without delay.

The Old Man had a big stout body and he had the habit of rolling his eyes up when listening to Mr. Wu Taegap's command, which made him look like an insolent old servant. But he was a good worker.

Mr. Wu Taegap did not say anything and the two servants went back to their quarters.

By sunset, hundreds of families were forsaking their homes, all of them headed for the south. Forming unending confused lines, these refugees trudged along the same streets through which so many military vehicles had shot the day before. Their rationale for going south seemed to be that the enemy's approach from the north made it the most logical and sensible course for citizens of Seoul to take. Among those remaining in the capital, the ones that believed in a casual street fight of short duration climbed up to Mt. Nam.

It started to rain before night and the refugees wet footsteps sounded heavy and gloomy in the darkening air.

That evening there was a presidential speech on the radio. It was to urge the citizens to have faith in the army and keep their posts of responsibility in their respective work places. He emphasized that there was no call for alarm.

Most of the people loved their president. They trusted him. Many who had thought of leaving, therefore, decided to stay after hearing his message. The president had given strength to them in their moment of weakness. None of them, of course, knew that the government had already fled to the south and the presidential speech was a recorded tape.

As time went on, Ihwa became very restless and worried for Ji-un that she could not sit still. She called Ji-un's school and even looked up the number of a professor with whom Ji-un seemed to have some contact in connection with his work for the Student Association. Neither of these calls, however, brought her any news of Ji-un. Lost and dejected, she went to see Tong-hun in his 'laboratory' across the yard.

"Can't you get me some news of things happening up there in Euijongbu or in Tongduchon?"

The radio in the anbang(a bigger room used chiefly by the mistress of a house but widely by other members of the house, too, for meals, chats, etc.) reported on the successful exploits of the National Army and repeated the message that the citiz ens should not worry. Ihwa wanted to know things that were not being reported on the radio.

Ihwa found Tong-hun looking grim and with his earphones on. In fact, she could not remember ever seeing him looking that serious. When he recognized Ihwa, he took off his earphones and came out of the room which was lit only by the dim light given off by tiny electric bulbs of red and green.

"I can't hear much on my contraption, either. But it's dead certain that our army has lost. I think we ought to leave right now," said Tong-hun. Then leaving Ihwa there, he went to see Mr. Wu Taegap hurriedly as if he did not wish to lose a minute. Ihwa stood in the yard for a few minutes letting the fine filaments of rain fall on her. The sky was streaked with red on the northern side which gave her a very ominous feeling. It was quite dark now. What happened to Ji-un, Ihwa asked herself for the hundredth time.

Tong-hun was walking back across the yard. Seeing Ihwa still standing there, he merely shook his head from left to right and then, without saying anything more, disappeared into his room with its red and green lights.

Ihwa had no wish to try to talk their father into taking the family out of Seoul. She could not go anywhere without seeing Ji-un.

"Turn all the lights off, and make sure that the gates are locked. Don't open them to anyone, even if somebody should come pounding on them," said Mr. Wu Taegap in a loud commanding voice. He seemed to think that if only these precautions were taken, there would be no trouble in keeping the enemy off.

When the truck carrying thirty or so students arrived at its destination, Ji-un jumped off the vehichle into the midst of the deafening sounds of gunfire. On their way there, they had passed several troops that were preparing for defensive combat but the vehicle on which Ji-un and his Student Association colleagues rode had not been stopped or searched at any stop but had run straight to the foremost frontline.

At first Ji-un thought that the first thing they needed to do was to find someone to whom they could explain their purpose in coming. Immediately, however, he realized that there was no sense in even thinking of such an action, because confusion and chaos reigned everywhere.

They saw a barricade built in the middle of the road. At the same time they heard an officer who seemed to have been giving out orders to the men from one side of the road shouting to them to drop down. His face was streaked with blood. Machine-gun and rifle shots were being exchanged by both sides and the bullets fired by the unseen enemy swished right by one's ears to hit the ground only a few yards ahead raising great puffs of dust. Wounded men were lying about here and there. Now the student volunteers could see the enemy soldiers hiding in the pine forest about three hundred yards away. At a glance, Ji-un was astounded to find their equipment and manpower far surpassing what could normally be expected of a border patrol force. The massive row of tanks lined up along the road next to the pine forest, which he did not need binoculars to recognize, was enough in itself to let anyone fathom the gravity of the situation and foresee the outcome of the confrontation.

It was during one of the quiet intervals between violent bursts of shooting that Ji-un took time to study the general state of things and draw some conclusions from his observation. The soldiers, in the meantime, were occupying themselves with their wounded comrades leaving, for the time being, their guns lying on the ground. Ji-un and his colleagues, too, helped by carrying the wounded to the truck they had ridden to come there.

"What do you think is going to happen?" Ji-un asked the soldier who had just helped him carry a wounded man to the truck. They were both running with their heads down low. The man to whom Ji-un had asked this question was a private with a boyish round face. His combat fatigues were soaked through with sweat and his expression was hard as a rock as he answered between clenched teeth,

"There's no hope."

Ji-un and the private picked up another wounded body. It seemed he was hit in the stomach which was a complete mess. Ji-un did not think he was alive. All the same he and the private carried him to the truck and loaded him on it along with other wounded soldiers.

The commander of the troop came rushing in, snatching the binoculars from his sweat-covered face.

"We are students of Seoul National University. We would like to help," said one of the students to the commander. There was no time to offer longer explanations.

"It's very kind of you all but. . . . " said the commander whose face seemed already branded with the ashen mark of death. Or maybe the death mark on this middle-aged major's forehead foretold the deaths of all fifty or so men fighting now under his command and possibly the annihilation of the entire army of the Republic of Korea. A major ran up to report on the number of wounded. One soldier was shouting that he could not call up headquarters. Maybe this one was the communications officer.

The road leading to the capital remained empty without any sign of reinforcements arriving. Yet, here on the border line, a war had started. When he finally realized this clearly, Ji-un felt all trivial thoughts and emotions inside his system coming to a full stop, to give way to an intense sensation of being alive and of the darkness and the drabness of ceasing to live.

Suddenly, one of the ill-thriving poplar trees by the roadside broke with a violent snap and its fragments flew in every direction. The shooting had started again. Picking up any weapon they could reach from the ground, Ji-un and his colleagues ran toward the barricade.

Ji-un felt shame about having come to this place of war and death in a mood of going on some consolation trip to a peace-time army. It was not as if he had not already thought about the possibility of risking his life in a war against the Communists. Yet he had not realized while coming here that he was already involved in that war.

Yes, it was a war, whether anybody thought it possible or not. What would the citizens be thinking now? Would they be getting correct reports by now? What about the government? Yes, what about the government? And the army? And Ihwa, yes, what on earth is happening with Ihwa? But all these thoughts were no more than fleeting shadows of thought. He was immediately fighting so hard that nothing but the act of fighting existed for him. It was as if in that state of extreme tension, his existence attained the unattachedness of one freed from all human preoccupations. He could no longer feel anything either. Neither the ominous sounds of gunfire nor the bullet that fell so close to him it nearly touched his arm, nor the sight of a human being falling wounded or dead in full view made him feel anything any longer.

Yet, to be absolutely truthful, even at this moment, he experienced a sensation which was as peculiar as it was unexpected. Upto this time, he had known war only through military training given at schools he attended and through books and movies. And from none of these had he been able to catch the very unique feeling he was experiencing now that he was in a real war. And he had no way of describing it.

With the downpour of heavy rain, the troop made a short retreat. The entire unit was now no more than several dozen men and one jeep and truck. It was getting dark. Although the unit had come upon another somewhat bigger at the point to which it retreated, the enemy came down upon it, all the same, possibly due to its low estimation of the power of the retreating army. A furious fight took place, which was on the part of the still heavily outnumbered ROK army a desperate last combat. Rain kept pouring down. Everything—even such things as time and place—seemed to have gone insane in that rain-trampled darkness torn by countless red flames.

By the time the tanks arrived, most of Ji-un's comrades-in-arms, both the soldiers and the students, were lying on the ground. The most these under-equipped and outnumbered fighters could do under the circumstances had been to postpone the southward invasion of the Communist army for only a matter of several hours. Ji-un had lost his gun in the turmoil of the confused fighting. He picked up a couple of grenades, therefore, and threw them toward the tanks. Huge angry blossoms of flames, and then, clouds of smoke rose up and the next instant Ji-un was running. He ran for the next trench because he had to fight on. Even while he was running, however, he felt as if part of him was falling. . . . as if his body was loosening up. But he did not stop because he had to run as far as the next trench. . . .

When Ji-un recovered his consciousness, he saw that he was lying on the floor of a hospital room. There were wounded soldiers all over the place, on the beds, the floor, and even out in the corridor. There were so many wounded and so little space that these men were lying nearly one on top of another covered with blood, dirt, and drenching rain water. Various moaning and groaning sounds were escaping from all this heap of human bodies. It was apparent that some of these wounded were no longer alive. Ji-un noticed that his left arm was bandaged. A breathtaking pain pierced him as he tried to lift up that arm. He knew, however, that it was not fractured seeing that he could move it at least. A minute later, he realized that he had a pain in his neck as well. He felt it with his right hand and found that there was a bandage around his neck, too. The bandage was wet and the hand that touched it came off stained with blood.

The window of the room in which Ji-un lay began to lighten. The noise of metalic things being roughly thrown about could be heard from somewhere. There was no more rain.

Something told Ji-un that he was lying in one of the rooms of the Attached Hospital of Seoul National University. He looked around more carefully to see if he could find any of his colleagues or the soldiers with whom he had fought on the border. He found no familiar faces offhand. Then he noticed that the one groaning sound which had stood out above the more or less collective sound of others a while back had started again, this time somewhat more urgent than before. Looking in the direction of this sound, Ji-un recognized the face of the young private who had carried the wounded with him back on the combat field. A wide white cloth was spread over his stomach and he was writhing with pain. Unlike others, he was not lying on the bare floor but on a stretcher on which he had presumably been carried there. He was now screaming for water in a voice which made Ji-un shiver.

Ji-un tried to get up but did not succeed because the pain from his wounds made him feel faint. He stayed still, therefore, closing his eyes in resignation. Machine-gun fire was heard from outside. It had been there ever since Ji-un regained consciousness. In fact, Ji-un had the impression that the machine-gun fire had continued since before he regained consciousness. Picking up these thoughts almost idly, Ji-un fell into a doze.

Suddenly, a great clamour enveloped the entire area mixed with sounds that were like the last cries of dying men. Then, all at once, shooting started from a very close by—right down the stairs from where Ji-un and the others were lying. It was coming from that ill-famed war weapon, the so-called taba-lchong (Russian sub-machine-gun).

A deadly silence ensued. A flash went through Ji-un's head, and one by one all the things that had been happening since he had set out for the border along with his Student Association colleagues fell into place in his mind.

The war had started and ended in defeat. Seoul had fallen into the hands of the Communists. There was no longer any doubt about the meaning of the shooting that was in progress downstairs. With all his might, Ji-un tried to stand up. His aim was to get the hell out of that place. Yet his body did not obey his will. And all this time, heavy, noisy footsteps had been approaching up the stairs and now the hard dry barrage of the alien firearm came right from the room next door.

The strange thing about this whole process was that there was such an overwhelming silence in it all. Except when the shots were fired, hardly any sound was made until the sound of some object, presumably, a human body, falling with a thud was heard. The door to the corridor had been left open. Ji-un could see that one of the men among the pile of wounded left there was looking in the direction of the shooting with large frightened eyes. As if to ward off some hallucinatory picture of a nightmarish scene, this man was making desperate jerky gestures with his arms.

Feet clad in leather boots were picking their way between the lying bodies on the wooden floor of the corridor. The squeaking sound that issued from the leather boots as the wearer took his steps resounded as if it were a sound huge enough to pull down the ceiling. Closing his eyes tight, Ji-un turned away from the sound. His feeling, thought, and every function in his system seemed to stop even before the cessation of the pumping of his heart took place. Only a dull sense of hate sizzling in the pit of his consciousness still remained.

Ji-un took a surreptitious look around the place, then very slowly extracted himself from the heap of dead bodies, head first. At the same time as his nostrils felt the open air, Ji-un saw the clear bright sky spreading out before his eyes. The bodies had been dumped on a grass-covered sloping surface. Blood-wet cadavers still pressed against him, as immovable as rocks. Yet these bodies had the trick of suddenly dropping a limb on Ji-un or sticking the tip of a toe into him.

Having been pressed down by the heavy dead bodies, Ji-un's arms and legs were nearly paralysed. Yet by painstakingly and obstinately applying himself to the task, Ji-un could wriggle out of the human heap inch by inch like an earthworm.

It looked as if the enemy who had shot down hundreds of soldiers and civilians could find no time for digging holes to bury them. They had merely dumped the bodies where the sloping grassland was gently indented making a sort of a terrace. None of the soldiers reappeared on the scene.

The sheer accident of a missed shot had given him yet another chance for life. Until the bodies had been dumped on this slope, Ji-un had pretended to be dead.

It was only in the afternoon that laborers with grimacing hard faces came along and started digging holes. There was among these men one wearing a white gown who looked quite young. . . . maybe he was a staff member at the hospital. He was giving orders to the diggers.

When the men started their work near the heap under which Ji-un was sprawling down after the exhaustion of his break-through, he pulled himself up into a standing position and, supporting his wounded arm with his right hand, staggered toward the white-gowned young man.

"Could you please lend me that white gown?" Ji-un asked him. Ji-un had become bold. He did not as yet know if the young man was a leftist working for the Communists. On the other hand, however, this was a risk he could not afford not to take because there was no question of walking out of that place looking as he did. He also counted on the fact that most of the medical students were non-political.

"Do you mean that?" the young man asked back, staring at Ji-un.

He had a broad face that did not look too fastidious. His white gown on the collar of which Ji-un recognized the blue badge of the university to which he himself belonged was quite wrinkled.

The medical student in the white gown threw a glance at the pile of bodies and then back at Ji-un. Unspoken words of understanding seemed to be exchanged between their two pairs of eyes. The young medical student now looked all around him, turning his body this way and that, to see if anybody was looking. Then he took off his badge from the gown and putting it on his jacket underneath the gown said to Ji-un,

"You'd better take off your badge, too. Better wear it outside, I mean."

Saying this, the young man quickly took off his gown and handed it to Ji-un, saying,

"There's a comb in one of the pockets. And you'd better wipe off the corner of your mouth."

"Thank you," said Ji-un.

The young man walked back to the diggers. Then seeing that two old laborers were looking his way, with their feet on the upper edge of their shovels, the medical student said authoritatively,

"Dig on. We don't have a lot of time."

Ji-un started walking in the direction of the hospital building. The grassy slope on which the bodies had been thrown was none other than part of the many sloping grassy areas surrounding the medical school compound. From where Ji-un started walking toward the hospital building, one could look out at the stone wall of Changgyong Palace across the tramway. Ji-un could see through the iron fence that divided the university site from the street a tank with a red flag rolling along the tramway.

Then there was the sound of rifle shots, cannons firing, and the reverberation of heavy vehicles on the pavement.

For a while the sky itself seemed filled with the wildest orchestration of war weapons. On the ground, a troop of thin, small-bodied soldiers were thumping along weighed down with heavy fighting gear.

Ji-un neared the front door of the hospital building. Communist officers in square-shaped uniform jackets and sharp-edged hats were walking to and fro near the doorway glancing at the stretchers carrying their wounded out of the building. Strong northern accents could be heard here and there.

Ji-un changed direction in the middle and started walking down the hilly driveway leading from the hospital building to the front gate. He did not hurry. Fear had left him for some time now.

As he was passing through the front gate, he was stopped by two bayonets.

"Just stepping out. Will be back right away," said-Ji-un to the guards in a calm voice.

They let him go and he walked out into the street.

Ihwa and her family, too, had spent their night in agony. When around midnight frightening tall flames soared up into the sky in the direction of the Han River, Madam Shim was so frightened that she fell into a faint. She woke up after a while but the great clamor of explosions itself had lasted for quite a long spell, reverberating far and wide. The tall flames which bathed nearly the whole of the city in a crimson dye had taken even longer to subside.

The incident had finally shaken the conviction of Mr. Wu Taegap who had believed for as long as he could that nothing would endanger the people in his household. The radio was no longer announcing government messages about how every citizen ought to attend to his daily work with equanimity. The fact was that from around nine o'clock that night, the radio station had stopped functioning altogether.

The footsteps trudging on in the rain had continued all night. Finally the dawn broke and it was then that gunfire of arms rang out up and down the street all at once. The submachine -gun rattled on continuously and at times the shooting seemed to be taking place right outside the wall of Mr. Wu Taegap's house.

All the members of the household had kept inside after locking the gates, trying to be as quiet as they could. From the Old Man who had taken a peep out through a cleft in the wooden gate, the family learned that the Communists had taken the city. Mr. Wu Taegap became very sullen after hearing this.

Yet, how could anyone believe that a different world had arrived overnight ? In no time, perhaps, the National Army will be back counter- attacking. As long as we don't get hurt in the street-to-street fighting, we will be all right. . . . This was what Mr. Wu Taegap still wanted to believe. In a dignified tone, therefore, Mr. Wu Taegap told his family about this prospect.

Yet the sounds of shooting and other sounds of disaster punctuated by occasional inarticulate shouts increased by the minute, plunging Mr. Wu Taegap's household into growing fear and anxiety.

Mr. Wu Taegap and his family ate breakfast in the main building. This was Ogyop's decision. Neither to this nor to the fact that the breakfast was served at an hour when normally no-one except Mr. Wu Taegap would be up and around did the members of the family raise any objection. They did not even seem conscious of such facts. Nor did they look as if they knew what they were eating.

"You must eat more, mother. You need to. You, too, Tong -hun, eat while you can, you know." Ogyop prompted them, with these words, to take as much food as they could and the rest of the family were almost mechanically swallowing down some food in order to obey her.

"All the houses are putting up flags," said the Old Woman to Ogyop, stepping inside the taechong which was itself a rather unusual thing for her to do.

As Ogyop stood up to go out to the gate to inspect the neighborhood, Madam Shim pushed her head out of the anbang where she had gone back in after breakfast and stopped her.

"Don't open the gate, daughter,"said Madam Shim in a weak, miserable voice.

"I will go and take a look," said Tonggeun, already walking out toward the gate.

Tonggeun came back after a while, dragging his feet in a pair of women's rubber shoes which were much too small for him.

"We are finished. It's red flags all over. Looks like our National Army uncles have taken real long leaves."

"Don't talk turnips, son," said Madam Shim mechanically responding to Tonggeun's attempt at witticism in her customary way. But her face was pale with tension.

"There's only one way to deal with this situation. We must improvise a red flag and raise it high. Otherwise, at any moment, our northern uncles may come down on us with their guns and bayonets, you know."

Tonggeun brought out such things as drawing paper and paint to the taechong and prepared to start the job. Then, as if remembering something, he turned to Ihwa and said,

"I don't think I need to go to this trouble. We can just use one of Big Sister's handkerchiefs, I think. We need one that's red all over."

"I don't have a handkerchief like that. Not one that's entirely red, anyway," said Ihwa, bluntly refusing to rise up to Tonggeun's light-hearted mood.

"I don't think it has to be all pure red, Sister. Just give me one that has some red in it."

"Tonggeun!" called Mr. Wu Taegap in his solemn, admonishing voice.

Sensing the meaning of this interjection, Tonggeun gave

a good-natured smile but proceeded to dip the brush into the water to wet it.

A while later, the chief of the Neighborhood Association came knocking at the gate. The purpose of this visit was to show a diagram of the flag of the People's Republic of Korea and hand out poster portraits of Josef Stalin and Kim Ilsong. He told the family to put up the portraits where everybody could see them easily and to make a flag exactly as shown in the diagram and to put in place of what they already had. As he said this, the Chief pointed at the make-shift flag Tonggeun had improvised with paper and part of a bamboo broom. Each of the portraits was the size of a regular door. After leaving these specific directions, the Chief of the Neighborhood Association went on to the house nextdoor. He was a young man who owned a small tailor's shop in town. Today, he looked as if he were going through a period of great inward confusion. Before he left for the next house, this man gave an apologetic smile as if seeking understanding and sympathy for what he was doing. Ihwa looked at the make-shift flag Tonggeun made. It was the first time that she had ever taken a look at even a replica of 'their' flag. And it was the first time, too, that she had heard the official name of that place which she had only known and thought of as 'the North.' She then looked at the two portraits which were about to be put up on the big pillars flanking the doorway to the taechong so that everybody coming in from outside could instantly see them.

By late afternoon, the family had to admit the fact that the world indeed had changed for them. At the same time, they sensed that in this changed world, painful and cruel things could happen to just about anyone at any moment. One thing was clear. They ought to have crossed the river and gone south.

Tonggeun who had been out to gather some information came back with a report on the so-called People's Trial. It was too pitiable and frightening to hear. Listening to Tonggeun about the proceedings of this terrible ordeal, Mr. Wu Taegap thought of his brother Wu Taeyong and his family. Whatever bad feelings might have been created between the brothers, he could never wish for any such terrible things to fall on that house.

All this while, Mr. Wu Taegap did not think about any of these terrible repercussions as something that could touch him and his family. Since he was a failed businessman without anything that could be called real property, he was rather inclined to believe that the Communists, who were reputed to sympathize with the moneyless, would consider him as one of their kind. Although he wasn't going hungry and lived in a fair-sized house, he could never be called a wealthy man. As he thought more about this matter, he became all the more convinced that the Communists would not harm him or his family.

Another communique was circulated by the Dong-hoe(subsidiary district office) urging all the houses to send a representative to the square. Sensing instinctively that sending the Old Man or any other in a similar position would not do, Mr. Wu Taegap's family decided to let Tong-hun go to represent the house. All of a sudden the authority of this institution called the Dong-hoe which they had up to now thought of as no more than an insignificant administrative unit came to acquire a threatening imperiousness.

Gunshots continued for reasons not as yet known to most of the citizens. Every time these shots were heard nearby, Madam Shim emitted a groan as if in sudden pain. Afterward, she looked up at the portraits of Josef Stalin and Kim Ilsong in turn, with eyes filled with uncomprehending uneasiness.

The owner of the tailor's shop came back to convey the order from the Dong-hoe that the house hand over all the grain they had in store. This time he was with a number of men none of whom looked familiar to the family. While the sacks of rice were being carried out of the house, Mr. Wu Taegap and Madam Shim stayed in a den at the back of a room hardly breathing.

Tonggeun and Tong-hun took turns in reporting what they had seen and heard in the outside world. From them the rest of the family learned such words as 'the subversive element' and heard about how the whole family of a boy they knew had been massacred and how dead bodies were lying about in the streets where no ordinary vehicles were running any longer. The boys also reported on how they had walked to their school just to see what was happening but had been turned away by soldiers guarding the gates with bayonets.

The existing order had been literally and completely destroyed, which in itself was perhaps not entirely to be lamented because a new order can always set in after an old order has been abolished. But in the present case, what was the order that could be expected? Was it something that held any hope for the majority of people? Was it at least something which would protect the people from an indiscriminate and undeserved violence?

Somebody was banging angrily at the front gate. When it was opened, two soldiers thumped into the yard. They were both around twenty years of age and had emaciated faces with tired eyes. They were both thin and on the short side, but maybe the rifles that hung down heavily from their shoulders were making them look smaller than they really were.

"Who's the head of this house?" One of the soldiers asked in a strong northern accent, the black blade of his bayonet glinting above his shoulder.

When the soldiers came in, Ihwa was sitting on the toemmaru(narrow porchlike protrusion on the outside of a room built of wood) with her legs dangling. Tonggeun was standing in the middle of the front yard and the Old Woman and the Old Man were lingering in the gateway. The soldiers had rushed in upon them so unexpectedly, however, that all four of them were frozen in their places unable even to make a sound. It was as if horrible incarnations of the general destruction and killing were suddenly in front of their eyes.

"Good afternoon. May I help you with anything."

It was Ogyop who appeared from somewhere smiling and speaking to these intruders in her sweet voice as if they were some friendly guests.

"Excuse us, miss, but we must take a look inside the hous-e,"said the soldier in a voice which was courteous enough coming from one who was incarnating destruction and mass-acre.

"Oh, I see. That's quite all right. Please follow me," said Ogyop and led them up to the step.

"I am sorry but we cannot take off our shoes."

"That's all right with us. Please feel free to look."

As they stepped onto the well-polished floor of the taechong in their dirt-covered boots, the other soldier who had as yet not spoken a word mumbled in a low voice, 'I'm sorry.'

The two soldiers looked inside the rooms through the open screen doors. It was impossible to guess at what they were looking for in this house. Something separated the people of this house and these soldiers so irreparably that there seemed to be less rapport between them than between aliens. Or maybe one could even say that there was less basis of comm-unication between them than between human and some other -than-human species.

Finally, the soldiers went to Ihwa's room where they stood staring at the books in the bookcase which nearly covered the whole of one wall. In fact, it was the only one of its kind in the house.

Ogyop seemed to have little passion for books. As for Mr. Wu Taegap, he was even less interested reading. And Madam Shim did not even read the daily papers. Tong-hun's reading was limited to books and magazines related to mechanics and Tonggeun was much like his father where reading was conc-erned. Yet all the family members were appreciative of the special value of this possession of their older daughter and Ogyop was especially careful to maintain the books and the bookcase in good state.

The dismal visitors stood facing the rows of books wordlessly for a while. Even the inventive and perceptive Ogyop seemed unable to fathom these men's motive as they stood nailed in front of the bookcase. Finally, however, Ogyop seemed to come up with an idea.

"We have these kinds of books, too. It's my older sister who reads them," said Ogyop in a deliberately casual voice, pulling out books with titles such as The Communist Manifesto and Das Kapital. As luck would have it, inside the front cover of the latter book, there were pictures of Karl Marx and Friedrich Engels.

The sight of these pictures seemed to light up the faces of the two soldiers for the first time. The one who spoke most of the time now said,

"Very good. We will go now."

The two soldiers saluted Ogyop and left the house.

As soon as the gate was shut behind them, Tonggeun said without even trying to lower his voice,

"What did they want? Why did they come here? And why did they leave suddenly like that?"

"I'm not sure. . . . But I think I know one thing. I don't think they can read," said Ogyop pensively.

After the flap caused by the visit of the soldiers had calmed down a little, Ogyop had the Old Man and other household servants carry the mother -of-pearl-inlaid lacquer chests to the storage house and she made the men line up these chests along front against the wall.

Next she confiscated Madam Shim's jewelry including her favourite jade pinyo, jade rings, and some golden buttons. Lastly she sent off the old couple and other members of the serving staff, including the young errand-girl, to their homes on indefinite leave. When the Old Woman and the young errand -girl started crying either from regret at the separation or from fear, Ogyop consoled them.

"I am only sending you away because it's best for all of us. I fear that more danger may fall on us if we stay together. I'll make sure that you are all called back as soon as things take a turn for the better, believe me."

Madam Shim was obliged to take off her silk chima and wear a chima of coarse cotton which Ogyop made the Old Woman lend her mother.

"What's happening to us? What on earth is happening to us?" she wailed as she put on the Old Woman's black cotton chima.

Nobody offered her an answer this time.

Cradling his bad arm with his right arm, Ji-un walked along the streets at an even tempo unperturbed by the gunshots that seemed never to stop.

In the sky, shells fired by the anti-aircraft guns were exploding furiously filling the entire expanse with sounds and incandescent flames. Since one could see not even a shadow of an airplane in sight, it was beyond comprehension why the A. A. guns were keeping so busy. Ji-un walked on glimpsing a fragment from an exploded shell spiralling down onto the paved road.

Not a single ROK soldier could be seen in the street. The city was completely defenseless. The incessant blank shots from the submachine-gun, therefore, were utterly meaningless, merely a nuisance. Now and then, Ji-un ran into dead bodies lying on the pavement. Some of them were soldiers in heavy leather boots. The rest were civilians. On the body of a dead woman, Ji-un saw an infant crying, clutching at the woman's lifeless breasts. The sight of the infant with the dead body presented a vision of a monstrous creature which carried life only in one protruding portion of its decaying body. By the entrance of a government building, the bodies of two policemen in full uniform were lying. These were ones that had been faithful to their duty to the last possible moment just as the government had urged through the last radio announcements.

A run-down automobile passed by with an enemy officer in its back seat. Within a few minutes, about half a dozen tanks rolled down the same way. A woman in army uniform was standing in the seat of a tank and shouting : Manse! Manse! (long live. . . . !)" One could see her curly permed hair sticking out of her helmet. The passers-by were looking up at this woman as if in a stupor.

When he heard her voice shouting long-lives, Ji-un felt as if a hot coal was scorching his eyeballs. This was a street which he had loved and where there had been freedom. True, depression and inertia had made life in this and other streets somewhat less than wholly healthy and happy. Yet there had been ample laughter and freedom up to only a few days ago. The country had finally overcome the inevitable confusion after the historic Liberation and seemed to be gathering strength to grow into a full-fledged modern state. People were ready to work in any kind of situation and they worked hard. The students were united in their desire to build a strong new society and their zealousness for the realization of this goal had been unparalleled. Yes, although the division of the country remained a national problem as yet impossible to solve, the majority of Seoulites had been content to attempt whatever development could be achieved within the given circumstances.

Ji-un felt a great pain in his heart.

Almost unaware, he was walking in the direction of Pildong where Ihwa's house was. His original plan was to see if she was safe and tell her about his own miraculous survival through two massacres. After that. . . . yes, after that, he would cross the Han River and go south. The ROK army was sure to come back up and he had to fall in with them for the counter-attack.

Suddenly a piercing whistle made Ji-un turn his head. A soldier in green trousers was halting every one of the small number of people passing his way. He was wielding his arms angrily with murder on his face. A barricade of sand bags came in sight a short distance away. On the other side of this barricade were parked rows of strange-looking jeeps and sidecars.

Ji-un turned back and took a detour to Ihwa's house which meant that he had to walk a much longer distance than he would have if he had followed the original route. Finally, however, he entered the alleyway leading to her house.

Before he went any further into this alley, however, he abruptly stopped short. This was because he caught sight of Kim Oshik a little way off in the alley.

Although Kim Oshik had gone to both high school and college with him, Ji-un looked at him now with a sense of fear spreading through his body. Kim Oshik and Ji-un had been close friends once, but ever since the former became a communist, Ji-un had come to dread him as an enemy. Even as a boy, Oshik had been thoroughgoing in everything he attempted and, after he joined the leftist movement, he had turned downright ruthless in carrying out whatever he had to do. Ji-un knew only too well what consequence would result from his being sighted by Kim Oshik at such a moment as this.

Kim Oshik was wearing a tie-less shirt, to one sleeve of which was attached a piece of red cloth. Observing more carefully, Ji-un could see that one of his feet was on the threshold of Ihwa's front gate. A communist officer with epaulettes on his uniform jacket was standing exchanging some words with Kim Oshik. The well-built big body of the latter looked full of self-confidence and his eyes, which were devoid of any human impurity, were meticulously moving as if on inspection. Oshik knew about Ji-un and Ihwa. Could he have come here to capture me, Ji-un asked himself.

Ji-un turned back sharply and feeling mortified and defeated began walking back along the road he had just followed. His direction now was the south. He would go and join the National Army. This was his foremost duty now.

Goodbye Ihwa, we will have to meet another time, he said in his mind. He could hear Kim Oshik's boisterous laughter as he walked farther away from the alley, tears flowing down his cheeks.

The bridges over the Han River had been blown up long before Ji-un reached the riverside. Fallen jeeps and trucks could be seen in the water and from some of the automobiles that had been overturned, the heads or limbs of the dead passengers were sticking out. Some bodies were lying face down. Apparently these had been shot from the back.

Even without the bridge, the riverside was being heavily guarded. Shots were being fired at frequent intervals up and down the riverside, from which Ji-un could surmise that some people were trying to swim across. Many who had come toward the river with the intention of fleeing south turned back on hearing these gunshots.

Ji-un looked down at his arm. Blood had oozed out of the white sleeve of the gown he was still wearing. There was a twinging pain in that arm even when it was immobile. And he was faint with hunger.

Even so he wanted to try swimming across. He did not wish to go back to town where characters like Kim Oshik would be strutting about. Taking a mental measure of the upper reaches of the river, Ji-un moved away from the bridges at a rapid pace.

At dawn of the next day after the visit of the illiterate soldiers, Mr. Wu Taegap was taken away by a group of two communist officers and three bearded men in farmers' work-clothes. The young owner of the tailor's shop and a staff member of the dong-hoe stood outside the gate casting surreptitious glances into the house from time to time. Mr. Wu Taegap was doing what he could with his total lack of eloquence to convince the men that he did not belong to the enemy camp but rather to their side, being deprived of property and money. He was no capitalist but was even in debt, he said. But none of this had any effect on the men.

"You'd better save your speech for later," one of them shouted. Instantly Mr. Wu Taegap's face turned dark red. Clumsily struggling to suppress his anger, he spat hard on the ground. Just then, Madam Shim broke into a loud wailing.

"What's this, do you want to go and be shot with him?" said one of the gang glaring at her. Madam Shim's weeping stopped abruptly.

"Don't be afraid, father. I will go with you," said Tonggeun.

"Nobody can come with anybody," said one of the bearded men this time, in a contemptuous voice.

"Go to Tangju dong and let your uncle know. Tell him to get away," said Mr. Wu Taegap in a low muffled voice turning his head slightly toward Tonggeun.

Then he was led out of his gate with both arms gripped by his captors.

With his hands pushed into his side pockets, Tonggeun followed them at some distance, trying not to be detected. Only after seeing them enter a tall building near the South Gate did he turn back and so running toward Tangju dong.

His uncle's house, however, was empty and all the doors were wide open. Recognizing a girl who had been working as a maid servant at his uncle's house, Tonggeun beckoned to her to come over.

What he could gather from this girl was that his uncle had taken an airplane out of the city with his family on Sunday.

"The people of the neighborhood took away all the furniture. The mistress took with her the more valuable things."

The girl who was still in her early teens chatted on absently while Tonggeun muttered inwardly : 'Fast as a kite, shrewd as a fox, you are, uncle.' And he shook his head a couple of times as if in genuine admiration of the feat performed by his fast-thinking and fast-moving uncle.

Days passed and yet Mr. Wu Taegap had not returned. To add calamity to disaster, the order came from the Dong-hoe that Mr. Wu Taegap's house, which was the house of 'subversive elements', must be handed over to the People.

On the day when this order was conveyed to the house, Ihwa stayed inside her room looking out at the scene taking place in their yard with a pale face. Unfamiliar faces were gathered in quite a crowd there, some shouting loudly and others kicking at doors with their feet.

"Hurry up! We want the house right now. Do you see this

gun?" said one of the men savagely and then fired a number of shots in succession against the door of the storehouse, making a ring of black holes in the wooden door.

"But this is all so sudden and we can't possibly. . . ." Ogyop was protesting in a low but determined voice.

"We will give you a little time. Make yourselves ready to go within that time." said one of the men who seemed a little more civilized than the rest. He then cast uneasy glances at a man who had an unusually bushy beard. Maybe he was one of the newly-made People's men who was still in danger of being condemned as a 'subversive.' He spoke without an accent, which meant that he was probably a resident of Seoul. Inside the sarangchae, men in leather boots were already stomping about making a lot of noise. Mr. Wu Taegap's sandalwood desk had been flung out onto the ground and all the doors had been torn off so that the sarangchae now looked like some kind of pavilion.

"Let's go, Ogyop, even if we have to live in the streets," said Ihwa.

"I know what you mean but we can't live in the streets indefinitely. We need a home...," replied Ogyop.

"But we can't keep on being insulted like this by those savages!"

"Lower your voice, Sister," whispered Ogyop precipitately.

Ihwa thought about the possibility of their father returning to the house to find all of them gone, but did not feel like discussing it now. Besides, as days passed, the family was beginning to give up hope of having him back so soon. We must leave at once, thought Ihwa looking at the vulgar triumphant faces that were, to Ihwa, more distasteful than their soiled clothing.

"But where could we go? We don't even have any relative's house to go and stay. Not even your uncle's after what happened. . . ."

"Mother," said Ihwa in a shrill voice as if she could not stand her mother's self-commiseration.

Just then something truly unexpected took place. It was that Tonggeun who had gone out of the house early in the morning, walked into the yard carryng a rifle on his shoulder and wearing a white towel as a headband around his forehead. On the towel was written 'Voluntary Army' in Chinese ink. With him were a few other boys of his age group wearing the same headbands.

After stomping into the yard in a jocular manner in the company of his 'Voluntary Army' friends, Tonggeun took a look all around the place, taking in the situation. Then he went to the well, scooped up some water with the gourd dipper and drank from it taking his time. The boys who came with Tonggeun followed suit. Then all together, they went out to the sarangchae.

Soon, sounds of loud chatting and laughter came from the direction of the sarangchae. Listening to them, Ihwa began to feel a headache. She held her head in both hands.

A while later, those of the intruders who had stationed themselves in the inner section of the house began to move out to the sarangchae. These were men who were more ferocious and ruthless than the soldiers from the north. They were, as one, unshaved(it seemed to be a mode among these communist new-comers to be unshaved).

"We'll have to let them use that part," said Tonggeun pointing at the sarangchae with his chin. "Couldn't make them give that up, too," added Tonggeun without particularly trying to lower his voice. "And I will do what I can to get them to release father. If he comes back, make him lock himself up so people can't see him. Don't tell the neighbors that he came back."

"But what about you, Tonggeun," said Ihwa. "What's going to. . . ." she could not finish the sentence.

"Can't be choosy, can we?" said Tonggeun showing his usual smile for the first time. "One day at a time, you know."

The boys who had stayed behind in the sarangchae thronged

back to the main house. Their faces were flushed with excitement as if they were in some thrilling gang fight.

"I will come again soon," said Tonggeun leaving.

Madam Shim did not say a word but tears flowed down her face as she looked at her son walking out across the yard.

Two days later, Mr. Wu Taegap came home just as Tonggeun had intimated. He was extremely weak but at any rate was the sole person among all that had been taken away from that vicinity that came back alive. It was under the cover of dusk that he came home and knocked at a side entrance to the main house. Immediately after coming into the house, he hid in a secluded room at the back of the house. During his absence from home, he seemed to have picked up some knowledge of what communism meant.

"I saw Tonggeun," he muttered after a long silence. He still seemed dazed from what he had just gone through.

"Where did you see him? He hasn't come home since yesterday."

Mr. Wu Taegap didn't open his mouth right away. But finally he said,

"In the street. He was with many other boys."

"Did he see you? Did he see his father?" asked Madam Shim a little breathlessly. But Mr. Wu Taegap kept silent again.

Just as Madam Shim said, Tonggeun had come home the day before. He did not, however, stay long. He hadn't even come inside the house. He had stood around the yard a while. Drinking the well water from the gourd dipper, he had said in his carefree voice, 'De-licious!' Then, he was gone. Gone forever from his family.

Ji-un, who spent the night in a warehouse with a view of the river, knew that he had to give up the idea of crossing it for the time being, anyway. The riverside was so heavily guarded no young men dared to be seen in that vicinity. To make matters worse, the wound on his arm began to develop an abscess. Remembering a female relative who had a house near Munsan, he decided to go to her. One summer during his undergraduate years, he had gone out there to fish and stayed overnight at her house.

Ji-un assuaged his hunger with a few tomatoes and eggplants he could pick from the vegetable patches he found along the road leading back to central Seoul. Passing through the downtown area, he went straight on north in the direction of Munsan.

The rank smell of cadavers rotting on the roadside stung Ji-un's nostrils. And there was so much heat from the sun that his skin tingled.

It must have been a very bizarre figure that Ji-un cut walking the country road in his borrowed white hospital gown. Yet nobody paid any attention to him.

The people who lived in the small village where Ji-un's female relative had a house were still trusting and peaceful. Ji-un's female relative whom Ji-un called 'aunt' was surprised and glad to see Ji-un come to visit with her. Since she could see no reason why Ji-un should be harassed by the new rulers, his 'aunt' preoccupied herself solely with worrying about his injured arm.

"A bomb hurt you, didn't it? Where're you living these days?"

"My boarding house is across the Han River. I couldn't go there because the bridge has been cut. I... I had no place to go."

"What a pity! But you did well by coming here. There's a hospital, too, in Samsongri which isn't too far from here. But first of all, you'd better change into some clothes of uncle's here."

Her husband, who was a farmer of few words, seemed to feel a need to interfere at this point. He said,

"You'd better tone it down a bit. This isn't something all the neighbors need to know."

Then he went out and picking up Ji-un's shoes off the stone step outside put them away so that none of the neighbors could see them.

Ji-un stayed in that house for over a week. Things were going well for the people of this farming village. The Seoulites who were getting short of grain were coming out here to trade valuable possessions for varying quantities of grain, almost begging to give away expensive items for a sack of grain.

One chima-measure of velvet (about two and half yards) was traded for one toe (about one liter) of rice ; one sewing-machine was comparable in price to two mals (one mal equals ten toes) of barley. And prices were set by the villagers who were procuring watches, trays with mother-of-pearl inlay, rolls of fine fabrics and many other things which they had never dreamed of owning. The latest common topic among the village women had to do with what new valuables certain houses of the village had come into possession of. And the women went round different houses to view the new exhibits.

"Look, they say this is diamond. They want to know how much rice we can give them for this ring. What shall I tell them?"

"A diamond ring? What will we do with a thing like that? Even a gold ring is little use nowadays. . . ."

"But. . . ."

"I say, forget it!"

The wife would then take the ring back to the grain-seeker saying something like this :

"Come back with a length of cotton or some such thing. We have no use for the like of this."

"What about sewing machine?"

"Well. . . . if it's a Falcon Brand, we could give you a little rice for it. But not any other make, you know. . . ."

Sometimes, the villagers added to their audacity toward the grain-begging Seoulites a boastful speech about how the 'friends' from the People's Republic of Korea were the allies of the workers and farmers like themselves.

Of course, the villagers themselves were not without some doubts about this categorization of the people into two clear

-cut groups with workers and farmers always on the right side and the rest of the people always on the wrong side. Yet, it was an assumption that could not harm folks like themselves, thought the villagers and therefore went along with the trend of the time.

The more educated of the villagers were going around with red bands around their arms testifying to their special advancedness in learning and informedness in the way of the world. These men made a point of gathering the villagers in the square several times a day and delivering speeches and teaching songs to them. On these occasions, the ones that had the red bands on their arms stood in one row facing the people as if they were teachers of an elementary school watching over the children.

"What did they say?" a parent would ask a son who had attended one of these meetings.

"Don't know. I just shouted a few 'manse's and came home."

"You mean they didn't say anything?"

"They say they will collect copper spoons from the houses."

In time, the feeling that a sacrifice was needed for the accomplishment of the 'great mission' spread in the air and thus it was that a hunt for the 'subversive elements' was triggered off in this inconspicuous farming community as it was in hundreds of other areas in and near the capital.

Even so, it was never an easy job to find the 'subversive elements' in such a simple-living farmers' community as this. And yet the red-banded enthusiasts had to find some such enemy of the people in order not to bring accusations of sabotage upon themselves.

The easiest way to recognize a 'subversive element' was to find out who lived more comfortably than others. Whether or not whoever it was that was a little more well-to-do than others had made his extra wealth solely by his diligence and by his quick thinking did not matter. It so happened that one younger-generation farmer who was a recipient of the Prize of Exemplary Farming awarded by the District Office became the first victim of the purge. This man owned a fairly large chicken farm and was raising a good number of pigs. But all this was purely the fruit of this man's own zeal and hard work. True, his chickens and pigs were fatter than those of other houses but it was he himself who had made that possible.

Another person who was brought into the list of the 'subversives' was the owner of the only tile-roofed house. However, this man was nearing his seventieth year and was, moreover, as poor as any of his fellow villagers.

On the day when these two men were taken to the Political Security Department, the villagers had followed them in a throng. The old man, who had enjoyed respect in the village, received many bows of farewell on this day. Nobody knew what happened to these men after they walked out of the Village Entrance that day flanked by officers from the Political Security Department. Thanks to the offering of these victims, however, the other villagers were granted a peace in which they managed to make their daily living on a more or less steady basis despite the turbulence in the outside world.

Although Ji-un tried to spend all his time inside the house, he began to feel restless when his arm was nearly healed. Lying down with one arm under his head, he would listen to the communist army songs the village children were singing, and his heart would become so full of frustrated fury that it nearly split.

A rumor from the capital said that the army notes which were circulating widely were the only currency that had any worth. The same source of information also conveyed the news that the broadcasting station was now back in operation while President Rhee was miles and miles away so that it was not likely that Seoul would be counter-attacked in the near future. Ji-un grew impatient. He wanted to see things with his own eyes, and he had to go south and join the National Army before the communists could move down south. It was almost certain that a good number of his comrades who could not go south in time were hiding here and there in the capital. He wanted to meet up with them if it was at all possible.

Wearing a straw hat and hemp shirt(just because everybody seemed to go about in this attire), Ji-un paid a visit to the capital. Whenever he ran into people, he wiped his face with the large towel he carried with him.

Ji-un wished to see Ihwa. The memory of her slender waist and supple lips was now an added pain and agony to him. Even in his dreams, he was persecuted by the thought of Ihwa.

New customs and manners were on display in Seoul streets. Every unused lot had been turned into a sort of a market where a mob of people were fighting to get at the merchandise which consisted of no more than a trayful of rice cakes, a scoop of millet, or a few boiled eggs.

The outer wall of Ihwa's house came in a view. With a pang and overflowing warmth, Ji-un recorded the sight into his consciousness. Just then, however, a woman's voice called out,

"Isn't that Comrade Ji-un? So you've been safe, haven't you?"

It was Sukja. She was wearing a white joksam and a black tong-chima(shorter, working-woman's skirt). Just as in the case of men, the attire of women(especially those in active service for the Northern Comrades) had become surprisingly uniform lately.

Trying not to expose his inner perturbation, Ji-un looked straight at the woman who was smiling at him with obvious pleasure. What is the meaning of that smile, asked Ji-un to himself. Sukja had been an active leftist. She was also talked about as having a relationship with Kim Oshik. Ji-un could not find any words with which to answer this woman's question.

"Have you come to see Ihwa?" asked Sukja again, without a smile. Ji-un said nothing.

"You'd better go in through that side entrance. You'll find her home. . . ."

". . . ."

"I am on my way to Suwon. I have to take care of some

business there for the women's league," said Sukja, raising one hand to show Ji-un something she was holding in that hand. It looked like a pad or a notebook rolled into a cylinder.

"I won't be back for a week. But what are you standing there for? Walk right in!" she said. She was smiling again, in a strange meaningful way. Then she went away.

As if nailed to the spot, Ji-un stood there without moving. It was a mistake on his part not to have recognized Sukja first and slipped away. Like Kim Oshik, she was hard and unscrupulous. Isn't a 'ruthless fight' 'their' common catchword, anyway, thought Ji-un with deep chagrine. But Sukja was coming back.

"Comrade Ji-un, I won't harm Ihwa. Do you understand what I mean?"

Ji-un noticed that Sukja's fair-skinned sharp -featured face looked angry and hard. He nodded to her, feeling relieved that she was letting it go at that this time. Sukja walked away without turning back once.

Ihwa threw herself into Ji-un's arms with such abandon that Ji-un could not believe that he was embracing the same woman that used to resist his embraces, if only mildly. She remained in his arms for a long time.

"I wanted to die. When you did not come back, I thought-. . . ."

"Ihwa, oh, Ihwa. . . ."

Although the door to the room where the two young people shut themselves in was locked tight, they could distinctly hear the voices that came from the sarangchae.

"Comrade Doctor, shouldn't this be sent over there?"

"Yes, comrade, you are absolutely right!"

The voices kept on reiterating the word 'comrade."

"Ogyop cooks for them. I don't know what to think of the situation we are in," said Ihwa and began to sob, still in Ji-un's arms.

"All this happened because we could not get away in time. But the point is to survive through this. I don't think this state will last very long."

"Let me come with you. I cannot stay on here. Besides, I will make myself sick worrying about you again."

Ji-un stroked her hair in silence.

"People from the university came here looking for you."

"You mean Kim Oshik, don't you?"

"Yes, he came twice. And Sukja, too. She comes here quite often. She wants me to join the Women's League."

"I ran into her in the alley just a while ago. She as much as said that she won't arrest me here."

"I'm sure she won't do that. She says she will make me join the League. She seems pretty confident about that, which means that she won't do anything drastic until she has used up her last card."

Ihwa told Ji-un about all the things that had happened during their separation.

"We had hoped that Tonggeun would make his escape somehow and come back home. But we haven't seen him again ever since."

"Even if he had escaped, I don't think he could have come back here," said Ji-un and abruptly he clutched Ihwa against his chest and began to pour hot kisses on her lips. It was time for him to leave.

"I must go now."

"Stay a while longer."

"I will get in touch with you again, by one means or another."

"Promise me, please, that you won't get hurt again."

"I promise. I won't get wounded again. And I won't get killed," said Ji-un with a smile looking at the shiny tears that had welled up in Ihwa's eyes anew.

By any standard, the life Ihwa's family were leading these days was most bizarre and complicated. From the outsider's point of view, this was an enthusiast's house with the elder son gone to the Voluntary Army and the rest of the family offering half of their living quarters to the People's Army. Thanks to these zealous services to the communists, moreover, the family were eating well without undue harassment from the new master of Seoul. The neighbors whispered about this to each other and all of them thought that this family were exceptionally clever.

Since more people were finding it difficult to get even two meals a day, it was not a great wonder that they should be thus befuddled to find this family eating refined rice to their fill three times a day.

When the truck loaded with sacks of rice came to their gate, Ogyop, who was at a loss as to how to procure rice after the communists had taken their store of grain away at the onset of their occupation of the city, had herself been not a little bewildered.

(...eleven, twelve, thirteen....)

The neighbors had come to the gate of the house and stood around and counted the rice sacks as they were being unloaded and taken inside the house. Unable to watch this scene any longer, Ogyop had fled into the house.

Finally, an officer of the People's Army walked into the inner courtyard.

"We would like to have our meals cooked here from now on," said the People's Army officer to Ogyop waving his hand at the pile of rice sacks. He was a captain and looked no older than twenty-three or four. Although it was obvious that he was from the Hamgyongdo area, he was trying to cover his accent with a deliberately affable manner of speaking.

Ogyop stood looking at him without answering but showing her distress in her expression.

The young officer looked a little dismayed now. Maybe he was feeling uncomfortable in the presence of this young woman who was gentle but had something in her that made it difficult for him to get close unlike the female comrades with whom he associated.

"I thought there were other yosong(female) comrades in

this house," said the officer seeing that Ogyop was hesitant to answer.

". . . ."

"There will be twenty of us at each meal. We will need to be served only twice a day. If you need anything, like bowls, plates, just let me know. I will have them ready."

". . . ."

"I can get help, too, if you say so."

The young officer wiped the sweat off his face. His was a sensitive-looking oblong face with a shapely nose and a small wart on the left cheek.

Ogyop remained silent. On the white forehead above her lowered eyes, one could read the inner distress which she did not try to hide. The young captain seemed unable to find another sentence to utter. He now merely stared at Ogyop without a word.

The young communist officer knew that he had a right to shoot this obstinate and uncooperative woman with the pistol he had on his waist. Yet for some inexplicable reason, he was feeling more at a loss than angry as he kept staring at Ogyop's clear-complexioned face.

"Comrade Doctor!"

Somebody was shouting in the sarangchae. At the same time, a young soldier about the age of Tong-hun leapt into the inner courtyard through the connecting gate between the main house and the sarangchae.

"Comrade Doctor, you must explain this. Headquarters says it doesn't know anything about this and says I must go to the police department. The police department says it doesn't know anything so I must go to headquarters. I need an explanation!"

His cheeks were flushed. Maybe he had been running from one place to another for the past couple of hours. Frustrated to the limit, the young soldier was speaking to a superior in a gruff, angry voice, thrusting out a stub of a paper toward the 'comrade doctor.' But the latter did not seem to mind the young soldier's impertinence. He merely took the paper from the other's hand saying.

"You got it wrong, comrade. I meant for you to go to the Political Security Department."

"Why then did Comrade Kang Soku tell me to go to headquarters?"

The two men disappeared into the sarangchae, talking to each other almost as if they were equals, not a superior to an inferior, or an inferior to a superior. A mean-looking man of around thirty or so walked in through the front gate. His name was Kang Soku. He had a broad face with oddly-set mean-looking eyes. The pupils of his eyes were at all times in the corners of his eyes and his lips looked warped. The tips of his eyes and lips were all abnormally pointed. His irascible voice, too, had an unusually sharp edge to it. He would issue a short laugh over some matter and then, as if springing back to his original nature, reassume his customary cold look. He was in the habit of moving in and out of the inner gate all day.

"You must not close this gate, ever," he had said to Ogyop one day.

This man seemed to be one of the higher-ranking officers. He carried, at all times, a short leather whip in his hand for what use one could not tell. He created an ominous atmosphere around his person so that nobody seemed eager to be found by him. Ihwa and her family soon came to memorize the name Kang Soku, Comrade Kang Soku, that is.

On the day when the rice sacks were carried into Ihwa's house, this Comrade Kang Soku had come into the courtyard through the gate holding his leather whip with both hands, and then seeing Ogyop and the young officer standing in silence had said in a cold blunt voice,

"Hurry up and cook something to eat. And you, comrade, what are you standing there for?"

The Pyong-ando dialect which had a charm and flair of its own in other people sounded merely hard-hearted in this man's diction. After saying these words, he glared at Ogyop with eyes in which the pupils were rolled up sideways into the corners. It was not that he bore ill feelings toward Ogyop personally. Yet under his glare, she felt as if the sharp edge of a knife were brought down on her spine.

(We must not aggravate these people…,) Ogyop thought inwardly.

Although Mr. Wu Taegap hid himself in a back-room without making a sound, there was no doubt that he would be discovered easily enough as soon as anybody on the communists' side should think of searching this house. As for Madam Shim, she was no better than a child under these stressful and extreme circumstances. On the morning when Ogyop had to cook vegetable gruel for breakfast because there remained no grain in the house, Madam Shim had looked very sad and despondent. This was not all. She even degraded herself by openly peeping into the bowls of other members of her family even while knowing that what was served could be sufficient for no one. She did not seem to give any thought to the fact that in order to give her a bigger portion Ogyop herself was eating even less than others. She behaved in such a thoughtless way that her daughters feared that she might howl like a child if there should remain nothing to eat in the house.

Ihwa's open animosity toward the people of the sarangchae was yet another problem Ogyop had to live with daily. Luckily, her sister rarely came out of the house. Yet at times she ran into their new lodgers by the well. Then she did not put in any effort to cover up her dislike for these people. She would scoop up the well water slowly and proceed to do something like washing her handkerchief while the thirsty men stood waiting for her to give them their turn. If Comrade Kang Soku should glare at her, moreover, she stared right back at him. Although other women were adopting the style of the new age, wearing coarse cotton hanbok(traditional Korean attire) with sleeves tucked up and rubber shoes on their bare feet, Ihwa did not change the fashion of her clothes in any way. She wore the same (now that the whole world was wearing drab colors) conspicuously bright-colored dresses that she used to wear.

"They won't dare to touch us," she said derisively. "Comrade Kang or anybody else can get as mad at us as they like but. . . ." Instead of finishing the sentence Ihwa had laughed in a shrill high-strung voice. Thinking that her sister was turning hysterical, Ogyop knitted her eyebrows in distress.

Ogyop felt that she needed to get along with her lodgers if only for the sake of her family. Getting into trouble with them meant being shot to death by them.

(And especially for Tong-hun's sake, I must not displease them,) said Ogyop to herself.

Ogyop was doubly worried for Tong-hun because this laconic last-born child of the house had already asked several times to be allowed to attempt an escape from the occupied city.

Suppose he does succeed in getting out of the city, where could he stay afterward?

Tong-hun said he would go to the house of a friend of his in some out-of-the-way town or village.

Maybe this was not so unlikely because except in the capital, people would still be helping and trusting one another, thought Ogyop.

"Once I'm out of here, I'll be okay. You needn't worry,"

Tong-hun had said to the family. Yet when finally he did attempt an escape, he failed and came back home. The People's Council office at the entrance of the alley, in the meantime, was paying special attention to Tong-hun as he passed in and out of the alleyway. One day, the Chief of the Neighborhood Association finally came to see TongÇhun.

"How about joining the Youth Corps?" said the Chief of the Neighborhood Association.

This owner of the tailor's shop had by now dropped his previous diffident tone and was speaking in a self-confident and even aggressive manner. He was sitting by the window of the People's Council office at all hours. Maybe, he was no longer running his tailor shop. His beard, albeit sparse and poorly-grown, was the most succinct proof of the change in his mental attitude and social status. Leaning back against the chair, he would give a perfunctory nod to those who greeted him as they passed the window behind which he sat. It seemed as if he had had a fast course in insolence from those in whom he had formerly noted(with a meek-natured nonchalance) a most outspoken arrogance toward other people. Realizing that it was not possible for him to make his outings into the city without being spotted by the Chief of the Neighborhood Association, Tong-hun stopped going out and like his father locked himself within the house.

"I hate the terrorist dictatorship. I cannot live a supervised life."

These words of her younger brother frightened Ogyop.

(I must get him out of Seoul, somehow...,) Ogyop thought.

She felt that she was responsible for his safety.

Carrying a hamjibak(large bowl), she walked over to the pile of rice sacks. She was about to prepare the first meal for their twenty lodgers without the help of either her mother or sister. Just then, however, she heard a voice call behind her back.

"Oh, isn't this our young mistress! How have you been these many days?"

It was the Old Woman, the person from whom Ogyop had never been separated from since her toddling days until this summer. Her dark-complexioned wrinkled face had tanned a great deal and she looked as if she had aged a number of years in the short interval during which they had not seen each other. Yet her face was beaming with joy at seeing Ogyop and she now came toward her young mistress with outstretched arms.

"Where's our manim(mistress)? And how is our nari(master), these days?"

Putting her hamjibak down, Ogyop held the Old Woman by both hands.

As of this day, the Old Woman was back with the family again. Since she was indispensible in preparing meals for the People's Army, the family did not need to hear criticism from others for keeping a servant.

Two days later, the Old Man, too, showed up. Yet he had become more stubborn than before. And the reason he came back to the house was merely that he wanted to check on his wife who had left saying she just had to go back to Seoul and see with her own eyes that the family were safe.

Once back, however, he seemed to feel that after all life in the city was less back-breaking than country life. Also, the Old Woman absolutely refused to leave the house once she felt that she had Ogyop's permission to stay.

It did not take long for the Old Man to find out about the self-confinement of Mr. Wu Taegap and Tong-hun. Maybe he was somewhat gratified by this discovery, maybe not. Anyway, he seemed glad that he had his fill of food and made himself useful enough by taking the food out to the sarangchae and unloading the foodstuffs from the truck when it came to the gate.

As for Ogyop, she went about her cooking meticulously and uncomplainingly now that she had help on her side. Looking at her work around the kitchen preparing food for the soldiers, nobody could detect any trace of fear or hate on her face or in her attitude.

(Maybe she would cook the food in just that way even if Kang Soku were the only person to feed. . . .)

Ihwa felt anger rise in her when she thought this. She was getting more and more fretful, merely wishing for the days to pass quickly. How long would these suffocating days continue. . . .

Finding no way of breaking out of the occupied zone, Ji-un went back and forth between Munsan and Seoul in extreme restlessness and despair. In time, he came to learn that market places where people gathered in great numbers were the safest spots for him. Even if he should run into any of 'them,' in one of these crowded places, he could fairly easily make his escape unless he were shot. And in any case it was not very likely that the people who might be interested in getting hold of him would be hovering about in the market places where there were only meager quantities of low-quality food. No, they would be too well-fed for that, thought Ji-un bitterly.

While mixing among the crowds, Ji-un sharpened his ears for any news or information. The citizens who were suffering from a severe shortage of food were fighting over a spoonful of grain and a single piece of summer squash. In one incident, an adult ate from a tray of rice cakes being sold by a very young child and then without paying the child for the rice cakes fled away. The child began wailing and, taking advantage of this commotion, another thief helped himself to the child's merchandise. When the adult, a woman of thirty some years, who had sent the child out to the market to sell the rice cakes, heard about this, she collapsed down on the ground looking inconsolably sad. And this was none other than one of those housewives whose daily occupation it had been until a short time ago to go to the market, with her basket dangling pleasantly from her arm, to pick up some nice things to cook for the family supper.

Attracted by the smell of cooked meat, people were gathered around a grill on which a layer of pulgogi pieces was cooking. Those who had money to spare paid one hundred hwan and partook of a piece of the meat. Almost none of them could afford more than a piece, and yet after swallowing down that single piece of the pulgogi, these people were tortured by a sense of guilt because of their family back home who could not have the luxury of eating a piece of cooked meat.

Was it going to be a communist world from now on? Was everything taken away overnight from the people in this city so that only what would newly germinate out of this devastated human domicile would belong to the dispossessed population?

It looked like a situation of utter hopelessness which every citizen ought to bemoan. And yet, amidst the overwhelming sense of despair felt by the whole city, there seemed to flicker a glimmer of hope and anticipation. Pyong-yang radio was daily reporting on the heroic exploits of the People's Army and yet somehow one could not help learning that the People's Army's southward progress did not break through the line between Chonan and Taejon.

And then one day a fleet of bombers were detected flying across the sky at a high altitude above the capital. Many citiz ens saw the bright silvery reflections these bombers scattered in the sunlight before they disappeared into the far sky. They were headed for the north, possibly for Pyong-yang!

Like many other people, Ji-un was squatting down on the ground of the market place looking up at these northbound bombers, hugging his knees with both arms. Although nobody spoke, it was clear that everybody was thinking the same thing. There was a faint smile of relief on the mouths of these people.

Just then, a young communist soldier—he was almost a boy —rode a bicycle into the market place honking noisily to make the crowd make way for him. Suddenly, he seemed to realiz e what it was that the people were so intently watching. Leaping off his bicycle, this boy soldier unslung the rifle from his shoulder. He aimed it at the distant target.

Next moment, the boy soldier's anti-aircraft shooting started making a great deal of deafening noise. Was this boy really thinking that he could, with his rifle, shoot down the B29 bombers that flew so high up that they were no more than silvery glints in the sun? The boy, however, gave up his grand A.A. attack after several shooting attempts. There was an expression of endless chagrine on his face as he glared up at the disappearing U.S. bombers. Ji-un, who had been watching this young communist soldier throughout his short-lived and fruitless military maneuver, smiled to himself with sadness and disbelief.

The boy mounted his bicycle again and rode away.

If only I had a short wave radio!, thought Ji-un. And I wish I had a safe place to stay....

Aside from the fact that the People's Army could not march beyond Taejon and that American B29 bombers had flown north, Ji-un had no way of knowing anything. It was, of course, the same for all the other old citizens of Seoul who had remained.

Yet even that much knowledge was a consolation and relief. And it was a good thing that this much was known to the general populace, thought Ji-un. The reason he was especially glad about this was that many of the original residents of the capital were joining up with the communists from a hasty conclusion that the communists were taking over the city for good.

(There will be more victims and sacrifices if this state of affairs continues)

Ji-un thought gloomily. The appearance of the bombers, therefore, had a special meaning for Ji-un.

The bombers came every day after that, at exactly the same hour. One day, they bombed an armory in Yongsan. Great damage was inflicted upon the inhabitants who lived near this spot and other citizens, too, suffered piteously because of the infernal explosions and smoke. This was all exceedingly painful and frightening, and yet the Seoulites definitely began to hope from this time on....

The occupying communists for their part were furiously proclaiming that the American imperialists were committing a savage and atrocious act of diplomatic interference. The strange thing was that despite the regular coming and going of these bombers, no visible change occurred in the political climate even after a spell of more than ten days of this aerial commuting. And the Pyong-yang broadcast merely announced minor damages inflicted by the American bombers and then went on to declare an unchanging resolution to march on southward.

Despair hung over the city once more.

And then one day, an abrupt policy to draft the Voluntary Soldiers was put through and a forcible mobilization of male citizens, especially the young, started.

Although it was called by a more amenable name, the new act was tantamount to arresting all male citizens except the very old and the children. The thoroughfares were completely blocked by check-points and so the citizens who had gone out to procure grain or those who were on their way to the market to obtain some eatables could not proceed to their destinations. And these men ended up by being captured and taken away by the Voluntary Army drafters even before they could find out what was happening to them.

At one spot a young boy who had been going home with his father carrying a small bundle of grain to help the parent was crying by the big sack of grain which his father had left there before being led away by the drafters.

The drafters came to people's houses at night and took boys and men away. Some of the eligible were caught in their hiding places away from home where they had come seeking a better refuge.

Nobody could be sure which places and which hours were the safest. In time, the streets became devoid of male pedestrians. Other than the communist soldiers, the 'enthusiasts' who were safe anywhere were the only male citizens who dared to be seen in the street. The rest of the male population hid away not only from the thoroughfares and streets but from the general view within their own houses. They hid themselves in such places as the hole between the roof and ceiling or some such secret recess elsewhere in their homes.

On the day when this mass arrest of the Voluntary Soldiers started, Ji-un was on his way from the city toward his temporary abode in Munsan.

As he looked from the entrance of the village, he noticed that a group of people were gathered outside the house where he was staying. One of the men was holding something which from afar looked like a notebook. Another man seemed to be shouting angrily about something. And then, Ji-un saw the 'uncle' gesticulating to the shouting man as if to say : 'Come inside and search for yourself.'

Without another minute of delay, Ji-un turned back and began to run. The village had become unsafe for him now. He went straight to a market place in the Fifth Avenue of Chongro.

The reason he chose this place rather than any other spot was that he had several days ago met one of the colleagues who had gone to the demilitarized zone with him at the onset of the war. This young man had told Ji-un on that day that he thought all the rest of the Youth Association members that had gone with them to the Thirty-Eighth Parallel that day were dead. This man himself had one bandaged arm slung on a strip of cloth wound around his neck. He was selling fried food in this market place.

"It's safest to be among the crowds. Besides, this camouflage is quite effective when you are being hunted by the lovers of the workingclass, you know," the man had said with a grin, urging Ji-un to eat some of his merchandise. And then as if in a soliloquy he had muttered.

"Bear up a while longer. Soon, the Allied Army will land at Inchon."

He seemed pretty confident about what he was saying.

"Where did you hear this? Is it from a reliable source?" asked Ji-un breathlessly.

"From a radio. Somebody who knew English heard this from an American broadcst on the short wave."

"So you didn't hear it personally. . . . " Ji-un had said sounding somewhat disappointed. And yet it was far better that he heard the news, or the rumour, than not hearing it at all.

"Well, you wait and see. They'll be here in three to four days. And why shouldn't they, I ask you!" The Youth Association staff turned fried food merchant had exclaimed without raising his voice.

Upon reaching the market place in question, Ji-un looked

all about for this man. He could not be found, however. Recognizing, instead, a middle-aged woman whom Ji-un had seen, that time, making and selling wheat cake patties sitting next to Ji-un's former colleague, he went up to her and asked her about his friend.

"Ah, you came to see that college boy?" the woman said unambiguously. And then she went on,

"They took him away yesterday. Those who came for the boy looked like students like him. Nowadays, you can't even trust your friends."

". . . ."

"It's no good running about at a time like this. You'd better go home and stay there. Unless, that is, you are safe to go where you like . . . ."

Saying this last part, the woman suddenly became wary in her expression.

(So he has been taken away. Probably they will shoot him. Or maybe he is dead already . . . .)

Ji-un seemed to see his one-time colleague's happy face as he was telling him about the prospective landing of the allied Army. Ji-un walked out of the market place feeling entirely dejected.

If all his colleagues that had gone to Euijongbu were really dead, Ji-un had no one else to look up now. Then suddenly, he remembered his college mate Haksu whose house was in Shindangdong. Last time Ji-un had seen him, Haksu was taking a home-rest to recuperate from tuberculosis. Ji-un was not sure at all that he could still find his friend at his old house in Shindangdong but he decided to give it a try.

It was Haksu's father who answered Ji-un's knock at their gate. The older man acknowledged Ji-un's bow with a noncommittal expression. Ji-un could tell that the older man's aloofness did not derive from his failure to recognize his son's friend but rather from his doubts as to how Ji-un stood in relation to the changed scheme of things.

"Is Haksu home? My name is Yun Ji-un. I would like to see

Haksu, if I may. . . . "

"You came to see our Haksu?" said the older man and then, still undecided, began pacing back and forth in front of his gate with both hands together behind his back.

At this moment, a middle-aged woman whom Ji-un recognized as Haksu's mother stepped out of the gate. She looked worried. Seeing the two men confronting each other in a strange wordless tension, she began to wring her hands in distress.

Ji-un felt extremely uncomfortable. So he broke the silence first,

"I am called Yun Ji-un. I and Haksu worked together at the Youth Association. Is he home?"

Saying these words, he was suddenly assailed by an uneasy feeling that perhaps Haksu had gone over to 'their' side.

Right at that moment, however, the pale outline of a face flitted across the other side of a small window by the entrance hall of this house. Ji-un saw that this face gave a quick smile as it recognized him through the glass. It was the face of Haksu's younger sister. Haksu had a way of telling a great many things about his friends to this sister and a great deal about his younger sister to his friends, especially to Ji-un. Ji-un and she, therefore, had shared a sense of closeness toward each other although they did not talk to each other very often. Now she walked out to the gate and greeted Ji-un warmly.

After Ji-un was led into the house, the front gate and the hall door were locked up tight again. Picking up a pair of men's white rubber shoes from under the wooden staircase, Haksu's mother put in their place a pair of women's jade-blue rubber shoes.

A minute later, a rustling noise was heard from above the ceiling at the top of the staircase and then Ji-un saw Haksu climbing down the stairs, his face sallow but smiling warmly.

"Hello, hello. . . . Am I glad to see you safe!" said Haksu.

"And I am glad to see you safe, too," said Ji-un meaning

every word he uttered.

"Entirely thanks to the most thorough surveillance network of my family, I might say," said Haksu somewhat self-consciously.

"You know the meaning of those rubber shoes? They are a signal. When the white rubber shoes are placed there, it means I should not move an inch. I mean I must stay up there as if I were sealed into it. But the blue rubber shoes are a signal for the 'all clear. It's my mother's idea."

Ji-un stayed at Haksu's house for two days. This meant that Haksu's family had to be doubly on their watch to keep the danger off. But this was not the foremost reason why Ji-un decided to leave the house. It was because of the ration of food at mealtimes that Ji-un could not impose himself on this house any longer. His eating one bowl of gruel meant a little less of it for each one of the family.

He said goodbye to them and walked out of their house. But he had nowhere else to go. He could not think of going to Ihwa's house. It was not only because of the communist soldiers lodged at the sarangchae of her house that Ji-un could not go there. Ji-un knew from his last visit that across the alleyway from Ihwa's house were the branch offices of the Youth Corps and the Women's League, one next to the other, and at the entrance to the alleyway was the People's Council office watching everybody coming in and going out of the alley. That Ihwa had been able to hold out without being dragged into some communist organization so far was due to the strategic position of her house vis-a-vis all these power-bases.

Ji-un headed for Munsan again, unable to think of anywhere else to go. On the way out to Munsan, however, Ji-un finally fell into the hands of the communists.

It was a long, long line of men young and old that was led to a building in Chunggu under the escort of People's Council officers. This unending human line grew even longer and bigger as more conscripted men and boys were added to it as the line kept on moving toward its temporary destination in central Seoul. After the head of the line reached the front gate of the building in question, the entire troop came to a slow halt after which only a limited number were made to enter the building at one time, forming a single line, while all the rest of the countless captured men were kept waiting outside.

Those who were ordered to enter the building saw a wide staircase in front of them which they were urged on to climb. Soldiers with bayonets were standing along this staircase so that nobody who once climbed up could climb down these stairs again.

(I must not go up those stairs,) Ji-un warned himself fiercely.

Upon reaching the first step of this staircase, therefore, Ji-un slid sideways slipping out of the line without being seen by the guard. The man who was walking right behind him raised his head and looked at Ji-un questioningly for a brief second but his worry-ridden face was turned away from Ji-un in the next second as the man continued to move on up the stairs following the line.

Ji-un stood around composedly. He had made sure that those men who were acting as guards in and outside of this building were ordinary-looking men without so much as an official badge. In short, these men looked no different from Ji-un himself.

As he stood by on one side of the staircase, the captured men kept on coming in through the front gate and climbed the stairs. By now, everybody seemed to be thinking that he was one of the guards.

Choosing the right moment, he walked rapidly up to the front gate. Then, saying suddenly, 'Move aside! Let me pass!' he pushed through the incoming line of people one hand raised to keep them from pushing him backwards. By and large, Ji-un was acting the part of a guard or a civilian officer trying to get through the incoming stream of human bodies in order to take care of some urgent business.

There was a second when one of the guards who were keeping watch over the inflowing line of men glared at Ji-un with bloodshot eyes. But he looked away instantly, his attention attracted by something else.

Under the circumstances it was not strange that these men did not have a very clear idea of who they were working with. The comrades, the organization staff, and the soldiers were very often unknown to one another. Everything was happening so fast that these men lacked the time to keep track of things such as one another's faces.

Ji-un walked about one hundred paces away from the building at a normal tempo. Then he broke into a run.

Luckily Ji-un was helped by a bombing that occurred right at that opportune moment. He did not doubt, however, that even if not been assisted by the bomb explosion in his escape he would have made it on his two feet alone.

It was a sultry and restless night. Ihwa woke up in the middle of the night. She was sleeping in the same room as Madam Shim and Ogyop and the door was securely locked. And yet, an indescribable fear and forlornness came over Ihwa, and also the rest of the female occupants of this room, every night. In the other back-room Mr. Wu Taegap and Tong-hun were sleeping together. Staring into the darkness of the small room, Ihwa thought about the communist soldiers that were occupying up the sarangchae. In her mind's eye, the squadron of northern soldiers in their sarangchae were sleeping in their uniforms and long leather boots, with even their thick belts still fastened around their waists. The soldiers were rolling about on the floor like so many of logs. Suddenly she felt a chill running down her spine and she turned in her bed as if to avoid the sight of the soldiers.

Soon her eyes became more used to the darkness, and she saw that a milky lightness was penetrating through the paper screen door, accentuating the designs of the slender frame-sticks interspacing the rice paper. Maybe it was the moonlight veiled by a layer of cloud.

It was then that Ihwa heard a low sound from the direction

of the backyard. Instantly Ihwa felt that maybe somebody had leapt over the hedge. Ihwa's head began to spin. Who would have the daring to roam about the streets at this time of night while martial law was freezing the entire city? Ihwa listened intently. There was no more sound from the backyard, now. But all of a sudden, Ihwa saw the silhouette of the upper half of a tall and bushy-haired man's figure reflected on her screen door. Hardly able to breathe, Ihwa stayed completely immobile.

For a few seconds, the unknown man stood in front of the room without budging. Then he moved on in the direction of the front yard throwing his silhouette on the screen door now. Ihwa could hear his footsteps from inside the room. The man did not come back to her door again.

"Stop!"

It was only when five to seven minutes had passed since Ihwa first saw the silhouette of the man that somebody shouted this in a voice that rang out in the quiet of the night. In the next second, two shots were fired : Bang! Bang! The sound of the foot-steps of a man wearing leather shoes approached and then went away. Ogyop and Madam Shim were sitting up in their beds awakened by the sound of the gunshots.

"What's happened, daughter? Didn't the sound come right from out of our back yard?"

"I don't know anything, mother."

Deliberately, Ihwa maintained her silence and kept on lying in bed.

"I am sure it's nothing serious, mother. Go back to sleep."

"All right, I'll do that."

Still Madam Shim did not go back to sleep but kept sitting and mumbling to herself now and then. From the room where Mr. Wu Taegap and Tong-hun slept not one tiny sound escaped. They, too, must be awake, thought Ihwa. Her heart ached when she thought of how anxious her father and brother must be and how strongly they must long to find out what had happened.

When the day broke, the Old Man left the house to find out about last night's intruder. He came back with the report that a man had been shot dead outside the house.

"There's a hut of a house near Teh Dong-hoe with an ilgak gae (a small sized gate). The dead man's a son of that house. What a wicked criminal they have for a son! That a man should act so shamefully at a time like this!"

The Old Man had lately developed a habit of expressing his opinion on all things.

"You've said enough words, husband," said the Old Woman in a mildly reprimanding voice, and then asked, "But what did the boy steal anyway?"

"Can't a man talk without a wife interfering?" said the Old Man in a piqued tone, glaring at his wife discontentedly.

Getting up without a word, Ihwa went out, dragging somebody's rubber shoes that had been lying on the stone step.

Although there were already people moving up and down in the alleyway at the front of the house, it was still absolutely quiet at the back which was connected to the mountain. As Ihwa stood there near the hedge, the east began to turn to a rosy color. She saw the prostrate body of a tall bushy-haired man whose back and shoulders were turning pink under the first sunlight.

Looking a little closer, Ihwa noticed that from a small cloth sack that was underneath the man's chest, a little rice had spilled out on the ground. She saw, also, that about half the rice grains scattered in the grass were dyed red by the blood from his wound.

(It's Yong-a's father!) said Ihwa inwardly.

Yong-a was a small girl who was crippled by polio. Ihwa had seen her often enough playing by herself in the alley. She smiled at Ihwa, showing a dimple on her pretty face, when Ihwa passed by her. Maybe it was because the child was friendless that she took to Ihwa who was but a passer-by. Or maybe she just liked people . . . . Often, Ihwa saw this big-bodied man approach and lift the child up from the stone step on which she had been sitting swinging her good leg playfully.

(So it was rice he wanted. . . .) thought Ihwa, suddenly overcome by an overwhelming sense of horror and confusion. The image of Yong-a's thin crippled leg flitted across her mind.

People were coming toward the scene of the shooting. Ihwa saw that the Old Man was at the head of the crowd and was leading them. Behind the Old Man followed a woman with an unusually round face which was at the moment bleach-white from panic. Among those who were following the Old Man, Ihwa recognized several who were their neighbors. She turned back and walked back to the house.

"What a thing to do for one who has good years ahead of him yet!," said the Old Man who had been to the dead man's house to help carry the body. "If he was so hungry, why didn't he join the People's Army?"

Ogyop stared at the Old Man while he talked on. Sensing her disapproval of her husband's harangue, the Old Woman fidgeted uncomfortably with an apologetic expression on her face.

Several days passed after this and one day the round-faced woman who had walked behind the Old Man on the day of the shooting showed up at Ihwa's house. This woman said she wished to help prepare the meals for the People's Army soldiers. The reason she gave was that she could think of no other ways of feeding herself and her family.

"How can she think of such a thing after her husband was killed because of the rice stacked in this house?" Ihwa nearly shrieked from anger at the woman's lack of pride. But Ogyop merely turned to the Old Woman and said,

"She has to look after her husband's old parents. And her child is sick from lack of food. Let her work here."

The woman came to Ihwa's house as soon as the day broke and went back home in mid-morning carrying on her head a hamjibak with left-over foods from the soldiers' breakfast table. She did the same thing in the evening, also. She packed the hamjibak with food, covered it up carefully so that no-one could see the white lumps of cold cooked rice she was carrying in it. As she walked back home with the hamjibak on her head, one could see that her face looked almost happy.

While her mother worked at Ihwa's house, Young-a, who usually came with her mother, sat in some corner of the courtyard amusing herself with one thing or another. Ihwa had to make sure that the child did not resemble her mother in any of her features before she could pick up the child in her arms. She carried the child to the toemmaru and played with her for a while.

Aside from the incident of the shooting, the neighborhood was tense because of the drafting of Voluntary Soldiers. The Chief of the Neighborhood Association who had once been such a meek-tempered shopkeeper now ransacked the houses at the head of the drafters.

No drafter came to Ihwa's house, however, nor did any visitor came to give this family the current news of the outside world. Yet, by and by, whatever happened on the other side of the high wall of the house came to be known to the insiders as well and Ihwa's family determined once more that they would hide Tong-hun all the more securely from now on.

The planes still flew across the sky everyday but no visible change was taking place in the capital. And then, one day there was a clamour of bombs exploding which continued for about an hour. Suddenly the Ihwa's family heard a voice calling from out in the courtyard,

"Mother! Mother! Where are you, mother?"

It was an unfamiliar male voice. Madam Shim opened the sliding door a crack and peeped out. It would have been natural for this family to lose all composure on hearing such a call all of a sudden. But the benefit of playing the role of 'enthusiasts' was that the family was tolerably insured against contingencies in the outside world. Rather, the danger lay inside the high walls, within the People's Army quarters, or in the inimical personality of Kang Soku.

Even so, Madam Shim could not bring herself to open the door wider than an inch or so. Putting her face against this aperture, she asked in a voice which sounded as weak as the chirping of an insect,

"Who's calling?"

Then, she seemed to recognize the caller. She said in a more natural voice.

"You're Unbo, aren't you?"

She now opened the door wide, relaxing.

The visitor was the son of the Old Woman. He had lived in this house for several years when a child, and after being sent to the Old Woman's parental house in the provinces to grow up there, he paid his visits on special occasions such as New Year's. He was now old enough to marry and had a strong big farmer's body like his father, the Old Man.

"I am glad you came, Unbo. I'll call your mother. Halmom (old woman)! But you must sit down. Why don't you sit on that toemmaru for a bit. . . . "

Madam Shim knew that she was supposed to use the affix 'comrade' when calling anybody, not only the Old Woman but also the crippled girl's mother who came to help with the meals. But Madam Shim could never utter the word no matter what. Since Ogyop expressly forbade her to call the servants by their old appellations, Madam Shim had kept herself from calling them altogether. The sudden appearance of Unbo before her eyes, however, made her forget about her precautions. Madam Shim was always happy to see healthy and strong young men. So she talked to the young visitor again in a familiar tone,

"So, how is life in the country these days?"

Unbo was in no mood for socializing, however, let alone playing the part of a subordinate. He had not even made the customary bow to the older woman, nor had he made any move to go and sit down on the toemmaru as Madam Shim had urged. Instead, he muttered a sentence which had nothing to do with the question Madam Shim asked.

"Looks like my father's not around, either."

Still unoffended, Madam Shim said,

"I'm sure he isn't far off. Sit down a bit on that toemmaru."

"Yangban fiddlesticks! Some people just won't admit it's a different world now," mumbled the gruff young man as if to somebody else hovering up in a far sky. Just then, there came the voice of the Old Woman.

"Oh, it's you? Have you offered your bow to manim?"

The Old Woman was coming from the backyard carrying a basketful of green vegetables which she had washed at the well.

Ignoring her words completely, Unbo said angrily,

"What do you think you're doing in this place? Is a servant always a servant and a slave forever a slave, do you think? Let's go home!"

"What's gotten into you, son? Come over here. I will take you to my quarters," said the Old Woman, not a little dismayed at her son's erratic behaviour.

"I say let's go. How could you let them turn you into a servant all over again? Didn't you say you would come right back? Devil take your. . . ."

"No, son, it's not like that. And over there are Comrade soldiers, you see. So, you behave now, or. . . ."

"Or what, mother? Oh, you really make me laugh, ha, ha, ha. . . ."

Then Unbo stopped laughing and snapped,

"It's not us that need to be afraid, mother. How can you be such a fool?"

Madam Shim shut the door. There was fear in her eyes. Now one could hear the voice of the Old Man, too, mixed with the voices of the mother and son coming from the courtyard. After a while, the trio seemed to be retreating to the old couple's quarters. Before they made their exit from the earshot of those listening in the room, the Old Man could be heard saying in a voice which had a tinge of malice, 'You have a point there, son. . . .'

A while later, the Old Woman came to Madam Shim along with her son.

"He says he would like to greet manim before he goes. He is just a boy with no thought in his head and. . . ."

The Old Woman winced at a sharp glance from her son but continued,

"It seems, manim, that this boy became a member of the Youth Corps or some such thing. And I told him that this house, too, is in a way close to people like that. I made my boy understand."

"I am sure you did," said Madam Shim vaguely.

Unbo was still glaring at Madam Shim with eyes cold with hate which made her very uneasy.

"I hear you've set your wedding day, but I believe it's difficult to go through with it now. Of course, there's no reason why a person should postpone his or her marriage just because. . . ." Madam Shim went on listlessly hoping in her mind for Unbo to say something that would ease her disturbed mind. But Unbo had no such intention. He looked away without answering, with his chin insolently tilted up.

"How can we think of a wedding when the world's turned upside down like this? When will it be like it used to be, I wonder...," said the Old Woman in the apparently deliberate tone of an innocent imbecile.

"In case you do have your wedding," said Madam Shim getting up and going to an adjacent room, "I have something I want to give you, although jewelry seems to be no use nowadays."

Madam Shim pushed aside her sewing case to one side of the shelf and reached for another basket that she had hidden at the back. Taking this basket down, she fumbled among balls of old socks and finally pulled out a small jar.

Carrying this jar in which she had hidden some rings and buttons, Madam Shim walked back to the other room. Unbo's words and attitude had finally convinced her that valuables such as these had truly become useless now.

"Let's find something to give the bride although it may mean nothing to her. . . ." So saying, Madam Shim picked out a ring inlaid with a pearl.

"I think pearl will be nice for a young bride. And I will give her this golden button. This is the peach-shape button. . . ."

Placing the ring and the button on her small white palm, Madam Shim smiled guilelessly, like a child. The milky smooth touch of the pearl with its faint iridescence of pink and blue next to the soberer beauty of the golden button was so pleasant to look at that Madam Shim could not help feeling joy no matter how worthless they were to the eyes of others.

Luckily, Unbo stretched out a hand and let Madam Shim put the ring and the button in it. He wrapped them in a handkerchief, taking his time, and then put them in the pocket of his cotton trousers.

"Goodbye, then," he said getting up to go.

"Goodbye. And come again soon. I know you would like to look in on your mother," said Madam Shim, somewhat relaxing now.

"Oh, oh, this is too much. . . ." stuttered the Old Woman who seemed too confused and distressed by everything that was taking place before her eyes to thank Madam Shim for her over-generous gift.

Unbo, who was taking all the time in the world, halted altogether when he reached the middle of the taechong. Then, turning back, he said,

"Can you spare one more ring with a red stone?"

Although this rather surprised Madam Shim, she quickly gave a smile and said,

"I certainly can, that is, if I can find a suitable one. . . ."

There was a platinum ring inlaid with a pea-size ruby. Since Madam Shim did not care for ornaments that were too colorful, she had hardly worn this ring. But as she remembered, it was a fairly expensive item in its time. She now handed it to Unbo with no hesitation or regret because. . . . didn't everybody say these things were worth not a penny these days. . . .

Later, Madam Shim told her daughters about this, adding, "Wonder where he learned about such things. . . . Can you spare a ring with a red stone, he said. . . . Amazing..."

But the daughters remained silent. Only Ihwa said inwardly, (This is what is meant by casting pearls before swine)

A young man wearing the badge of a medical college walked into the courtyard of Ihwa's house where there was a great commotion. Just as on any other day during this period, the communist soldiers were walking in and out of it incessantly, and there were large baskets of washed rice and vegetables lying about while Yong-a's mother and the Old Woman sca mpered around between these obstacles. After entering the courtyard, the medical student glanced in different directions as if he were looking for someone in particular. Then, spotting Ogyop who was looking out of the kitchen, he went toward her and asked in a low voice,

"Are you called Ihwa?"

"No, I'm not. But... who are you, if I may ask?"

The young medical student did not answer this question but said, instead,

"I'd like to see her if it's at all possible."

Seeing that Ogyop was hesitant, he added,

"I've come on an errand from someone. I have something to convey to her."

"Let me give it to her. I am her sister," said Ogyop quickly in a muffled voice.

Kang Soku was standing on one side of the courtyard sho-oting his slant-eyed cruel glare at the two young people. No, it was definitely not a good idea to call Ihwa out to the scen-e. . . .

"I see. Then. . . ."

But the young medical student, too, seemed aware of Kang Soku's ferocious stare. Making what looked like a spontaneous turn toward the communist officer, the young medical student walked up to him.

"So how's everything around here?" he said in a bold familiar tone, giving a broad smile.

Kang Soku merely twitched his lips once. He seemed to be one of those men who came into the world solely to hate. There was no room in his face for other people's good will or warm feeling to enter. No wonder, then, that he was completely impervious to the friendly greeting of an unknown young man of the enemy land which could well be false affability or the prologue to some intrigue. . . .

The young medical student, however, did not seem to mind Kang Soku's cold derisive response to his display of friendly feeling.

"You know, we got hold of some penicillin. What a lark!" said the medical student peeping into the soldiers' quarters with an air of camaraderie. Kang Soku was looking the other over from head to foot with suspicion. Yet, the mention of penicillin seemed to provoke his curiosity.

"Where's your clinic? He asked and then drew a couple of quick circles in the air with his leather whip from which he never seemed to be parted.

The young gave him some place name and number.

Just then, a captain who had a black wart on his left cheek walked into the courtyard. He was an exception among the soldiers lodging in Ihwa's sarangchae in that he alone looked somewhat human, unlike all the others who shared the common traits of being expressionless and impervious to communication. Maybe it was only the endearing black wart on one cheek that was making this man the sole exception.

When he saw Ogyop, he turned around self-consciously to face Kang Soku so that only his back was shown to Ogyop. While the captain and Kang Soku talked with each other, the young man from the 'clinic' stood with them at such ease that anybody would have thought he was their own man.

After the captain and Kang Soku disappeared into the sarangchae, the young medical student handed a folded note to Ogyop. He smiled to Ogyop once more and then went away.

Upon reading the note, Ihwa asked,

"Is the man who brought this gone?"

Her tone of voice showed that she was ready to run after him.

"He's gone. Should I have let you meet him?"

"No, that's not it. But... look at this!"

So saying, Ihwa broke into a sob covering her face with both hands. Then, her face became full of smiles in an instant and she said.

"Ji-un's alive! And I've been almost sure that he'd died. . . . "

The note was from Ji-un who wrote that he missed her and wanted her to come to see him at her convenience. There was a map showing how she should find the place, which seemed to be a three-story building at the back of the Capital Theatre.

Ogyop was happy for her sister whom she watched with her serene quiet smile. . . .

"I must go. But what shall I wear?" said Ihwa with agitation in her voice and movements.

After escaping from the building which was the Municipal District Office of Chunggu, Ji-un kept on walking for a long while. He wanted to remove himself as far from the dreaded area as possible and quickly, too. But where could he go?

The drafting was still going on at various spots in the thoroughfare so that Ji-un had to pick back streets and alleyways as he kept on walking toward a destination which did not exist. He had to find a place to hide in before sunset and before the curfew, but where?

Exhausted, he sat down on the stone steps by the road and wiped the sweat off his face. Suddenly a deep quiet sorrow which was incongruous with the urgency and violence of the circumstances surrounding Ji-un swelled up, as it were, from the bottom of his being. Biting his lips, Ji-un sat immobile, his eyes fixed on the white paved road.

Somebody was climbing the stone steps where Ji-un was sitting. Then about half way up the steps, this person halted and came back down.

"So we meet again. Do you recognize me?" said the person in a coarse but friendly voice.

Rolling his eyes upward slowly, Ji-un looked at the speaker who was standing in front of him. Then, he sprang up like a bolt grabbing the man's hand.

"You did me such a great favour that time. Thank you very much again. I see that you are still keeping yourself busy with work," said Ji-un eyeing the armband the man was wearing on one sleeve on which was written : Red Cross Relief Force. Hearing this, the man smiled good-naturedly, saying,

"A mere safety provision, you might call it." Then, he continued, "Are you in a hurry? Won't you come in with me for this is where I live."

He pointed at a gloomy red-brick building which bore the sign of a private clinic.

"No, I am not in a hurry, but. . . ." Ji-un could not find the right words to utter. He was merely overcome by such sadness and desolation as could not be put into words.

The person who had lent Ji-un his white gown on the grassy slope in the university campus site in early summer was now stalking ahead of him, pushing open the front door of the clinic. Inside were the consultation and waiting rooms at the entrances of which was a mixed crowd of soldiers and civilians with minor injuries. A nurse was scurrying along the corridor.

The medical student led Ji-un up the stairs to a room on the third floor and opened the door. The inside where there was nothing but an iron-frame bed and two chairs looked like one of the recuperation rooms of this clinic.

"This is where I lodge for the time being," said the medical student. "Take a seat." Then, in a more formal tone, he said again,

"My name is Pak Sanggyu. I'm in my second year at the College of Medicine. You are Mr. Yun Ji-un of the Student Association, are you not? I did not recognize you then because everything happened so unexpectedly. But watching you walk down the slope, I remembered. I heard you deliver a speech at the college entrance ceremony and also last summer."

"Well, I am glad to meet a fellow alumnus, then. Since I became a fugitive, I haven't been able to see any of my associates at school and it's been very hard to bear. . . ."

"Is it all right for you to roam about like this, though? I bet any Seoul National University student who has kept up with student political activities to any extent will recognize you right away."

"I ought to have crossed the Han River. I went to the riverside that day but it was too late."

Ji-un smiled bitterly recollecting the scene on the grass-covered slope where he had begged to borrow this man's white gown. Pak Sanggyu, too, smiled shaking his head mildly as if in sympathy.

"I would like to remind you earnestly that there's a lot of danger for you here in this city. We medical students can perhaps hope to get through unharmed by keeping ourselves busy with bandages and ointments, but not you or any other rightist political science students. You know your colleagues Chang-ik and Kohun? Do you know how they died? They were shot down in front of the Capitol Building. They were passing by trying to shade their faces with their hands or maybe with a handkerchief. But they were spotted by Kim Oshik, of all people, and. . . ."

"Did Kim Oshik shoot them?" asked Ji-un in a sinister voice.

"It's certain that Kohun was killed by a bullet fired by Kim Oshik. But about Chang-ik, there's a rumor that he was killed by 'their' submachine-gun."

There was a silence between them for a few seconds. Then, Sanggyu glimpsing the other's grief-distracted profile with pitying eyes said,

"I am sure they won't last long."

The explosive vibration coming from planes flying at a high altitude made the panes of the window clatter. It was the hour when the planes normally returned from their northward flight.

"If only the ones flying those planes were not so slow-motioned!" said Sanggyu somewhat plaintively, turning his face toward the sound.

"But if they hadn't made any move at all̃ I mean the Allied Forces could have stalled longer on the pretext of discretion, you know̃ if so, where would we have been? I am, therefore, exceedingly grateful to these slow-motioned allies of ours. At least they are now taking some action which the North Koreans cannot have taken into account. But I think I had better move on, now, before the curfew. It's been very nice to meet you today," said Ji-un raising himself and picking up his straw hat.

"Which way are you going?" asked Sanggyu.

Ji-un did not know how to answer the other. After fumbling for likely words to utter, Ji-un ended up by emitting an awkward laugh.

"I don't really know," he said, finally.

Sanggyu semed to guess the situation and tried to persuade Ji-un to stay.

"You know 'they' (Sanggyu seemed to have a special taste for referring to the communists only in this indirect way) are swarming in the building nextdoor and come here to this clinic at all times, too. But to tell you the truth, a place such as this is actually one of the safest hide-outs at a time like this. 'They' can't tell us one from another in a place like this. And the People's Council and so on which are usually the greatest threats to people like you have little call for sending their agents here, you see."

Sanggyu explained to Ji-un that his father who was a medical practitioner and his older brother who was just graduated from the college of medicine were taking the burden of treating the wounded soldiers and civilians in the heat of mid-summer while he, Pak Sanggyu, was having it relatively easy moving back and forward thanks to the protection of the armband (he pointed at his armband) under the unofficial title of the 'communications man'. "I go to school, friends' houses, and other places. There's almost no place I can't go. So, you can let me do all your errands, too. As for you, however, don't ever go out of here."

Then he said apologetically that the food one could get at the hospital was quite uneatable.

Ji-un thanked him for everything. If he had not run into Sanggyu, he was not sure how much longer his will to live through this difficult time could have held out. He felt that he had come almost to his wit's end where he could only look down into a bottomless pit of despair.

Going inside the family's living quarters at the back of the clinic, Sanggyu brought out a number of things Ji-un might need. He then gave directions to Ji-un concerning even minute points so as to make Ji-un's stay there as comfortable and safe as possible. Ji-un thanked him inwardly with a sincere appreciation of his kind-heartedness. Contrary to the impression he gave of being carefree and easy-going, this man was a superbly careful and efficient thinker. Thus began Ji-un's life at the clinic. Since the patients were hospitalized in rooms on the second floor and the third floor was taken up mostly by the kitchen and a couple of compartments which were used partly as storage and only partially occupied by people, Ji-un did not need to worry too much about being found out. Yet, there was a need for him to be ready to act as one of the patients if the occasion should call for it. Part of what Sanggyu brought from the inner living quarters of this building were props Ji-un would need to play the part of a patient who was hospitalized there.

Ihwa made outings twice a day. Every time, she carried a carefully prepared lunch box hidden in a basket made of split bamboo.

"So this is what they mean by 'being on the enemy's payroll,'" joked Ji-un sitting up and opening the lunch box. At times, Sanggyu joined Ji-un in disposing of what the latter procured by 'being on the enemy's payroll.' Ihwa made a detour through the market street after leaving her home in

Pildong to go to the clinic. Often she looked back to see if she was being followed by Sukja or Kim Oshik. At times, too, she deliberately took narrow alleyways to get to the clinic. There was always complete confusion in the market place which Ihwa usually crossed on her way to and from the hospital. The merchants were mostly those citizens who were too poor to eat the food they had obtained with a great deal of difficulty. These people, therefore, were selling what they themselves needed to keep alive. Ordinary housewives turned overnight into merchants and peddlers, and children, too, helped the adults in these newly-ventured enterprises. They seemed to have forgotten their immediate past when their sole daily concern was being educated to be good children. Now they were no different from real orphans and beggars for whom the existential fight at the market place was a most natural occupation.

"Sweet beans! Sweet beans!"

"Saccharin! Genuine Saccharin!"

The children sang out as they stood along the passages within the market place with their tin containers or square wooden trays hanging from a strap round their necks.

Saccharin was very popular those days because sugar was next to non-existent.

Sitting behind the row of children were adults who were selling thin gruel or noodles although nobody could tell from exactly what base material they had been made. The customers peered to find out which merchant's bowl of gruel or noodles contained the bigger portion of nourishment before they sat down in front of the merchant of their choice to partake of their alimentary merchandise. The women who came out with their trays of food to sell kept their hardened expressions even while they served the customers because their minds were laden with worries and anxiety for their husbands and sons whom they had left at home hidden away in the ceiling or some hole under the floor.

A woman walked up in the direction of Ihwa. She had a

familiar face. Looking again, Ihwa recognized her as a student in the music department of her university. She had, until only a short time ago, been quite a famous campus figure partly because she had an excellent singing voice but also because she was pretty and glamorous with a very well-developed body. Also she was the subject of numerous juicy campus scandals which at times involved even the professors in her department. She was also an object of competition and envious gossip among the boys of the nearby universities.

She behaved as if she were the treasured daughter of some American millionaire, always expensively and fashionably dressed and adorned.

This young woman, Ihwa saw, was now coming toward her carrying a large wooden tray on her head. She was wearing a black mongdangchima (shorter-length skirt fit for a working woman) and white joksam and rubber shoes on her bare feet. Her hair, which seemed to have gotten long enough somehow, was plaited in two and done up around her forehead in the northwestern style. With one hand she was steadying the wooden tray on her head and Ihwa could see how the end of her sleeve was folded up in the manner of one who is in the habit of working with her hands. She seemed in a hurry. Without so much as looking aside, the one-time college primadonna passed by Ihwa looking straight ahead.

(So you follow the fashion even in the midst of all this) thought Ihwa with bitter admiration.

One could never find women with made-up faces in the Seoul streets nowadays. The only women with make-up were women soldiers in the People's Army.

At times, Ihwa ran into a troop of these women soldiers on her way to see Ji-un at the clinic. They filed out of the same alleyway in two rows at about the same hour.

These women soldiers were wearing dark-green jumper style skirts which came down to just above their knees. A pair of long black boots covered the rest of their legs and over their shoulders they were wearing black leather straps crosswise and around their waist was fastened a broad belt of the same leather as the boots and the straps. On the whole, their way of dressing, which Ihwa had reason to believe was influenced by the Russian style, was exotic and had its own charm. Their faces, however, destroyed any sense of harmony their attire might have managed to create.

The faces of the People's Army women soldiers were made up thickly with cosmetics in a most unbecoming way. No matter how friendly one felt toward these women, their facial make-up was sure to induce a sense of revulsion in the onlooker. Could it be that such western cosmetic commodities as Coty facial powder or lipsticks had been distributed among these women? Could it be that the North Korean government had repaid the patriotic service of these women whom they had so arduously educated and trained to be an exemplary advance guard force with these particular items looted from the war?

In any case, there was no doubt that these women soldiers occupied themselves very diligently with consuming their newly-acquired cosmetic materials. On their coarse sun-blackened faces, the white powder was smeared thickly (almost like thick white paint on a wall). The eyebrows drew black mountain peaks and the cheeks were painted the color of an apple. The troops of these women soldiers always smelled nice and fragrant.

Feeling disconsolate, Ihwa paused for a second and examined them. They looked about her own age. Ihwa thought how they had been of the same nationality as she was, using the same language and following the same ways and customs, only until some years ago. Yet, now that she looked at them, she felt that there could be nothing between her and these women that would tie them together.

Walking in rows, they threw uneasy awkward glances at Ihwa. Maybe they, too, were feeling how this woman they saw so near them was intrinsically different from them. The young woman with clear complexion and sparkling eyes was staring back at them with a proud and mildly pitying look. The daughters of the communist republic in their Slavic attire looked away as if to avoid beeing stared at by the alien female.

Why are they looking away, wondered Ihwa. Are they not trained to be as fierce and as cruel as they like? Isn't it bizarre that these women who have painted their faces all over with cosmetics looted from the slaughter grounds called the war are acting as if they, too, know how to feel awkward, and even ashamed?

At times, too, Ihwa came across two or three dozen boy soldiers marching in line. These always looked straight ahead, never turning their eyes to look at the young woman walking on the sidewalk. The sight of a woman seemed rather to make their facial muscles more rigid and their eyes all the more immovably fixed on the head of the soldier walking in front.

To eyes that were used to the easy carefree manners of American soldiers who would smile, wave a hand, wink, or even call out a greeting as they passed by in irregular step, the tense, awkward behaviour of these boy soldiers looked somewhat facetious. Yet their rigidity had, none the less, an admirable quality to it. It was apparent that these young soldiers had been strictly trained to behave themselves when they marched down to Seoul(to liberate their compatriots from the monstrous exploitation of the English and American imperialists).

Looking at these young soldiers, Ihwa thought of Tonggeun and Tong-hun and she felt like crying.

Boys are (even in free societies) bound to walk more or less along the line drawn out by grownups. They are obedient like lambs and their hearts are filled with untainted passion. Gradually, however, they learn to think for themselves. Just as Tong-hun is finding out by himself that nothing is worth giving up liberty for, Ihwa said to herself inwardly. 'And just as Tonggeun chose the road of risk and adventure all by himself'

Yet, these boys from the north who were under-nourished,

small-boned, emaciated, and cheerless were destined to walk only the road mapped out for them. If any of them should begin to think independently for himself, he would surely be severely punished for it. The faculty of original thinking was a thing that had been totally removed from them so that they would perform their given roles unthinkingly and efficiently as if they were parts of a machine. They were trained to obliterate any human propensities that were not necessary to perform their socially-given functions.

(I want to live like a human being. I want all people, all boys to live like human beings...) Ihwa thought as she walked on without hurrying.

As the bombers flew across the sky of the capital more and more frequently, it became increasingly difficult for Ihwa to take food to the clinic for Ji-un. One trip to him often took nearly half a day. It was a rule during these days for the air-raid alarm to go off just as Ihwa had passed the entrance of the alleyway from which the women soldiers marched out. Although nobody looked at watches or clocks, one knew that these alarms were as punctual as timepieces.

The soldier who kept order in this section of the streets blew his whistle as soon as the air-raid alarms went off to make the pedestrians halt and seek shelter under the overhanging eaves of the houses by the road. His attitude, Ihwa noticed, grew more blunt and edgy daily.

In the beginning, however, this man whom Ihwa judged to be a military-policeman(from the green uniform he was wearing which looked like the horse-riding oufit conspicuously different from the uniforms of ordinary soldiers) was friendly and polite enough in his manner of speaking and behaviour. He would then say, "Comrade, come this way. It's dangerous here. Please hurry."

To older people and children, moreover, these guardians of order were especially considerate in marked contrast to the policemen of the Republic of Korea who thought nothing of gruffly hollering to the passers-by, 'Hay, you!,' 'Get out of here!' or some other such unceremonious words. Yet lately, the People's Republic military-policemen, too, had become less friendly and more impatient than before. One noticed sometimes that their blood-shot tired eyes had a murderous glint in them. Blowing their whistles harshly, they shouted, 'You, comrade, move away! Hurry up!"

The only difference between the attitude of these military -policemen and the Republic of Korea policemen was that the former still used honorifics in their speech. Except for this one point, they had become very much like the previous unceremonious traffic officers of the capital.

"The adopted manners don't last long. Of course, you can't call their way of speaking and behaving only a pretence. I admit they may have some genuinely good points. So maybe they are acting this way now because their self-esteem has been shattered by their failure to march down to Pusan 'at a run' as they boasted in the beginning," Ji-un had said when Ihwa told him about the change in the attitude of the People's Republic traffic officers' manners.

For those citizens who were obliged to take in shelter during the air-raid alarms, however, the increased visits of the bombers were not entirely bad news. Rather, they secretly waited for these bombers to appear and their hopes grew as the planes came oftener because it meant to them that the day of their deliverance from their present life of deprivation and bondage was not far away. The citizens standing in the shelter looked up at the sky without trying to hide their joy. The presence of the irascible military-policeman in his green riding outfit fretting nearby did nothing to stop their feeling buoyant. The bombers showed up punctually at the same hour and dropped their bombs on certain limited areas. When leaflets announcing the change in time or place were be dropped, the news spread in no time despite the terrifying pronouncement by the People's Army headquarters about punishing whoever picked up and read these leaflets or repeated what they read to others with instant death by shooting. Those residing in danger areas had to move out of their homes with their bundles of bare necessities leaving everything else behind. Bedridden patients and little children, too, were seen spending nights in the open. Yet none of them complained of discomfort during this period.

The contents of these leaflets sometimes turned out to be baseless. Yet, in a way, the very fact that false rumors could spread so widely within a short time was an added proof that people were craving for freedom and humanity even in the midst of the darkness and despair in which they lived.

"It is clear that they don't want to hurt the citizens. They are trying to fight only against 'them.'"

"They must have the belief that human lives are precious. That's where they are different from the ones that are here now."

People commented in this way on the selective methods of bombing the airplanes seemed to be following.

Ihwa felt as if she now knew only too well what it was that Ji-un had so passionately tried to explain to her about ideological questions. It was possible, of course, that people would come out with a number of different ways of looking at the same matter. For one theory to get the better of another, it would have to be built carefully and impregnably so that no other view could invalidate it. But to Ihwa at the present stage, no theory or explanation was necessary. Just as a human body knows by instinct what atmospheric composition and what level of temperature are most amenable to it, Ihwa knew what was the best thought for a human being to have and nurture. She knew it all now. No doubt communism with its efficient organization might be credited with a degree of rationality. Yet it was not of the sort that could served to help people get better as human beings. Ihwa sealed this precious realization in her heart.

Every time the explosion of bombs caused the windows in his temporary abode to clatter, Ji-un smiled with satisfaction.

"Our friends are slow in making a start. Think of the incident of Pearl Harbor! Their way is to take their time in approaching. But they will win out in the end," said Ji-un fondling Ihwa's hand, his gaunt face with its over-grown hair looking happy.

Ji-un never failed to finish the lunch box Ihwa brought him down to the last grain of rice.

"What an ugly arm this is!" said Ihwa poking at the plaster cast lying open on top of a small table at the head of Ji-un's bed. This was to be put on Ji-un's right arm and then to be slung on the sling hanging from Ji-un's neck in case of any sudden intrusion by outsiders. On the cast was smeared some tincture of iodine and some additional red coloring to simulate a blood-stain.

"Won't this bring you more trouble, though, if they findout?" asked Ihwa.

"Once I get caught, I will just have to go. At this stage, there's no such thing as my getting into more trouble or less trouble," said Ji-un grinning as if it were all a good joke.

"Don't talk like that," said Ihwa.

But what Ji-un said was true and they both knew it. They looked into each other's eyes which were shadowed with gloomy thoughts. Then they smiled and embraced.

One day, it took Ihwa several hours to come to the clinic carrying her usual lunch box. She had to stand in the shelter for a long time until the air-raid alarm was called off.

As usual, Ihwa went up the stairs and made a turn in the upstairs corridor to approach the room where Ji-un was. Just then, however, something that caught her eye made her heart thump and caused her to halt abruptly.

Ji-un's room was at the mid-point of this part of the corridor Unlike other rooms where one could see shoes lying about outside the door, the room Ji-un was using looked as if there were nobody inside. Its door was locked from inside at all hours so that Ihwa had to knock in a certain way to make Ji-un come and open the door for her. Even Sanggyu, who was doing the work of a doc on account of the great number of wounded that poured into the clinic, made a coughing sound or hummed a tune as a signal for Ji-un to open the door for him.

The reason Sanggyu and Ji-un were taking such strict precautions was that the former felt it too great a risk for Ji-un to be seen by those whom he referred to as 'those rascals in the next building' who some times came to the clinic, or by the patients hospitalized on the second floor.

That Ji-un's room had a deserted look, therefore, was not a surprise. On this particular day, however, Ihwa saw that a definite change had occurred to this room. For one thing, the room was locked on the outside with a padlock. And then a narrow, long table resembling a kitchen counter had been drawn up against the door blocking it lengthwise.

(What could have happened? Where has he gone?")

Ihwa ran down the stairs. Her heart beat so violently that she felt as if it would explode.

Sanggyu was sitting opposite two communist officers in the downstairs examination room. By shooting him an urgent glance, Ihwa made him turn his head toward her. He hurriedly came toward her and pulling her, not up the stairs, but in the opposite direction from the staircase, whispered into her ear,

"Go up by way of the kitchen. It's dark on those stairs. So be careful. Look for the room with the medicine chests. It's Room 201. Enter that room and knock on the door behind the white curtain. He'll open the door for you then. We had a little commotion last night," said Sanggyu hastily and gave a faint smile only then.

Following Sanggyu's direction, Ihwa climbed the dark staircase that led upstairs from the kitchen area. Her heart was still beating rapidly. As she finished climbing the stairs and stood on the second floor, she had a glimpse of a large room which she had noted to be always crowded with people now looking completely vacant. She sensed that something serious had happened last night.

Going into Room 201, she knocked at the door which was hidden by the curtain. The door clicked open and Ihwa saw that it was none other than Ji-un's original room.

"Ah, is that you?" said Ji-un in a strangely calm voice and smiling. Ihwa felt that despite his deliberate effort to appear calm, Ji-un had been waiting impatiently for her to come this morning.

"What happened last night? Did anyone come?" asked Ihwa breathlessly, taking his hand and putting it on her chest. Asking these questions made her tremble all over again, and therefore going back to the door hastily, she made sure that it was tightly locked.

"Yes, somebody came, the Great King of the Underworld. He came right up to my threshold," said Ji-un, laughing a little, and then continued, "I thought I would never be able to look at this pretty face again."

Ji-un held up Ihwa's chin in his fingers and gave it an affectionate shake.

"Tell me," said Ihwa pulling his hand down. "What happened? How could you escape getting caught?"

"Yes, my pretty, I will hand in my report. But I must ask you first, Ihwa. Wouldn't you think it a good riddance if I disappeared?"

"What are you saying?"

"I mean won't you in one corner of your mind feel relieved if I am no longer around?"

"Why should I?"

"Because you do not like me too well. You are being good to me now because this is an emergency period and I have become a helpless beggar. That's why you come to me with food and sympathy. But you can't help disliking me in part of your being. Isn't that so? Tell me honestly. Isn't it very difficult for you to love me entirely?"

His voice denoted that he was no longer joking good-humouredly. Ihwa saw that there was a film of shiny water over his eyes as he said these words and this realization made her feel suffocated.

(That's right. In one corner of my mind, I was frightened by you. That's why at times I fought to get away from your embraces. But it was not because I disliked you. I cannot tell you what it was.)

(I know. It was just that I did not want to show you my shortcomings. I was afraid that you might laugh at me. I felt that you thought more highly of me than I deserved. I dreaded being pushed down into the pit where I originally belonged. There's another thing. I feared physical contact. Maybe it was simple bashfulness because I had not been prepared for anything more than a kiss or a squeeze of a hand, just like a child. But you were always impatient. You oppressed me with your agressive urgency. And I rushed to escape from your approach even before I had time to think what I was doing. . . .)

Ihwa knew that she could bring out these explanations or excuses from her choking heart but she did not try to do so. For one thing, she felt that she was different now from how she had been in the past. Not that she was, as Ji-un implied, more inclined to be sympathetic toward Ji-un because of the plight he was in (Ihwa honestly thought it was too unjust of Ji-un to think so), but she was aware of the fact that her former fears, whether of being disgraced in her lover's eyes or of being desired physically by him, had virtually disappeared. She no longer felt any urge to show off her merits to Ji-un. And as to her réservedness about physical contact, she knew that she had become more mature in that respect over the past several months. These days, she often found herself caressing Ji-un on his head or neck and was quite submissive, too, toward Ji-un's violent embraces.

But why would Ji-un say such a thing at this stage of their intimate relationship, wondered Ihwa. He looked calm enough on the surface, but was he very restless inwardly?

"See, you can't answer my question," said Ji-un. But his tone had become playful again.

"All right, I will give my answer with this if you ask me that kind of a question again," said Ihwa picking up the plaster cast from the bed-side table and raising it as if to hit Ji-un with it. But she put down the cast immediately with a slight grimace at the unpleasant sensation her fingers felt at its touch.

"Yesterday, there was no time to put that on, even," said Ji-un. "I had just fallen asleep when I felt something terribly oppressive weighing down on me and woke up. They were there already, right outside the door."

Ihwa's face turned pale listening to Ji-un's account of last night's adventure. There was a soft knocking at the door through which Ihwa had entered. It was Sanggyu who walked over and took a seat beside the two lovers.

"Were you very surprised?" Sanggyu asked Ihwa with a smile.

The story Ihwa gathered from both of them was that a little after midnight three communist soldiers and a number of Youth Corps members had come to search the clinic. They had started ransacking the second floor rooms first. By the time Sanggyu and the other staff of the clinic had come upstairs, the doors of the second-floor rooms were all flung open.

Although Sanggyu was worried sick on account of Ji-un, he did not dare to go up to his floor for fear of attracting unnecessary attention. Maybe they will go away after searching just the second floor rooms, thought Sanggyu hopefully.

"The third floor? We don't have any patients up there," Lee the pharmacist was saying to the searchers at the foot of the staircase leading to the third floor. As if this explanation prompted them to make up their mind, the soldiers and the Youth Corps men started climbing the stairs to the next floor.

Sanggyu threw a surreptitious glance at Ji-un's door. Then he pretended to walk past that door to go somewhere else in the same direction and, in passing the door, put a padlock which he had prepared in advance on its outside latch. He had thought up this device after he saw on the second floor a patient who had a real wound in one arm being dragged out. The padlock was still swinging slightly when the men put their flashlight up to Ji-un's door.

"The room's unoccupied," said Sanggyu moving on ahead of the others. It was as much risk as he could take. Cold sweat ran down his back as he confirmed that the searchers were still lingering in front of the door. The yellow disk of the flashlight was flitting up and down the door bruskly. One of the group took a step onward. As if this were a signal, the rest of them began to move leaving Ji-un's door behind. The search ended up with the men taking all the patients away with them under the pretext of 'checking up.'

"There were very sick patients among them, too. Dr. Kim went over to see what's up but hasn't come back yet. I wonder what's keeping him...," said Sanggyu who was wearing an armband with 'Liaison Officer' printed on it instead of the usual red-cross armband on his short sleeve. Straightening the armband around his shirt sleeve so that one could easily read the words 'Liaison Officer,' Sanggyu went over to the window and looked out as if to take in the general situation before going out.

A dull metallic sound reverberated from afar. And then there was the explosion. Ihwa remembered the reason why it had taken so long for her to get to the clinic this afternoon. Pulling out the lunchbox from the basket, she said,

"You must be hungry, aren't you? I was held up near here. We were chased back to the shelter by another alarm as soon as we stepped out of it. I didn't know it was this late, though. Are you cross with me? I heard from somebody that people are apt to fall into ill humour when hungry. Do you think that's right?" said Ihwa.

"That sounds plausible," said Ji-un in a deliberately sober tone.

"Where's your other armband?" Ihwa asked Sanggyu, propping her elbow on the windowsill and ignoring Ji-un's intention to tease her.

"I lent it to a man who lives nextdoor to us."

"Is he a doctor?"

"No, he just borrowed it to use as a free pass, you know," said Sanggyu laughing a little "And this I found in our storage house the other day. I wore this at a school athletic meet when

I was a boy."

"Won't somebody catch you out, walking around with a fake armband like that?"

"I don't think so. Everybody's thrown together in any old way these days and nobody knows who he's working with or what anybody's wearing around his arm, for that matter."

Suddenly the window panes shook violently as if about to shatter and a deafening explosion ensued.

"That was a good one!" exclaimed Ji-un with the hand holding his chopsticks arrested midway to his mouth.

"Don't say such a thing. People may hear," said Ihwa in a frightened voice.

Sanggyu told the other two about the radio broadcast he said he had heard early that morning in the roof-top storeroom of the clinic building, under the cover of blankets for safety.

"It seems both sides are meeting in a very heavy battle somewhere. The report these boys here are making about destroying a whole division and capturing the division commander alive does not seem far from the fact. If the National Army failed in Taejon and again in Kimchon, I don't know how the tables are going to be turned," said Sanggyu in a voice which was serious for a change.

It was true that people were whispering the rumour that the Allied Army was scheduled to land in Inchon within a few days, but there was no way of knowing if there was any foundation to this hearsay.

"In any case, it's best to be cautious. I think it would be better if you didn't run around the streets the way you do," said Ji-un turning to Sanggyu.

"I think so, too. But, how can I just sit and do nothing? I must scurry around and find out when these sonofabitches will be wiped out. As a matter of fact, I think I will go right away and try to see Professor Han, at least," said Sanggyu and went down showing clearly that he was not going to follow Ji-un's advice, after all. Together, Ji-un and Ihwa talked about Professor Han for quite a lengthy while.

Professor Han who taught political science at the National University roamed about the streets all day long fearing that he would be more likely to be caught if he stayed home. Since he was almost at retirement age, it was not to send him to the Voluntary Army that the communists would be coming for him. But they were looking for him to arraign him as a subversive element. He carried a sheet of newspaper with him and when he felt too tired to walk he spread out the sheet of newspaper on a stone step or on the ground and sat down on it. He was educated in America and therefore was fluent in English so that he could understand the English broadcast he caught on the wireless. Thus he had made himself a reliable source of information during this dark time of confusion and bewilderment. According to Sanggyu, however, this man of science and talent had gone through some sort of metamorphosis (or maybe it was simply a somewhat colorful manifestation of his senility) and was now talking about nothing but Mt. Kyeryong and Chonggamrok (a popular book of apocalypse). This was very disheartening for Sanggyu who could no longer expect to hear juicy news from the professor even if he should have the luck of running into him in some market place. He was the first one in the academic circle to find out and spread the news that General McArthur had taken command of the Allied Forces. Yet for reasons that were not clear (maybe he was disappointed by the general's failure to bring about quick results, or maybe he decided not to fret over things which he could do nothing about), he began to lose interest in following the political events but increasingly immersed himself in the study of Chonggamrok (maybe he thought that it was a better way of passing time and forgetting hunger). Nobody knew his true motive for acting so strangely. Sanggyu came home exasperated every time he met this political science professor turned believer in Chonggamrok, but Ji-un was pleasantly diverted by what he heard about the professor.

As soon as the bombing stopped, Ihwa stood up to go home. "I am going to be very busy if I am to make another trip back and forth after going home this time."

"That's all right. I won't eat another meal today. So stay a while longer."

"No way! You must eat as much as you can and store up the energy."

"Because the rice comes free, you mean?" said Ji-un and the two laughed together merrily.

"I don't want you to walk the streets by yourself so much. I abhor the idea, actually."

"It's because you haven't been out in the streets lately and so don't know what it's like. The streets these days are filled with women. You don't see men any more, least of all young men."

"What about the People's Army heroes? I bet they stare at you all the time."

"What a childlike thing to say!"

"I don't care. I just don't like it."

Ihwa stretched out her arms and smoothed out the wrinkles on Ji-un-s grimacing forehead with the tips of her two hands and then she left his room to go home.

Days went by with a great deal of noise yet bringing little progress. Air-raids continued but without bringing about any new prospect in the political situation. A new rumour that the communists were planning to maintain the status through the winter circulated along with the conflicting rumour about the imminent Allied Forces' landing in Inchon.

If no reinforcements arrived until winter, most of the citiz ens would perish. Some would be taken away by the communists and others by their stooges. Some would die of hunger, others of air-raids. These thoughts and fears were enough to drive the citizens into extreme bad temper. Yet, it was only toward the airplane that they could vent their ill feelings.

"Good-for-nothing noise-makers! What do they do except splitting our ears, I say!"

If no change occurs, what would those who were hiding under the floor or up in the ceiling do?

Yong-a's mother who kept coming to Ihwa's house to prepare meals for the soldiers said one day,

"We have Yang Su-il up in our ceiling."

She laughed heartily after saying this. Then she offered the explanation that Yang Su-il was the name of her nextdoor neighbor. Although Ogyop told her not to talk about such a matter in a loud voice, the woman merely chuckled as if it were only a very amusing story. She said,

"I thought a cat had gone into our ceiling, you know."

It was not just this one man but countless heads of families and sons who were hiding under a floor or under the roof, half suffocated.

Shouldering a heavy rifle, Tonggeun trudged along the path at the foot of a mountain. The smell of grass made his nostrils tingle and above him he saw bright blue sky through the fragrant pine needles.

It was pleasant to walk on in this way. All about him were boys of his age group many of whom were actually his school friends, walking in a cheerful mood. It was true that some of the group walked in silence and looked sullen. The majority, however, were full of high spirits. At the head of the line walked a couple of People's Army officers and it was apparent that a similar number would be following at the tail.

The group spent two days in an elementary school building in the suburbs of Seoul before marching out in a row early that morning. None of them knew where they were going nor was there any need for them to know. Rifles had been handed out to those who declared that they knew how to shoot a gun (they constituted half of the present group which consisted of approximately two-hundred boys). The rest were made to carry wooden cases, two men to a case, or to carry a club or a sharpened bamboo stick on their shoulder.

During the two-day camp at the elementary school playground, the group had had a number of training sessions.

The Comrade Officer who had a narrow face and some education addressed the boys in these words:

"Courageous and Patriotic Comrades! I believe you all know how atrocious the western imperialists are. Yet, Rhee Seung-man did not hesitate to collaborate with American and English imperialists in league with his corrupt puppet regime. . . . "

The boys had sat on the wooden floor of the Meeting Hall with their knees pulled up, looking at the speaker making exaggerated gestures to match his vehement terminology. Just until a short while ago, these boys had loved and respected the old president of the Republic of Korea, their own country. They not only thought him a patriotic hero but also felt an affection which had a certain degree of intimacy, even. When they had a chance to see the presidential car pass flanked by outriders, the boys paused in their steps and said something like this,

"Grandpa has been somewhere. Where do you think he went today?"

It was not just the school kids who felt this way toward the old president but others such as bus girls or the younger generation. Bus drivers, too, showed their affection for the old man by exclaiming, 'It's grandpa! It's grandpa!'

To hear the narrow-faced communist officer speak slightingly of the president was not a little painful for the boys. This was because few among them were true sympathizers with communism and its long history of struggle and resistance.

"...must deliver them from the oppression and exploitation of the bourgeois social system which has been enslaving you all for so long..."

Feeling a sense of alienation at the words spoken by this People's Army officer, Tonggeun wondered why it was that he felt uncomfortable at the faultless enunciation from which the officer had eliminated all traces of his northern accent. What bourgeois oppression is he talking about, wondered Tonggeun, because as far as he could see there had not been any bourgeoisie as such in the Republic of Korea. After the Land Reform, nobody could be said to enjoy affluence in the form of private property and the majority of small property

-owners were no better than his own father Mr. Wu Taegap. He turned his eyes toward Chol who was a close friend now sitting beside him. He was listening intently to the communist officer's speech.

(Well, it's natural because he is by nature vulnerable. But he is wrong if he thinks that communism is such a lark...) thought Tonggeun.

Yet, Chol was an honor student and had a meticulous fastidiousness when making a decision to act.

(But what is there to think about or debate at any length in this issue? All they want is to establish the working-class regime through violent action...) thought Tonggeun looking at the speaker who at that moment was banging the top of the lecture-table in front of him to emphasize a point he was making.

(I wouldn't care if there was nothing more to it than the working-class people strutting about a little. Anybody else can strut about and I won't care. But why do they kill off anyone who doesn't please them? Why do they think that killing people indiscriminately is a righteous and legitimate act? This is what I can't take no matter how anybody puts it ...) Tonggeun thought on.

He was intending to escape at the first likely chance. He also thought that he would need to make it very soon. But at the same time, his judgement told him to wait until he was some distance away from Seoul so that his desertion from the Voluntary Army would not be known to the communists in the capital, least of all to those residing in his house and their associates. If they should find out about his deception (of falsely joining the Voluntary Army and then deserting it), they were quite likely to take it out on his father whom he had rescued from their clutches under his disguise of a zealous sympathizer with the communist cause. There will be repercussions on the rest of the family, too, thought Tonggeun thinking of Ogyop's graceful form in her customary hanbok attire and of her serene thoughtful eyes.

(You must not worry about me, Little Sister) said Tonggeun inwardly.

He abhorred communism. Yet he was not totally devoid of curiosity as to how their regime operated. This was a manifestation of the same strain of idle curiosity about things that had governed his personal life from his childhood making him take piano lessons or build the annex to his father's outer house.

Deep in thought as if comparing what the speaker said with his own observations, Chol was listening attentively to the speech nodding his head pensively at frequent intervals. Seeing his face shine brightly at some point, Tonggeun surmised that maybe the speaker pronounced some outstandingly eloquent exposition of a communist theory at that moment. He was very fond of this friend Chol, but even to him, he did not tell of his hidden plan for escape.

A thunderous clapping woke Tonggeun up from his reverie and he heard somebody shouting from the back, 'We agree!' Many more voices mimicked him, shouting, 'We agree,' 'We agree.' Tonggeun waited a while and then hollered, 'I agree!' His voice was stronger than that of any other boy. But there was an unmistakable joking tone in that call.

Chol turned to him and said in a serious voice,

"You'd better be careful. Somebody may misunderstand your motive."

They walked all day long and spent that night at another elementary school building in a provincial town. Then they marched again the next day.

"Do you think we will really fight the National Army?"

"I don't know. . . . But aren't we moving northward, now? And there's no more National Army left in that direction. I bet they have fled almost as far down as Pusan at this point."

"Even so, there can still be fights between the two armies, don't you think? Even if the communists have succeeded in chasing the National Army as far as Pusan. Unless, of course, the retreating army makes a leap into the South Sea."

"If that's how things stand, fighting would be out of the question, don't you think?"

"Why are we marching on in this way, then? Where are we going?"

"No need to fret. I am sure there are lots of things remaining to be done even now."

Among the boys who had belonged to different classes in school, there were some who were from a different school altogether. They had come to be in this platoon for the sole reason that they were standing close to the majority of boys who came from Tonggeun's school and who were now marching together. These boys who came from another school looked uneasy and at break time or during meals, they huddled together in one corner. Then there were a few who were passionately pro-communist. These sang the song, Red Flag, at the top of their voices and called out the slogans without staying quiet even for a brief while. These were either pro-communist from before the capture of the capital by the People's Army or turncoats who lost no time in aligning themselves with the communists. They manifested an excessive zealousness for communism and seemed to relish using such terminology as 'our brave and noble comrade soldiers.'

More than half the boys had been mobilized against their will, however. They had gone to their schools that fateful day only to see what was happening but ended up by being picked up by the drafters right at their own schools. They had not protested because everything took place so unexpectedly that they had had little time to fathom the situation. Also, even if they had had the intention and presence of mind to protest, they would not have known how to do it. As more days passed since they joined the Voluntary Army albeit involuntarily and they moved farther and farther away from the capital, however, the boys grew more morose.

Tonggeun belonged neither to the group of enthusiasts nor to that of the potential protesters. He behaved as nonchalantly as he always had.

The boys had thought, at first, that they were definitely northbound. Yet what they found out in the course of several days' march over and around mountains was that they were moving southward, after all.

"Are we not approaching Suwon? I think that shiny thing over there is the reservoir," said Chol pointing at the plains in the distance on the morning after their group camp in the mountains "I couldn't care less! All we need to do is go where we are told and liberate the victims of western imperialism through ruthless fighting. Am I not right, comrade Chol?" said Tonggeun.

His friend Chol did not say anything.

It started to rain toward the evening. The distant plains which Chol had guessed to be Suwon had long disappeared from the boys' sight. None of the boys seemed to know where they were. Those who were walking with their rifles on their shoulders began to feel the weight painfully. Everyone could see that the uniform jacket of his school friend walking in front of him was drenched with sweat. Although every boy was exhausted, one felt that somebody at the head of the line was increasing the speed of the marchers. Now, even Tonggeun panted, forgetting his customary standoffish style.

When the group reached the valley, they were given a brief rest. Sitting on the grass with his rifle lying across his knees, Tonggeun watched a light-green insect crawl up the stalk of a wild plant.

Chol took out an old-fashioned pocket watch in a round golden case which looked identical on both sides. Opening the watch case, Chol exclaimed,

"It's stopped! I forgot to wind it up."

"It's a regular antique, isn't it? How did you come by it?"

"I ought to have left it with my father before I left. But it's just as well that I didn't. Maybe I will keep it as a memento. And I think I will set the hands at six o'clock... because it was at six o'clock that I left my home," said Chol setting the time and then putting the watch carefullyinside his pocket again.

One of the enthusiasts among the group was seen to run up to a People's Army officer. These enthusiasts were the only segment of the student volunteers who had any communication with the People's Army representatives. The rest of the boys were like aliens in their relationship with the 'comrades' from the north.

The rain became heavier than earlier in the evening. As if alarmed by this, the commanding officer issued the order to march on. The boys stood up and formed a line.

Suddenly, however, the piercing sounds of machine guns were heard from up the mountain ridge and some of the boys saw the roundish shapes of helmets moving among the trees. Instantly, the bullets from the machine guns shot several of the boys to the ground.

Almost unawares, Tonggeun rolled himself to a nearby natural shelter made by a depression in the ground and fired his rifle several times in the general direction of the helmets. In a little while, however, he regained enough consciousness to look around him letting go of the gun. He saw that the cannon which a number of boys had had to transport together up to this point was firing venomously in the direction of the ridge. He could also see that boys were getting ready to fire their rifles with their bellies flat on the ground behind some rocks or bushes on this side.

Then Tonggeun's eye caught sight of Chol engaged in shooting about five yard to his right. He was pulling the trigger confidently and correctly just as he had done in the military training classes in which he was always the object of praise from the training officer.

"Chol! Stop it," shouted Tonggeun peremptorily.

His friend did not seem to have heard him, however. Tonggeun picked up the rifle he had dropped on the ground near him and flung it farther away and then lay down on the ground on his back.

I will stay here like this until the National Army come down from the mountain ridge and captures the survivors alive, said

Tonggeun to himself as he tried to make himself more comfortable in the shelter.

Again, Tonggeun was walking along the mountain path. This time, however, he was a private soldier of the National Army in his newly-acquired fatigues and helmet. He walked on at the tail of a line of soldiers who were covered with dirt and sweat from the last combat. He was carrying an M-I machine gun which was legitimately his and a Russian-made submachine gun which he had looted during combat.

The sloping path strewn with rolling stones was not the easiest course to follow although Tonggeun tried hard not to slip. His new comrades who had just survived a desperate fight with him, however, were trudging on stolidly ahead of him without a word.

Tonggeun had himself fought numerous desperate battles by now and had become more or less indifferent to his own life and death. Yet, looking at these taciturn soldiers who had come out alive through so many dangers of war, Tonggeun could not help being moved by some inexplicably powerful emotion. It was a desperate fight every time which usually ended with most of the soldiers dead. Once only Tonggeun and the sergeant who was the squad-commander came out alive from a battle.

The Voluntary Army unit to which Tonggeun and his schoolmates had belonged had met a complete defeat that day. Several dozen of the boys who had been captured alive received the treatments they deserved. After a due course of chastisement, the boys were handed over to the draftee training center to be fitted out as National Army soldiers.

The boys had pleaded that they had been half-forcibly dragged into the Voluntary Army by the 'enthusiasts.' Their explanation, it seemed, was favourably received by the National Army interrogators and thus it was that the boys ended up in the training center.

Tonggeun's lot was no different from that of other boys up to the time he was transported to the Center in an Army truck.

Yet, from this point on, he managed to shape his destiny according to the dictates of his heart. By one method or another, he succeeded in being picked, ahead of other captured boys, to join a combat unit and fight against the People's Army.

The first place the Voluntary Army draftees had been taken to seemed to be an area near Chonan. The National Army which was in the process of reorganizing after being scattered, however, was repeatedly forced to retreat until the troops went as far down as Kimchon along with the new draftees who did not yet know how to aim their rifles properly.

The United Nations Army which had met failure in the defensive and offensive fight in Chonan, also, made a fast retreat to Taejon and even here they were thoroughly defeated by the People's Army who came down upon them in an unrelenting offensive.

After Kimchon, a battle took place on the Nakdong river bank. The smokes and flames from the fire of thousands of guns had blacked out the sky and the river had been veritably dyed red with blood. Still, the fight continued.

The National Army which had been hastily reorganized did not have the power to meet the enemy at division level. The most they could do was attempt guerrilla-style warfare with small units scattered sporadically and fighting the enemy separately. Even so, these soldiers fought fiercely and the same desperate battles took place day after day between the river and the steep mountain slopes.

Tonggeun fought in the company of these die-hards.

As a soldier on the battlefield, Tonggeun performed his duty quite competently. Although he appeared to be somewhat absent-minded, his movements were agile and in action he was as bold as if he were unable to reflect on the danger his actions involved.

On the day when he had survived a combat along with the sergeant, he and the sergeant had run into a group of enemy soldiers while roaming in the mountains. Since neither of them had bullets or anything else with which to put a fight, they were instantly captured.

Instead of killing them right away, the enemy soldiers(there were four of them) first tied them to the trunks of pine trees as if to show off their cruelty. Then they joked and laughed in front of them.

When finally their rifles were pointed at them ready to be fired, a fighter came down along the ridge like a falcon and shot the enemy soldiers dead with his machine-gun.

When the sergeant woke up, Private Wu Tonggeun was writhing in on attempt to free himself from the ropes that were binding him around the chest and tied in knots round his wrists. While the sergeant watched, the ropes were untied and fell on the ground. Seeing this, the sergeant tried to untie himself in the same manner but for some reason he could not budge out of the ropes.

"How did you do it? Did they maybe tie you up loose?" said the sergeant, watching Tonggeun work on the ropes that were around his ankles. Tonggeun merely smiled and going over to the sergeant, helped him get his freedom back.

After this event, the sergeant often nagged Tonggeun to teach him how to free oneself from the ropes.

"It was by chance that I could do it," said Tonggeun.

"No, it can't be, I think you are a strange boy," the sergeant, who looked no older than twenty, said to Tonggeun and then, lowering his voice went on,

"Are you not the only one of us who went into the field a number of times but came back each time without as much as a nosebleed?"

"I never sought safety. And yet it's just as you say," said Tonggeun.

"Yes, and that's exactly what I mean," the sergeant mused in a pensive tone.

Tonggeun thought of Chol from time to time. He had kept on shooting that day although Tonggeun had shouted to him to stop. And he was shot to death. That boy had joined the Voluntary Army thinking that he would best understand what communism was by jumping into its midst. Yes, he had gone over to the communists as if he were matriculating from school. . . . Just as if he could get out of their company after studying them at his leisure. The war, in the meantime, was not progressing well at all for the National Army. Neither the American force garrisoned in Japan which was flown over only to be repeatedly defeated so that it had to fall back on stalling tactics nor the great defence the US division led by Major General Dean put up after arriving on the battle scene could keep off the red army that was crushing them like a red tide. How much more blood would have to be spilt yet? And was this a war that held any hope for anybody? Nobody could answer these questions.

From Tonggeun's point of view, the mere fact that freedom was still breathing in the form of these brave soldiers was endlessly gratifying, because had he not almost believed that any hope for a free society in this land was utterly shattered and had he not envisioned a country filled solely with slaves of communism? Since he was in this frame of mind, he did not really care too much about whether the National Army could really win the war or end up by being wiped out altogether. If he had that kind of leisure, he utilized it by sleeping his accumulated fatigue off. And now and then he thought of his home and family, especially Ogyop. Drawing her face in his mind's eys, he thought to himself that people, no matter who, would behave well toward her. Because that's the only way anybody could behave toward her, said Tonggeun to himself. Still he was worried.

Tonggeun and the other soldiers were returning from a clean-up operation up in the mountains. Tonggeun was following the troop at the end of the line. Although his combat fatigues were torn in places and the string was ripped off from his helmet, Tonggeun had come out of this bloody desperate fight without so much as a nosebleed again. He was thinking now that the sergeant would probably nag him to teach him how to untie a rope if they had some free time tomorrow.

Yet how tired he was! Every time he took a step, he felt as if his knees would give way like those of a horse about to fall on its bent knees. His most ardent wish at this moment was to go back to their barracks as fast as they could, unload their rifles and lie down.

Suddenly he thought he heard a low moaning sound. He continued his half-dazed walk concentrating his remaining energy on taking yet another step.

In the next instant, however, he heard another sound which was unmistakable this time. It was a sound emitted by a human. He could not decipher the meaning of that sound but could tell that the sound came from behind the rocks piled up a little way from the path the soldiers were following.

Tonggeun walked over to the pile of rocks behind which was a thicket dense with grass. A communist soldier in a ragged uniform was lying prostrate among the overgrown grass. He was a small-bodied man. Tonggeun saw that his hands and feet were twitching weakly.

After making sure that the enemy soldier was unarmed, Tonggeun gave him a kick to see the reaction. To his surprise, the prostrate body sprang up into a sitting position and then with his knees flat on the ground and his two hands folded against his chest, the soldier began to mutter something rapidly.

From the way the enemy soldier acted, it was easy to see that he was frightened. But to discover him there and listen to his strange muttering startled Tonggeun no less. For one thing, his utterance was such as Tonggeun had never before heard. And then, his manner of utter abjection in front of Tonggeun as if he were praying to Buddha was a most bizarre sight for him.

The man seemed to have a wound somewhere. Tonggeun could see that the front of his uniform jacket was wet with blood. Looking at him, Tonggeun was surprised by the fineness of his upturned countenance.

He had an oblong face, handsome nose, gentle big eyes, and

dark eyebrows that arched gracefully over his beautiful eyes. Tonggeun saw that the face he was looking at was that of a boy younger than himself. Maybe he was Tong -hun's age. The fairness of his skin could be on account of the bleeding from his wound. Continually babbling something, the boy was trembling all over.

After looking down for a while on the stranger who spoke in an alien way, Tonggeun finally woke up to the fact that what the wounded boy was muttering was Chinese. He also gathered from the boy's gesture that he was imploring Tonggeun not to kill him and also was indicating with his finger that he was wounded on his side.

Tonggeun had heard before this that Chinese soldiers were participating in this war but this was the first time he had laid eyes on one. But how could a boy such as this be enlisted in an army? This boy he was facing was far more like the pampered son of a noble house kidnapped by a barbarian tribe.

Tonggeun aimed his rifle at the boy's temple. He did not really intend to shoot him but he felt like intimidating the alien boy a little in this way. Scared into a frenzy, the Chinese boy rubbed his hands fervently, kowtowing again and again.

"What a miserable jerk this is!" said Tonggeun lowering his gun. But what should he do about this Chinese boy? Blood was trickling down from his side and it seemed that he was wounded in the legs as well. It was almost certain that he would die if he were left here.

Tonggeun began to turn back to rejoin his company when the Chinese boy made frantic gestures as if to clutch at him shaking his head violently. Maybe his wound gave him too sharp a pain. He fell back on the ground as soon as he struggled to move forward. But he pulled himself up again and desperately rubbed his hands together in supplication. His mouth was making unintelligible sounds all this while.

"Hey, you jerk, what do you want from me?" shouted Tonggeun.

Then the alien boy nodded his head apparently misunderstanding Tonggeun.

"What a luckless jerk. . . ." said Tonggeun and then, putting his rifle down on the ground, he bent down with his back toward the enemy soldier. And he said,

"Get on there, you sonofabitch!"

Balancing the wounded boy's bottom against the barrel of his rifle, Tonggeun began to walk. His knees, which had been too weak to support his own body, now gave him such trouble that he found it difficult to take even one step forward. The Chinese soldier was stretched limp on his back. And from the way his fatigue jacket was getting wet on the back, Tonggeun supposed that maybe the boy's wound had started bleeding more copiously.

Panting and staggering, Tonggeun made his painful way on until he could spot the helmet of the last man in the line of his comrades disappear around a bend down in the valley. He had to make haste in order not to lose his unit. He was standing at the edge of a cliff. He could see that a kind of a steep path cut down toward the valley. If only I did not have this sonofabitch on my back, thought Tonggeun, I could have tried to jump right from here. Slowly, however, he staggered toward the steep path. Just then, a tremendous dull noise resounded throughout the mountains. It was the sound of a cannon firing. Tonggeun saw a great flash on the mountain slope opposite him and then the next instant the shell that had been fired before this one exploded right behind Tonggeun. Making a fearful clamor and confusion, the mountain ridge on which Tonggeun had been standing carrying the wounded alien soldier rose up in the sky to fall back in cascades of dust. Then there were more sounds of cannon firing and more explosions. . . .

When the shell exploded behind him, Tonggeun had instantly judged that he might live if he jumped down into the valley. It might be the dead angle.

But instead of making a leap into the valley, Tonggeun took the path down the steep slope that led to the valley, without thinking throw the burden on his back.

Another shell flew over. It exploded at Tonggeun's feet. It was the end of Wu Tonggeun's life. His head, chest, and limbs rose up into the sky all in seperate pieces.

Just as she walked out of her alleyway into the street, Ihwa ran into O Sukja.

"Were you coming to my house?" asked Ihwa.

"Yes, I was, but I see that you are going out. Let's walk a little way together, then. We can talk while walking," said O Sukja turning around.

The two women walked side by side. Ihwa saw that O Sukja was wearing a black velvet skirt. Her face was shining with vitality. Although her eyes lingered on the basket Ihwa was carrying on one arm, she did not ask the latter where she was going.

"So how are you these days? Quite busy, I suppose?" said Ihwa without interest.

"Yes, I lead a very busy life. How about you?" asked Sukja looking straight into Ihwa's eyes with a meaningful smile on her lips.

When the air-raid alarm went off, the two women took shelter under the eaves of a shop building with a closed door. Immediately, there was the sound of bombs exploding followed by a bout of machine-gun shooting somewhere close to the shelter where Ihwa was standing with O Sukja.

"I want you to come to the clinic and help," said Sukja during the quiet interval.

When Ihwa first heard the word 'clinic' from O Sukja's mouth, her heart sank with a thump because she thought that the other woman was talking about the clinic where Ji-un was hiding. Even after she realized that O Sukja was talking about some other clinic, however, Ihwa's heart beat rapidly for some while on.

"We are getting increasing numbers of wounded. We need more hands," said the female communist party member in a lowered voice, looking after a fighter plane that tore across the sky with a screech just above the shelter.

"I don't think we could be much help for the wounded soldiers, though," said Ihwa uncertainly.

"You will only need to do what you see others do. That will be no problem," said Sukja.

The planes which had flown off a while ago came back this time in groups of two or three. As the planes screeched over the roof of the closed shop building, Ihwa and Sukja had to press themselves against the wall and block both ears with their palms.

"It won't do you any harm to listen to my advice, Ihwa. To be a medical student is a very powerful qualification at a time like this. It's not just anybody that is eligible to work at a military clinic. It's better to be working with the army now. It may take a little more time but we all know how this war is going to. . . . " It was impossible for O Sukja to finish her sentence because of a tremendous explosion that filled the entire atmosphere. Ihwa half expected Sukja to curse at the airplanes flying above but she did no such thing. Her face remained immobile and expressionless.

"Do as I tell you to, foolish girl. A time to study will come later, but now is the time to save our necks, even for you, Ihwa," said Sukja and then as if amused by her own words, she smiled briefly.

"I suppose it's all right to look after the wounded soldiers, but to tell you the truth I am a bit busy myself these days," said Ihwa cautiously. But O Sukja was not going to give up on Ihwa. She said in an obstinate voice,

"You know Pungmun Girls' High School in Angukdong? Well, that's where the Seventh Military Hospital is now. I want you to show up there one of these days, even tomorrow. When you come, ask for me. Or, you can look up Professor Ko who gave us a chemistry course, remember?"

Ihwa did not say anything.

When the 'all clear' siren went off with its repetitious broken sound, the two friends left the shelter and walked along the street again, "Kim Oshik has gone to Pyong-yang," said Sukja, suddenly changing the subject. When she said this sentence her voice sounded happy and excited.

"Is that so?" said Ihwa without mirth and looked at her friend. Maybe she, too, was planning to travel to Pyong-yang one of these days, thought Ihwa.

"Is he coming back here?" asked Ihwa.

"Yes, but not too soon, I don't think," answered Sukja still in a buoyant tone.

Ihwa was afraid that Sukja might mention Ji-un's name in the course of their conversation. Until they reached the crossroad where they said goodbye to each other, however, Sukja kept her mouth stolidly shut on that subject.

"Dont' forget that I came to see you today," said Sukja as they parted. She said it with a smile and yet Ihwa could not help noting a tone of warning in Sukja's last utterance. This oppressed her.

Another air-raid alarm pierced the sky and pedestrians in the street hurriedly huddled on either side of the street. Ihwa saw that Sukja, too, was being held up by the air-raid alarm not far from where she was.

Across the street was the office of the District People's Council. Through the open window of the dingy building in which the People's Council office was, Ihwa could see the inside of the crowded office where there were not even any partitions between the desks. Men were either sitting or standing at different spots in this one-room office and next to the window was a man sitting sideways so that his profile was visible to Ihwa. Standing in front of him was a boy of about thirteen or fourteen.

The boy was saying something to the man imploringly. But suddenly the man stood up from his seat. In his hand he held a club and with this he began to hit the boy repeatedly. It was a frenzied cruel beating that the man was giving the young boy. His eyes were bloodshot and his mouth was foaming.

Screams too painful to listen to came out of the boy's small body. He tried to avoid some of the blows by moving his shoulders this way and that. Then, finally, he collapsed on the floor as if unable to withstand the savage beating any longer. His body began to roll and his limbs scratched the air in convulsions. Now the sound the boy emitted was no longer the sharp scream of a while ago but a sinister subhuman groan.

All the men in the room were now standing astonished by what was taking place before their eyes. However as if they were certain that nothing they could try would be able to calm down this cruel man, or maybe because this kind of thing was not really so exceptional here, they all went back to whatever they had been doing before the incident.

These communists who made a point of calling everybody a 'comrade' were trying to advertise the fact that people were all equal whether they were men, women, old, or young and that nobody had the right to persecute anybody. If so, these were all the reasons why even the People's Council personnel should treat everyone as their equals and friends unless they were the so-called 'subversive elements.' One did not know what crime the boy had committed but one could at least be sure that he was no 'subversive element' because, if he had been, the punishment would surely have been something worse than the kind of private linching that was happening.

As if exhausted by his own atrocity, the man shouted to the boy,

"Get out! Sonofabitch!"

Then he kicked at the boy who was still rolling on the floor. One could see that the man's shoulders were moving up and down from the exertion of kicking the boy.

Still groaning piteously, the boy picked up a square-shaped bamboo basket from the floor and scampered out of the People's Council office falling more than once and almost crawling. Soon he disappeared in the direction of the market place.

This scene which filled an onlooker with unfathomable despair and hate seemed to be a rather fitting, albeit cruel, counterpart to what was happening in the sky : a tremendous sky-splitting clamour that reverberated throughout the entire atmosphere.

All this while, Ihwa stood watching, her body trembling. Maybe it was not particularly novel to see a human being beat up another human being. Maybe there was no country in which this kind of a thing never happens. An incident such as had just been witnessed by Ihwa and other citizens could very well be happening in other places under similar circumstances. Yet Ihwa did not have the leisure to reason with a cool logic at the moment. As if to seek a direct answer to the excruciating question that the inhuman scene raised for her, therefore, Ihwa shot an intense hate-filled glance in Sukja's direction.

On Sukja's fair-skinned face, bitter disappointment was only too easily discernible. Ihwa thought that maybe the fact of her watching this scene was the cause of Sukja's embitterment. Sukja was beginning to walk along the sun-bleached whiteness of the deserted street during the air-raid alarm. All at once she was stopped by the traffic officer in green pants who frantically blew his whistle at the young woman. Sukja talked to him briefly and then resumed her solitary walk. The movement of her shoulders as she walked seemed to indicate the intensity of her anger.

When Ihwa returned home from her twice-daily visit to Ji-un, she saw her mother sitting out in the taechong talking with the captain who had the black wart on his left cheek. Her mother's hair which used to be so shiny and well-groomed looked dull and unkempt. Her mouth with its smudge of red crayon was now one pale color on which Ihwa noticed new vertical wrinkles added to the old ones. In short, her mother had become an ungainly old woman during the past several months. The black skirt and white joksam both made of cotton seemed to hang on her small body like a monk's robe. Still, her voice carried a little of her habitual cheerfulness as she talked to the young communist officer.

"Are your parents living in your hometown?" she was asking

the man with the black wart.

The young captain was sitting on the edge of the taechong with his feet resting on the shoe stone. He seemed to be answering the old woman's conversational questioning with politeness mixed with ambivalence.

It seemed strange to Ihwa that this young man was being so vague and abstract about a topic which should be so close to his heart. Why was it that she felt an impenetrable veil covering this man's answer to her mother's inquiry about his own parents and home? In fact, this was a characteristic Ihwa noticed in other soldiers residing in the sarangchae also. Was it because they had a different emotional structure from us? Or was it merely a difference in the way of expressing it? Even Madam Shim who had such a childlike trusting mind looked somewhat bewildered by this young man's attitude. (Why are people acting so strangely? Why can't one talk to people in a natural way?) Madam Shim seemed to be wondering.

"Whereabout do you think my son is, I mean the one who joined the Voluntary Army?" Madam Shim made another attempt at conversation. Ihwa did not stay to hear the young officer's answer to her mother but went around the main building to her temporary quarters at the back. She told herself, however, that her mother ought, from now on, to be kept from talking to strangers. One never knew what her mother would say to whom. . . .

The communist soldiers in the sarangchae were all gone by ten o'clock every morning. Nobody in Ihwa's family knew where they went at this hour. They came back in groups of twos and threes in the evening. Ihwa and her family could not even tell if the people that returned in the evening were the same people that went out in the morning. The only steady parts of the group whom the family could recognize were this young officer with the black wart on his left cheek, Kang Soku who was, for some reason, always referred to by name, and the driver of the truck that was at all hours parked outside the front gate of the house.

(Why was this man staying at home today?) wondered Ihwa. She did not like it although except for his devious-looking expression and communist officer's uniform, Ihwa found him likeable enough.

Looking into the back room where her father was residing these days, Ihwa saw that he was bent down on the floor practicing his calligraphy.

Taehyon chojo yokeup-u/ Sohyon choljol yosao/
Chojo choljol chakjapkang/ Taeju soju nak-okban

What good could 'Pipahaeng' do for one while the world is being turned upside down by bombs, sub-machine guns, and bleeding people, said Ihwa to herself bitterly, but she was sorry for her father all the same. Her brother Tong-hun was sitting in a corner looking at a diagram of some machinery in a book.

Suddenly, Madam Shim said something in a raised voice. She was imploring. Startled, Ihwa got up to go to her.

"No, he's not home. He isn't. He's gone somewhere," her mother's voice was saying.

Ihwa went out to the taechong. The captain with the black wart was no longer there. Instead, the owner of the tailor shop was standing in the courtyard with a note pad in hand and a cold smile on his lips.

"Is that right? But if so, you ought to have filed a report," said the one-time tailor's shop owner, repeating what he had already said to Madam Shim. Ihwa sensed that the man said it over so that she might hear it clearly. Yet, he deliberately avoided looking at Ihwa.

"But what is there to. . . . " Madam Shim's unsteady tone betrayed the fact that she was hiding something from her interlocutor.

"What is the matter?" said Ihwa curtly, cutting her mother's rambling sentence short.

The Chief of the Neighborhood Association glanced toward

Ihwa but did not say anything.

"He says Tong-hun should join the Voluntary Army," said Madam Shim in a tearful voice as if to offer an answer on behalf of the man.

"What do you want from us?" said Ihwa again trying to sound firm.

"Why do you ask? Didn't you know that every house has been searched? We've been making an exception of this house on account of the People's Army comrades who stay here. That's why I have come personally to talk to you, don't you see?" The tone of the man's voice sounded upset. Outside the gate were a couple of Tong-hoe staffs peeping in and apparently waiting for the Chief of the Neighborhood Association to come out. Ihwa judged that maybe the tailor shop owner wanted to show off his weight against this house which had become an off-limit area for him and his associates since the house became affiliated with the People's Army personnel. His eyes which had formerly been humble and friendly were now filled with an uncanny obstinacy grown out of an over-developed self-confidence.

"You know how your father stands toward us. So be careful or. . . ." said the man in a threatening voice. He was no longer the good-hearted neighborhood tailor who used to mend clothes for the family.

Ihwa felt frightened. And she was furious. Her face turned white from excessive anger.

(A stool pigeon!)

To Ihwa, this man was a subhuman existence that lacked autonomy and personality. He had been converted to an 'enthusiast' not by any belief in communist ideology but by a taste of power. He was no more than a miserable crumb at the outer perimeter of a power circle. Yet what little power he was enjoying was the first of its kind he had ever known. Extreme contempt for the man mitigated her anger to a degree.

"My brother is not home," said Ihwa.

"And I am asking where he is. Should I go in there and look

for myself, maybe?"

The event ended up with the Chief of the Neighborhood Association leaving the house, after all, without further pursuing his belligerent purpose. And Ihwa and her family owed this to the communist officer with the black wart. It was while the confrontation between the Chief of the Neighborhood Association and Ihwa was taking place in the front yard that the communist officer who had retreated somewhere came back in and going to the kitchen door said to Ogyop,

"May I have a cup of water, please."

He drank the water with relish, and then still holding the cup in hand, he turned to the Chief of the Neighborhood Association saying,

"What is it, comrade?"

He was trying to smoothe out his strong northern accent so that his tone of voice would sound congenial to the other man.

Although as a representative of the People's Council, the former tailor had no reason to be intimidated by an army officer, the Chief of the Neighborhood association forsook his arrogant manner in front of the captain and replied in a shamefaced meek voice that he had dropped by to notify them of the draft for the Voluntary Army. He even gave a servile smile when saying this.

"Ah, you came about Comrade Tongguen? But he already joined the Voluntary Army. He is a very good communist," said the communist officer in a rather sharp voice as if accusing the other of not knowing these facts yet.

Ihwa was not a little surprised that this man who had a hard expression on his face and was so impersonal in his conversation with her mother could remember her brother Tonggeun's name. Were his feelings, then, operating in a way people like Ihwa could not comprehend, but actively all the same?

"Oh, I see. That's very good," said the Chief of the Neighborhood Association deliberately overlooking the fact that the communist officer was not talking about Tong-hun, the person whom the tailor had come to get but Tonggeun whom the latter knew to have gone with the Voluntary Army. He then wrote something in his note pad with his head bent over and his hand with the pen moving busily. After he finished writing in the note pad, the one-time owner of the tailor shop now turned instant enthusiast left Ihwa's house, after saying his goodbyes in an amicable manner. It seemed that even he could not overcome an instinctive fear of the communists.

(Where should we hide him?)

This was the only thought that kept Ihwa's head spinning right now.

Just before the sun went down, Ihwa went to the underground shelter where Tong-hun was hiding. She was carrying a lump of 'fist-rice (fast food made with cooked seasoned rice)' and a bottle of water.

This underground shelter was at the end of a clearing fenced off with barbed wire from the grassland where Yong-a's father had been shot to death. The shelter was dug into the mountain slope where large stones offered natural buttresses for it. It had been made so long ago that weeds were covering its entrance so that even the family of Mr. Wu Taegap who had had it built had forgotten about its existence for a long time.

Although one could go there by a shortcut through the back entrance along the path by the well, Ihwa chose the detour that went around the house from the outside through the front gate. The sight of their sarangchae with its crowd of communist inhabitants came into her eyes as she walked along their outer wall. Since the ground level of their outer house was lower than that of the main house, however, the wall served quite well as a screen so that Ihwa could pass by without much fear of being seen by the soldiers.

As a rule, Ihwa tried to go to Tong-hun only after all the soldiers left the house and before any of them returned. So that she might not look suspicious even to people other than the soldiers in case of her running into them on her way to and from the shelter, she carried such things as a bucket or a kettle to make people believe that she was getting water from a small well right next to the shelter.

The entrance to the shelter was so narrow that only one person could pass through it at one time. Both inside and outside this narrow entrance were various-sized rocks thrown about in a spontaneous way.

The catch word was the sound of water being scooped up from the well. One of the rocks then moved a little to one side and Ihwa pushed the food through this aperture surreptitiously.

This was Tong-hun's new hideout. It had been not easy to take him out to any place far from home under such vigilant surveillance as that which the communists were putting up. And then, too, who would, at a treacherous time like this, risk offering shelter to a relative or a friend's son even if one could succeed in transporting Tong-hun to some faraway area?

"I will die rather than be dragged into the Voluntary Army," Tong-hun had said on the day he went into this underground shelter.

After pushing in the food and water, Ihwa repeated the usual warnings about not lighting the lamp, not making a sound, and so on. Then she comforted him, saying this would be over very soon, now.

"I won't," or,

"I see," said Tong-hun to Ihwa's words of warning and comfort, but Ihwa could see that there was no heart in his voice.

At times, Tong-hun pushed a rock further aside than usual so that he could look at Ihwa's face. The face Ihwa saw through the small hole among the rocks was pitiful.

Yesterday, he had asked Ihwa to bring his electrical gadgetry to the shelter. Ihwa promised to do it for him only after she could obtain from him a firm promise that he would never handle them after dark.

Before leaving Tong-hun, Ihwa warned him once more, "You must never play with them at night, all right?"

"All right, Sister."
"Are you not cold?"
"No."
Some insect began to make a noise among the grass. As if this were a signal to begin a chorus, numerous insects joined the first one in making all kinds of noises from their shelter among the grass and bushes. Ihwa had the sensation that she had not heard the sound of the insects for many years, no for far longer than that. The western sky was dyed the color of blood and torn streaks of black cloud were racing across the sky, making a doleful picture.
"Listen to this, Big Sister," whispered Tong-hun pushing the earphones fixed to the end of the electric cords out of the hole.
Ihwa listened. To her surprise, a chorus of the national anthem sung slowly by old voices was flowing out of the earphones.
"Oh, my!" whispered Ihwa.
"Sad, isn't it?" whispered back Tong-hun using a diction uncustomary for him.
Ihwa's first impulse on hearing the chorus was to laugh out loud, but instead she found herself crying, quiet tears streaking her cheeks.
There was no way of reconciling her split feelings. Maybe she had got too used to the military songs of the communists, their march music that seemed to have been made to dance to, and their non-military songs with their slavic melody patterns, to react to the singing of the national anthem in a rational way. To her in her present frame of mind, the singing of the national anthem by an unknown group of old people sounded as if it were a melody that flew down from a time in a very distant past.
But what a farce it was! What good would singing the national anthem do if the government had forsaken the people to seek refuge in a far place all by itself? Still, listening to the singing, she could not help being so moved that her heart ached

and tears kept on flowing from her eyes. At the same time, the image of the old president for whom Ihwa had had respect and affection with his cabinet members at his side loomed up in her mind's eye. Sad and perplexed, she thought of the meaning of the phrase 'nanguk(troubled country).'

Ihwa recovered her senses soon enough, however, and reprimanded Tong-hun for his recklessness,

"You mustn't do this, Tong-hun. I told you it would be over very soon, now. If you get caught doing a foolish thing like this, it's really the end of everything, do you understand."

Ihwa's voice trembled as she said the last words of her admonishment. There was no answer from Tong-hun but Ihwa could hear a rustling sound from which she knew that Tong-hun was crawling back into the deeper part of the shelter. New tears welled up in Ihwa's eyes.

Ihwa picked up the bucket and turned to go home. The bloody sunset had turned into a drab grey while Ihwa had spent time with her brother. Ihwa's heart ached and the pain grew with each step away from the pit shelter where her baby brother was hiding as if he were a runaway outlaw. She did not wish to go on living in this kind of a world any longer.

She halted abruptly as she came close to where the outer wall of her house began.

"Mother! Is that you, mother?"

It was her mother.

Even after she was certain that the person who had been squatting among the grass was none other than her mother, Ihwa's pounding heart did not calm down.

Madam Shim was of a character that did not know how to act with plan and determination. For one thing, she did not have the ability to keep secrets effectively. At the least guile the other person used on her, Madam shim unresistingly exposed whatever she had meant to keep to herself. That was why Ogyop and Ihwa decided not to tell Madam Shim about Tong-hun's move to the old shelter to hide. Likewise from the Old Man, Old Woman, and Yong-a's mother, too, this fact was kept secret. To these household helps, Tong-hun was known to have gone to the country. As to Madam Shim, it was not in her to force her daughters to tell her where they had hidden her son.

Seeing her mother rise from the bush, therefore, Ihwa's first thought was whether her mother had seen her talk with Tong-hun in front of the pit shelter. Even if her mother could not have guessed her trip to the location of the shelter exactly, she might have sensed that something was going on around that spot, and it was not good that she should have. She would ask any number of senseless questions as if she were a very young child just starting to learn to talk and she might even go and take a peep into the shelter without her daughters' knowing about it.

"What have you been doing here, mother? When did you leave the house?" asked Ihwa in an impatient voice.

"I just came out to take the air. Is that why you came out, too, daughter?" said Madam Shim smiling unsuspectingly. It did not look as if she had been watching her daughter. She was scraping against her chima with her fingers, presumably to pull up her under-clothes, and then, turning her head toward the bush, spat heartily. From her mother's behaviour, Ihwa surmised that Madam Shim had squatted down among the grass to do her private business in the open air. And why not, as long as she came to take the air, thought Ihwa, and then said to the older woman,

"Let's go back in, mother."

"Yes, but wait a second, I have to. . . ." said Madam Shim and then stooping down, gathered up in one hand a fistful of weeds which she had apparently picked before Ihwa appeared and went on picking more from among the grass with her free hand.

"These blades can cut your hands," mumbled the old woman as she went on picking.

Ihwa wondered why her mother was picking the weeds but did not say anything.

"These days I can't listen to the radio comedies or have a nice chat with your father. Tonggeun has gone with the Voluntary army, and now even Tong-hun has gone away somewhere. I am so lonesome. . . ."

". . . ."

"Daughter, do you know when Tonggeun will come back to us?"

Asking this question, Madam Shim raised her eyes and looked at Ihwa. Hearing no answer from her daughter, however, Madam Shim went back to picking the weeds. After she has gathered what she considered a satisfactory amount of weeds, Madam Shim started for home walking ahead of her daughter.

The Old Woman and Yong-a's mother were busy carrying trays with steaming bowls of rice to the outer quarters. The rice was cooked on the temporary furnace they had made in the middle of the frontyard since the usual outdoor furnace in the backyard was occupied by the big pot of slow-cooking meat soup the soldiers would be served the next morning. While the rice had been cooking in the frontyard amongst the steam and black smoke, a number of hungry people, an old man in ragged clothes, a woman, and children had gathered outside the open gate looking in.

Ihwa's face turned red from anger and shame. She walked past them to go across the frontyard and stepped onto the taechong. In the pantry next to the kitchen, Ogyop was bent over a large bowl of cooked vegetables.

The sight of her sister intent on preparing food for the soldiers, too, made Ihwa angry. It was not as if she did not know that Ogyop's unquestioning service to the communist soldiers was what kept the family out of harm's way and in fact even Ji-un was benefiting from Ogyop's selfless behaviour. If she had not been there to protect the family, Mr. Wu Taegap and Tong-hun would long ago have been captured by the communists because they had nowhere to hide, and Ihwa and Ogyop herself could not have been exempt from getting involved with the Women's League or some such thing. Besides, where would the family have gotten food and what about Madam Shim who was so incompetent and helpless?

Yes, Ihwa knew all this, and yet she could not help being infuriated by Ogyop who seemed to have, at least on the surface, neither fear of nor aversion for the communist soldiers. Why does she work so hard to please the palates of those soldiers? Yes, why? Doesn't she know that it will do nothing to augment her happiness?

Ihwa pushed the back door of her room open because the smoke from all the cooking that was going on filled the room. The Old Man was passing the doorway carrying a load of ribs on his back. Ihwa knew that the sullen-faced Old Man was boldly stealing foodstuffs from the 'People's Army Comrades' to trade for things like a watch, a clock, or fabrics. She knew also that this was why the old couple's son made frequent visits to the house from the country and that the Old Woman's face looked uneasy on these occasions. Yet, these things were not important. The Old Man was being called 'Comrade Chon' by the soldiers at the saranchae. Yong-a's mother was 'Comrade Son' and the Old Woman was 'Comrade Grandmother' for them. Comrade Chon no longer made way or rubbed his hands by way of a greeting even if he should run into Madam Shim or Ihwa in the courtyard or gateway. This attitude was faithfully replicated in his son who was always rank with some foul smell. None of these things mattered at all, however. All the same, seeing the load of ribs on the Old Man's back, however, Ihwa thought of the scene she had witnessed at the market place this afternoon.

The communist soldier she had seen at the market place was the youngest she had yet encountered. He had small round eyes that looked very black and his uniform top came almost as low as his knees. Still like any other soldier, he was shouldering a rifle and wore a helmet on his head. This army equipment, however, made him look more boylike and pathetic than he might actually have been. He was talking to a meat merchant and showing him a wrinkled sheet of paper.

"Read this. And give me the meat. Really you must. . . ." the boy was saying, his cheeks swollen with discontent. But obviously he did not feel it easy to say anything harsher than that to the merchant nor could he use the bayonet at the end of the rifle on this man who was after all beloved comrade citiz en of People's Republic. Even so, he seemed exasperated that this man did not understand the importance of donating some meat to the People's Army who were risking their lives to rescue the people of the south including the merchant himself.

A lump of meat was lying on a wooden tray dripping blood. Meat was so expensive that most shoppers merely threw it a glance and passed by. Still, now and then, a person would come up and ask for a bit of the meat. Probably, these were those who would make paper-thin fillets of the meat they were buying, and then, after barbecuing these fillets with seasoning, sell them for one hundred won a piece.

Maybe the man was originally a merchant. He had a self -confident way with him either because he was versed in business techniques or because he was rich enough to be selling this kind of coveted merchandise which was hardly accessible for most shoppers. Therefore he was shouting in a rowdy pompous voice,

"Meat! Anybody for meat?"

While shouting, the merchant slapped the lump of meat with the flat of his knife as if to beat time. Although, with a patroniz ing(or sarcastic) smile, he glanced at the paper the young communist soldier held out, he was not really trying to read what was written there. Along with the sheet of paper, the young soldier was holding out several pieces of reddish paper. They were army notes, he said.

The meat merchant jeered more openly when he recogniz ed the army notes for what they were. Without paying any more attention to the young soldier who was growing more angry and impatient, the man shouted once more,

"Meat! Anybody for meat?"

Shouting at the top of his voice, the meat merchant threw a jeering glance up and down the boy in the soldier's outfit.

Many people were standing around watching this scene standing around. The boy with the rifle who might have come down to this market place from nearby Namsan continued standing under all these stares.

Ihwa felt as if she could understand why the man who sold the meat was so unafraid of this young soldier. First, the boy would not have harmed him in any practical sense. Second, the soldiers stationed on Namsan were having an extremely difficult time lately on account of the increasingly frequent visits of the planes. They no longer attempted counter-attacks with anti-aircraft guns as they used to earlier and seemed merely intent on avoiding attacks. As if there were no way of getting out of that area of concentrated bombing, the soldiers were huddled among the pine trees as if confined there. Such an incident as the by-standers were witnessing this afternoon was an indication of the confusion and disintegration occurring among the communist troops guarding the capital. And that was why the people who were watching the wrangling between the boy and the merchant had meaningful smiles on their faces.

But Ihwa had not felt like mocking the young soldier like the other by-standers. Not that she was sorry that the merchant did not give the meat to the young soldier so that some communist soldiers could have a feast, but she felt sorry for the boy who was being jeered at standing there.

(Are these soldiers beggars that they send out this boy to demean himself in this way? Is this the way the army treats its faithful followers?) Ihwa had said inwardly moving away from the crowd.

I must be a half-wit, thought Ihwa, her eyes still fixed on the darkening backyard through which the Old Man had disappeared with his loot of stolen ribs.

Why am I getting mad with innocent Ogyop and then feeling an uncalled-for pity for an enemy soldier? Perhaps I lack the ability to judge things objectively and to accept facts without feeling emotional about them....

Ogyop must be unhappy, too, underneath, thought Ihwa and this realization consoled her mind somewhat.

Ihwa walked out to the taechong. Footsteps and voices could be heard from the sarangchae. The soldiers seemed to be back. Yong-a's mother was crossing the frontyard toward the soldiers' quarters carrying a large tray.

Sitting at the edge of the taechong, Madam Shim was fondling something on her lap, with her head lowered. Ihwa looked and saw a number of grass dolls on the floor next to her mother's lap. These dolls were made with long grass blades that were tightly and smoothly put together to make the shape of a head and then finished with tresses of hair made with finely split grass blades. These tresses were twisted into pigtails which could then be wound up to make a knot at the back of the head. Madam Shim had decorated some of the grass-dolls' heads with a piece of crimson cloth or with a tiny pinyo. Among the heads there was even one which had a knot at the top of the head in the style of the women of old times. A dark red taenggi(hair-tie) was adorning this doll's hair, sticking out on both sides of the knot like two wings of the letter V. Madam Shim had these dolls lying side by side on the taechong floor beside her and was in the process of arranging a pigtail on a new doll.

"Would you bring me the scissors, daughter? I can't remember where the sewing basket is," Ihwa had heard her mother holler to Ogyop a while back and she had felt irritated with her mother who never knew how to do anything without somebody else helping her no matter how busy that person might be. Yet she had no intention of letting her mother know of her irritation. Instead she said to hermother calmly.

"Mother, I want you to stay out of the bushes at the back from now on."

"But why?"

"I can't explain. Just trust me and don't go there. Something terrible will happen if you do. Do you understand me, mother?"

"All right, I won't go there."

It was at times convenient for the family that Madam Shim was not inclined to inquire into a matter with persistence.

Daily, Ji-un grew more restless in his life of confinement and Ihwa could see it only too clearly.

It was not too bad when Sanggyu was in the room with them exchanging jokes. But when they were left to themselves in that locked-up room, a heavy suffocating silence often oppressed them insufferably.

Ihwa tried to make conversation, diagnosing Ji-un's depression as the result of lack of exercise. She explained in detail how the lunchbox had been prepared, or, taking out the book Ji-un had asked her to bring, she told him about what she had heard and seen in the outside world. Yet with none of this could she cheer up Ji-un or herself when the low mood possessed them.

Ji-un, it was true, tried what he could to show his appreciaton of Ihwa's troubles and respond to her efforts to make genial conversation. Yet his inner impatience prevented him from keeping this up. In a way, it was the same with Ihwa. She could no longer comfort Ji-un by saying that this state wouldn't last long now. She, too, was worn out by waiting too long.

Sanggyu, who went about continually to gather information, came home each time without much news and shaking his head depressedly.

More than a month had passed since the rumor about a counter-attack by the allied forces had spread. As if to prove the credibility of this rumor, moreover, the city was being strafed by the fighter planes everyday. However, Taejon and Kimchon had fallen into communist hands and finally the area along the Naktong River as well has been taken by the communists. It was not certain how many reinforcements had been brought in by the allied army but the communist radio was daily boasting about the victorious exploits of their army.

Across the Naktong River was Taegu and next was Pusan which was the end of everything. No wonder Ji-un is being so fretful, thought Ihwa.

"I want to go out there and fight. Even if I should fall and die there. . . ." said Ji-un looking as if he were going to explode from utter frustration. Often, Ihwa saw that his eyes were bloodshot.

One afternoon, he seemed more fretful than usual. He kept silent obstinately and did not even finish the lunchbox.

Bombs were being dropped somewhere. With gloom-filled eyes, Ji-un looked out of the window which had a view of a part of Namsan.

Ihwa remembered that of late Ji-un did not try to take her by the hand or embrace her. An all-annihilating sense of frustration was taking everything away from him including his capacity for joy and hope.

Ihwa stretched out a hand and put it on the chest of Ji-un who was leaning back against the headboard of his bed. Then pouring all her warmth into her two eyes, she looked him in the face. She wanted to see him regain his vitality. Poor Ji-un, he was like an animal locked up in a cage too small for him, while in the south, his colleagues were fighting courageously on the side of the free world . . . .

Ji-un was now closing his eyes. When he reopened his eyes, however, he suddenly grabbed Ihwa by the wrist and sprang up into a sitting position. He was breathing hard. His shoulders were moving up and down jerkily and his eyes were glaring in a very strange way. Ihwa felt that she had never seen him looking like that. Then that thought frightened Ihwa. She moved her lips, trying to say something, but no words came out of them.

Letting go of the wrist he had been grabbing, Ji-un stepped down from the bed. Then standing a few paces from Ihwa, he stared at her, emitting harsh breathing sounds. The impression he gave was that of a falcon about to snatch a chick. Or he looked like a predatory animal about to pounce upon its prey. He took one step toward Ihwa. The top of his blue pyjamas was open showing the muscles of his chest that was heaving rapidly.

Ihwa staggered backward, frightened. Her two eyes were searching his face in bewilderment. What she found there were only anger and hate.

But why? Why? Why was Ji-un acting this way?

Deep wrinkles were dug on Ji-un's forehead which must have come from his excruciating agony and restlessness, and yet, to Ihwa at the present moment, even these wrinkles were a thing of utter incomprehensibility. There was only on inhuman harshness on this face making it so unknowable for her.

Slowly, her long-forgotten dread of this man came back to life, articulating itself more clearly as the seconds passed by. She remembered how he had locked his tongue into hers and refused to remove it and how she feared this act of his although she was not unaware of the fact that she would have to accept its ultimate meaning sooner or later.

In dread and resistance, Ihwa moved one more step backward. Right at this moment, however, Ji-un sprang on her and pushed her down on the floor. Pulling the skirt of her dress downward, Ihwa looked at him imploringly. And inwardly, she begged him.

(Ji-un! Ji-un! Please don't make my fear of you grow. Please....)

Ji-un put one knee against the floor. His face was dark red and his lips were glossy with a strange oiliness. Without uttering one word, he grabbed at Ihwa's slip. Ihwa resisted. The lace came off with a noise from the bottom of Ihwa's slip.

It was too much. What Ji-un was doing was too savage and too cheap. In black despair, Ihwa went on resisting Ji-un with all her might.

She could not think of anything any longer. She could not feel anything any longer. Wetting herself with tears, she kept on fighting Ji-un with her hands and feet.

Feeling her panties torn off her, Ihwa slapped Ji-un on the face. It made a sharp noise. Abruptly, Ji-un stopped and let go of her as if he were suddenly waking up from a nightmare.

He stared at Ihwa with eyes in which the pupils were dilated. And then turning back sharply he banged his forehead against the wall, clutching at the wall with his hands which were spread wide on the wall. In all he presented the picture of a man in great torment and bottomless despair.

Ihwa pulled the rest of the lace off her slip with a violent hand. She threw the strip of lace into the basket and tossed the lunchbox Ji-un had left unfinished into it as well. Then she left the room. It was really too much. It was absolutely too cruel for him to have acted that way. . . .

Like someone in high fever, Ihwa dashed through the street blindly. She wanted to cry with abandon like a child and make a lot of noise. Her fury was so strong that it was hard to keep it from bursting out. In spite of everything, however, she could not hate Ji-un wholeheartedly because she loved him. And maybe, in a sense, she loved him now more than ever.

(And yet. . . .)

Ihwa did not know what to think from this point on.

(And yet . . . . And yet . . . .)she kept on reiterating the same phrase and sobbing sorrowfully. The image of Ji-un leaning forward against the wall with his wide-spread hands clutching onto it flashed back into her mind again and again.

"Comrade, comrade, you are in danger. Step in here, please," the traffic officer was wielding his arm to try to stop Ihwa who was running like one who did not know what she was doing. The young communist officer in green trousers did not seem perturbed at all even when he saw that Ihwa's face was covered with tears. His expression was as neutral as if he were looking at a lump of wood or stone.

In the distant sky, planes were going through acrobatic movements soaring and then falling perpendicularly to turn the world beneath into a sea of fire. Their wings glinted with a dull leaden glare.

The crimson flames and horrid sounds of explosions were creating the illusion of some apocalyptic miracle taking place under the low-hanging grey sky.

The beautiful arches that were appearing in rapid succession even reminded one of some well-practiced movements exhibited during an athletic event.

Ah, how frustrated and despairing Ji-un must be! Ihwa's thought kept on going back to him.

(But he treated me so cruelly, as if he hated me. . . .)

Tears rolled down her cheeks again. Her anger toward Ji-un had not gone away.

Ihwa pushed open the front door of the clinic very quietly. With a quick glance in the direction of the examination room, Ihwa climbed the stairs rapidly.

Her cheeks were flushed. It had been with a very serious determination that she had come to the clinic today. Last night in bed, she had come to realize what it meant to drive Ji-un, who was already so depressed and helpless, further down into deeper sorrow.

(If only I could cheer him up. . . .)

Why should she grudge him anything? To keep her innocence under the circumstances seemed utterly meaningless.

Yesterday, Ji-un had frightened her one degree too much. He behaved too impatiently. Yes, it was just so. But that was all.

Even Ihwa had not believed love to be all spiritual without a physical side to it like in a children's play. In one corner of her mind,she had merely desired that their relationship be maintained at that level for the time being. Yet in the other part of her consciousness, she had known that it would have to progress toward that ultimate state where love would be more serious, perhaps more despairing, but, exactly for that reason, more undivided.

Only her personal idea of physical love had been such that

a romantic serenity, sweet and unhurried whispers, and a gradual yielding to an embracing darkness each had a part to play.

But now, said Ihwa, halting to take a deep breath on the landing of the staircase, I will try and overcome any shocks that might come from the discrepancy between my wishful idea of love and love as it can most easily become if not checked by a tremendous conscious effort. This was a time when bombs were falling like rain. Maybe this was not a time when a person could criticize Ji-un's style of loving as gross. Yes, maybe, it was her own lack of understanding that stopped her from seeing this point. Forgetting the fundamental aspect under the force of personal emotion was a defect she had.

Ihwa halted again in front of Ji-un's door. She bit her lower lip lightly with her upper front teeth and let a smile float up into her eyes. Then she pushed the door open.

She had dressed herself elaborately for this visit. She was wearing a silk dress of a dark moss color and her hair showed the effect of her careful brushing and grooming. A faint fragrance of jasmine drifted from her skin.

Ji-un will welcome me without a word, looking into my eyes from the bed with his large, still slightly angry eyes, thought Ihwa. Maybe, he will glare at me with his mouth twisted with anger. . . . But I will make him laugh no matter how mad he is with me. . . . And Ihwa pushed the door wide open.

But Ji-un was not in the room.

A white sheet was neatly spread over the empty bed and Ji-un's straw hat was gone from its usual spot on the wall. Ihwa sensed that something had happened.

Kneeling down, Ihwa peeped underneath the bed. She could not find Ji-un's shoes there. Instead, the pair of slippers which Ji-un had been using inside this room were left on the floor where Ihwa's knees touched them.

(Ji-un has gone away. . . .)

Covering her ears with both hands, Ihwa stood dumbfounded in the middle of the empty room. She did not know what she should do. Her heart beat so fast that she felt as if her chest were bursting. A large group of bombers flew above the roof of the clinic building, making not only the windows but also the very floor Ihwa stood on go into a convulsion.

(Where did he go?)

She was so shaken that she felt dizzy.

Picking up one of the slippers, Ihwa clutched it against her chest. This gesture brought Ji-un's presence so close to her being that she seemed able to feel it physically. She looked all around the room. Then she did the very thing that a person in despair often does, trusting in fantasy.

(Maybe he has just stepped out somewhere. . . .)

(He could have gone to our house to see me. . . .)

Ihwa knew only too well, however, that for Ji-un to have gone out meant almost certain death.

Picking up the basket with the lunchbox from the floor, Ihwa put it on the bedside table. Ji-un's cheerful voice saying, ' Thank you, thank you, what would I have done without you,' and his face looking into the basket came to Ihwa's mind and brought a sharp pain. Just then Ihwa heard footsteps outside the room.

"Oh, hello," said Sanggyu opening the door without knoc-king. Looking in, Sanggyu made a puzzled face.

Staring at him with dull eyes, Ihwa said nothing.

"Hasn't he gone to your house?" asked Sanggyu, and then, without waiting to hear Ihwa's answer, asked again, "You mean you haven't seen or heard from him since yesterday?"

Ihwa shook her head and still did not say anything. She did not have enough presence of mind to pretend equanimity in front of Sanggyu.

(He will not come back. I know it,) this was what Ihwa was muttering inside.

Stepping inside the room, Sanggyu closed the door. With a serious face, he began to examine Ihwa's expression. His two hands were pushed inside the pockets of the doctor's white gown he was wearing. Ihwa's eyes noticed that there were blood stains on the outside of the pockets. Maybe, it was the blood of someone wounded during the latest visit by the planes.

"He seemed extremely high-strung yesterday evening. He went out in that state. Since he was in a great hurry to leave, I did not have any chance to ask him questions. Do you know if he had had any visitors during the day?"

"I am not sure. . . ." said Ihwa, finally breaking into tears. She covered her face with both hands and gave herself up to violent sobbing.

"You mustn't upset yourself. I am sure he had some urgent business. He will come back in the evening," said Sanggyu trying to calm her down.

Ihwa did not say anything.

"It's not as if he went out not knowing the danger it meant. So he must be in control of things. Please don't worry too much. When he was leaving, I was so busy with the patients that I could not spare much time for him. There were more than ten wounded coming in at the same time and most of them were kids, you see. But if I had known things would turn out this way, I would surely have taken time to ask him where on earth he was going," said Sanggyu in an apologetic tone as if it were his fault that Ji-un was gone.

Ihwa raised her face finally and asked,

"Hasn't he left any word? Like when he would be back. . . ."

Sanggyu did not answer at once but remained silent and pensive-looking for some while. Then he answered,

"He asked to shake my hand before he went saying he owed me much. Then he said he had to go out for a while but I should not worry even if he did not come back here because one could not predict one's actions in these times, he said. He was laughing when he said this, so I thought he was joking."

"He complained of suffocating. He said he would like to go out and fight even if he gets killed trying it," said Ihwa in a low voice but her thought was fixed on the scene that had taken place in that room yesterday afternoon.

"Don't worry yourself too much, anyway. He will be very

careful. I will let you know as soon as he returns," said Sang-gyu.

Ihwa thanked him and left the clinic. The basket on her arm felt different today as she started on her trip back to her house. Then she realized that it was because Ji-un had not eaten the contents of the lunchbox inside the basket.

She staggered from exhaustion. Yet she felt as if she could run into Ji-un if only she went on roaming the streets instead of going home. It was a foolish thought but already, just by imagining such a happening, Ihwa's heart beat excitedly. Yet in the very next instant after experiencing this excitement, Ihwa felt so dejected that her world became dark again because it seemed impossible for that kind of a happening to take place.

She began to walk in the opposite direction from her house, somehow passing right through the bombing and the off-limit areas. Since she only went back and forth on the road from her house to the clinic durmg these many weeks, the streets she now walked looked strange to her. The strangeness came not only from the fact that she had for so long not seen these streets but also from actual changes that had taken place in the form of ruins made by bombing, the sight of the homeless and the wounded, and the communist soldiers that seemed to be everywhere one turned one's eyes.

Ji-un was nowhere. Passing by a school yard, Ihwa saw that a crowd of drafted people—they were picked up either in the thoroughfare or in their own houses where they had perhaps relaxed their vigilance for the night—were looking out of the second-floor windows with uneasy expressions. These people were gathered in a throng at each window gazing at some points beyond the locked front door and iron gate. Maybe Ji-un is among them, thought Ihwa.

In the next instant, however, Ihwa remembered what Ji-un had told her about his bold escape from his drafters in the earlier part of the war and this thought made her smile in spite of herself. I am sure Ji-un is not among those, said Ihwa to herself with more self-assurance. He must be somewhere very very far away, thought Ihwa.

Wounded soldiers walked past Ihwa in succession. One of them was cradling one arm that was wounded from the shoulder down in his other good arm. The soldiers seemed to have walked a long rough way. Their faces were mud-colored and sallow and their chests were heaving painfully. Their soiled khaki uniforms were drenched in sweat and their feet had strips of cotton cloth around them in place of shoes.

After she saw several of these wounded soldiers pass by her one after another, Ihwa stopped and looked after them as if to find out in which direction they were going.

A school yard with a red cross flag came into sight. On the whitewashed roof, too, one saw the red cross mark distinctly against the white backdrop . Ihwa recognized it to be the site of Pungmun Girls' High School. It was no other than the military hospital O Sukja had told her to drop by some time back. As Ihwa watched, several wounded soldiers entered the gate of the school one by one.

Some of the wounded were limping but most seemed to have been wounded elsewhere but their legs. Those who did not have the strength to walk must have been left to their fate, thought Ihwa. How they must have bled, and what great pain they must be suffering!

Ihwa felt her sorrow and dejection overtake her again. She roamed about the streets on her tired, increasingly unsteady feet until sunset.

Ihwa went back to the clinic the next two days. Ji-un never came back. Only the plaster cast that was supposed to be put on his arm in an emergency welcomed her, its two parts spread out on the bedside table.

Maybe Ji-un had been taken prisoner already in some remote place.... Or maybe he has been wounded and is lying in the grass somewhere.... Maybe he is dead....

The thought that Ji-un could have gone away from her for

good gnawed at her heart incessantly.

Driven into a desperate situation from which he had no means whatsoever of escape, Ji-un had perhaps turned fierce and wild. Maybe it was my mistake that I treated him so harshly. Although at the time I had no other way of behavin-g....

Ihwa could not withstand the loneliness that kept rushing into her insides. Now that she thought back, the very fact of her having seen Ji-un every single day for over a month was nearly unbelievable. How comforting it was to know that Ji-un was there at the clinic in safety. And how it had helped her live through this confusing and painful time.... Having lost Ji-un, all the strength flew out of her body and scattered in every direction.

Like a somnambulist, Ihwa wandered about in the streets everyday.

"Our most courageous armoured corps and infantry along with our Partisan comrades have after a heroic battle won the victory. The enemy troops are beginning to flee across the Naktong River. The number of dead on the enemy's side is.... Ninety were captured alive including two interpreters.... Hail to our Great Leader Kim Ilsong! Hail to the heroic soldiers of the People's Army...." A loudspeaker was announcing to the passers-by.

One day Ihwa returned home and ran into Kang Soku who said to her in a jeering tone,

"Where do you go every day, Comrade Ihwa?"

Ihwa walked by him without answering. She hated the look of the man and abhorred his unctuous voice.

Lately, the captain with the black wart had been coming into the inner courtyard frequently. He smiled to Madam Shim showing his white teeth or asked Ogyop for a drink of water.

As if induced by the captain's frequent visits to the inner quarters, Kang Soku, too, had showed himself quite often on this side of the house of late.

Kang Soku's purpose in coming over seemed to be mainly

to talk nonsense to the family with his mouth sarcastically twisted(actually this could have been an unintentional habit he had). He would say,

"I see that Comrade Ihwa doesn't show enthusiasm for our cause. . . ."

But Ihwa did not deign to talk back to him.

Although he did not refrain from making nasty remarks or giving a mean look to the women of the house, he took Ihwa's habitually contemptuous attitude toward him with nonchalance. He would fasten his eyes on her back as she walked away from him.

"I say, where have you been? I want to have a chat with you," said Kang Soku again. He seemed determined to get a word out of Ihwa today.

Ihwa looked at him and saw that his eyes were bloodshot. Did anything happen while I was away, Ihwa asked herself quickly. And then she stared at him without blinking. Her face was burning because of a sorrow and fury in which such a character as Kang Soku had no part.

Reading her expression, Kang Soku twitched his mouth and continued.

"Why don't you go out to the Women's League and help?"

Although Kang Soku did not pursue the subject beyond this but contented himself with contemplating Ihwa mockingly. Ihwa herself felt a chill run down her spine when she heard what the man said.

When she entered their common room, Ogyop told her that there had been a summons for her from the Women's League.

Later in the evening, Ihwa was whispering to Tong-hun in front of the pit shelter.

"You mustn't worry, Tong-hun, even if I don't come here for a few days, all right? I will probably be staying in a place which is safer than home. I will, of course, direct Ogyop to take over what I have been doing, but all the same I am very sorry to leave you for now. . . ."

"I will be all right."

"Have patience, Tong-hun. Will you do that for me? I am sure this won't continue forever. And I will come to see you now and then."

"Don't worry."

After a brief silence, Tong-hun said,

"Looks like these soldiers are going to cross the Naktong River before morning, doesn't it?"

"Well, I don't know. But that may not be so simple. They took long time to get to the Naktong River from Taejon, didn't they? And US reinforcements are arriving on this side all the time, it seems."

"I hope you're right."

Turning back from the shelter, Ihwa shed hot tears. She said in her heart, please forgive me, Tong-hun.

"Main Complaints : Buliet wound, shell wound, bone fracture in the upper arm, severe bleeding."

"Main Compalaints : Bullet wound, abrasion on the shoulder, rupture of right forearm. . . ."

Ihwa was sitting at the window of the registrar's office wearing a sanitary gown on top of her yellow dress. The line of wounded soldiers who were covered with blood, sweat, and dust stretched out to the front yard. The soldiers who received the preliminary examination slip from Ihwa after she rapidly filled it out walked along the corridor, trembling from excessive pain, toward the classroom with the sign : examination room. Those who had been to the examination room went to the corner allocated to them and lay down on the blanket spread out on the bare floor.

Although everywhere in this clinic, one saw blood and death, and screams and groans of pain never ceased, still, as a military clinic, this was not a bad place. The doctors and other medical staff were doing their best for the patients and food rations were quite generous.

The only trouble was that there were so many wounded soldiers coming in continously that the doctors at times could not take care of them properly no matter how quickly they went about their job. Yet, many patients were recovering and the supply of medicine was efficient. Gradually, Ihwa immersed herself in the routine of this new life.

At the sound of the bell, all patients excepting those who could not move gathered at the auditorium and had their meal. They were given soup, meat, and as much rice as they could eat. The staff, that is, the army doctors, and the civilian doctors and the medical students like Ihwa who either volunteered or were drafted ate separately at a long table.

The mixed smell of blood oozing out of the bandages, chloroform, and food created a peculiarly pathetic atmosphere in this makeshift eating hall and in some inexplicable way this peculiar atmosphere helped stabilize Ihwa's ravaged mind. The feeling that she was contributing to mitigating the pain of these wounded men gave Ihwa the courage to overcome her own grief.

Ihwa tried not to think of Ji-un. Still, whenever she saw som e-one suffering from severe pain, she could not help thinking of him. Was it not possible that Ji-un, too, was suffering from this kind of a wound somewhere? Once her mind accepted this possibility, it seemed quite certain that he was wounded and suffering great pain without anybody to help him. She felt as if she could hear him groan.

"Your name and serial number. . . ."

"Your unit?"

Writing down the soldiers' answers to these routine questions, Ihwa sometimes had a momentary illusion that the wounded soldier in front of her was Ji-un.

But she could not give herself to such 'wasteful' sentimentality for long. The soldiers who had covered hundreds of miles on their own feet were mostly in a desperate state. When her eyes looked at a young soldier—almost a boy-with a face tense with pain but looking undaunted despite everything as if he still believed in some lofty human values, Ihwa said to herself that she must not think about anything but this boy soldier's wound.

"Fracture on the right forearm, burn on the face. All right. You can go now."

With emergency cases, she wanted to cut out even this much preliminary formality. The foremost duty seemed to be to get the patient treated by the doctor. She tried, therefore, to minimize the time the wounded had to spend at her window.

When, at the beginning of her life in this clinic, she returned to the tatami(straw mats covering Japanese rooms) room now serving as the female helps' lodging but presumably the 'night-watch room' in its original function, Ihwa could not help feeling a huge emptiness rushing back into her heart. Unexpectedly, however, this changed after a matter of several days. Soon, Ihwa found herself falling asleep as soon as she got into bed, exhausted with fatigue. Although the other four women who roomed with Ihwa looked like students themselves, none of them seemed to feel it necessary to tell the others who she was. They just shared the room at night without getting into each other's way. Of the women soldiers in green jumpers, Ihwa found not even one in this place. When Ihwa ran into them in the streets, she had imagined them to be military nurses. Maybe they had been military police or something else, thought Ihwa. The only women outside the five rooming in this tatami room together were several old women working in the kitchen.

One of the other four women who roomed with Ihwa took turns with Ihwa at working in the registrar's office, but the rest helped the doctors to treat the patients. Maybe these women already had their medical practitioner's licence. But to Ihwa's knowledge. one at least was still a student at the College of Nursing.

In her free time, that is, when she did not have to sit at the registrar's window, Ihwa often followed this woman whom she judged to be a student nurse into the treatment room. Without any explanation, Ihwa helped this woman in her work.

They were always short-handed. Soon, therefore, one of the doctors gave Ihwa orders to do this or that thing in the course of treating patients. This meant that Ihwa invited herself to be on the list of nurses. And life became even more full of toil than before for Ihwa from this time on.

As she saw more of them, Ihwa found out that the soldiers' faces which she had thought so similar before were actually distinguishable one from another. Likewise, she became familiar with the names of the doctors. And now she did not feel too much alienation when called 'Comrade Ihwa.' Seeing Ihwa take her seat at the table at meal times, the soldiers, most of whom were closer to being boys than young men, threw bashful glances in her direction. As soon as their eyes met hers, however, they hurriedly looked away in embarrassment.

From their point of view, Ihwa was very different from the warrior type women these soldiers were accustomed to having dealings with. She was beautiful, simply, like a flower. Still, when Ihwa smiled at them, they had no means of comprehending the meaning of her smile. Something unbridgeable was lying between Ihwa and the young soldiers.

The clothes Ihwa wore underneath the sanitary gown were in light colors such as yellow, blue, or pink. She did not tie her hair tightly at the back or make hard-knit pigtails to be pulled up harshly into a knot on top of the head like the northern women but let it fall down softly just above her shoulders in a very charming way. That Ihwa did not pretend to be a believer in proletarianism, that she did not act as if she had had that belief sincelong before the outbreak of the Korean War and the subsequent occupation of Seoul by the Proletarian Army was another incomprehensible for people residing in this 'paradise of the proletariat.' It was also reckless behaviour on Ihwa's part. But Ihwa had no intention of throwing away the pretty shoes she already had in order to wear the sneakers that seemed to be the standard footwear of women in this clinic.

From among the soldiers who wore their uniforms or fatigues even after their hospitalization at the clinic, there was one who gave Ihwa an endearing impression. This one always sat at the end of a soldiers' table that was placed at right angles to the long table where Ihwa ate with other members of the staff. When the soldiers came in a row, too, he followed at the end of the line.

This soldier looked around seventeen and had a pleasant and charming face although he still dragged his wounded leg. He attracted the staff's attention especially on account of an extraordinary episode in which he was involved.

The boy was attending a middle school in Chungchong Province(a southern province) when the war broke out. He had joined the National Army in the early stage of the war as result of possibly on-the-street drafting. After a few days' intensive training in how to use a gun, he was sent to the frontline, where he suffered a fracture of a thighbone in the first combat he entered.

When he regained consciousness, he was being transported in an army truck along with other wounded soldiers. A heavy rain was pouring on all of them since it was an uncovered truck they were riding in.

Soon everybody on the truck was drenched with rainwater and the piled-up bodies of the wounded hit or scraped against each others' wounds as the truck rattled along an unpaved road.

Several died on the way.

The middle-school boy from Chungchong Province woke up and then fell into unconsciousness again many times during this trip. During the intervals of wakefulness, however, this young boy managed to make an important discovery, which was the fact that the truck was not headed for Pusan orTaegu but for the north. What astonished him more than this was that the soldiers moaning and groaning next to him were not sergeants or privates or captains from his unit but soldiers of the People's Army.

The key to this mystery lay in the mistake made by an orderly on the communist side who, confused by rain and darkness, mistook the middle-school student(who had his head shaved according to the school regulations) for one of their own in the process of separating the communist wounded from the wounded of the National Army at the site of the combat between the two armies.

The staff members of the clinic, therefore, could not help smiling when looking at this boy and the boy for his part smiled back as if he himself could share the sense of the absurd and the comic the staff members were experiencing at his expense.

None of these circumstances, however, could change the fact that he was now a member of the People's Army. It was too evident a fact for anyone to deny. When his wounded leg healed completely, he would be sent back to the battlefield as a 'heroic member' of the People's Army.

Maybe it was his face and disposition or maybe it was his age(somehow, this boy's youthfulness stood out among all the boy soldiers in the communist army of which there were a great number), but for one reason or another, every staff member seemed to like him.

When he first ran into Ihwa in the corridor, he had looked very pleased. Looking at his face and observing his manner, Ihwa had said to herself that this one did not have the look of a communist soldier.

After she heard the true circumstances from him, however, Ihwa began to treat him with an unconcealed friendliness. When she saw him come into the mess hall at the end of the line and take his seat at the end of the soldiers' table which was at right angles to the staff table, she gave a slight nod to him by way of greeting.

The taciturn greeting Ihwa sent this boy soldier was perhaps an incongruity in the rigid and fierce atmosphere which the communist soldiers created wherever they might be. For even during mealtimes, the communist soldiers were tense and far from communicative. Indeed tenseness and rigidity seemed to be a hereditary thing with these soldiers which they were born with like an outermost layer of hard skin encasing their whole being.

To be unguarded among these well-enforced beings was an unwise and highly risky policy. Ihwa knew this only too well. And yet, whenever Ihwa contemplated this matter, the picture of the red cross drawn on the whitewashed roof came to her mind and she told herself for the hundredth time that her life would have reached its end on the day when the communist ideals and the spirit of the red cross betrayed each other.

Her hopeless and agonizing longing for Ji-un, too, would have come to its end in the event of such a schism.

Ihwa was not afraid, therefore.

The boy who became a People's Army soldier because of his hair-style responded to Ihwa's greeting from the far end by touching his forehead with his right hand in a quick salute.This gesture he made reminded Ihwa of a similar body movement made by American soldiers.

And his spontaneity and trusting nature were of the same material which formed Ihwa's own outlook.

And this outlook was an extremely dangerous one.

Although in principle Ihwa ought to have found the personalities of the medical or sanitary officers heterogeneous, in actual fact, the civilian doctors and medical students, all of whom were residents of Seoul, caused her to experience in a way, a greater alienation than the communist personnel at the clinic.

Granted that it was difficult to tell the 'enthusiasts' from the'non-enthusiasts,'the voluntary staff, from the drafted ones, or a person who came there out of a humanistic motive uninhibited by ideological considerations from all the rest, each of these civilian staff members was too far separated from the others.

Even when these civilians were thrown together by themselves without any of the communist staff watching them, they never made conversation. If, against their will, a conversation got started, they made sure that it did not continue. Out of extreme precaution, they even avoided letting a gathering of two or three occur.

Their caution seemed to derive not only from their fear of the communists but also from distrust of each other. The heavy silence and rigid expression, one noticed among the civilian staff were more complex and impenetrable that those manifested by the communist soldiers and medical staff.

Ihwa did not know in what part of the school building the male civilian staff was lodging, but she could be sure that even in those quarters, the opaque walls between these people would never disappear.

As more days went on, Ihwa became quite used to the screams, the groans, the sight of blood, and the smell of pus. Even when she nearly bumped into a stretcher with a corpse on it, she was not frightened. All the time, she tried to move as precisely and as nimbly as if she were a mechanical tool. She knew that this was the only way to keep the screaming, groaning and the smell of blood and pus away from her. When she was helping in the operating room, she worked in complete tension, as if she were a soldier at the battlefield, so that nobody could touch her.

The bombing by the allied army in the meantime was getting more severe in the capital. Large flames and black pillars of smoke rose over the city at all hours. Thunderous explosions continued from the early hours to the middle of the night, shaking the very earth under people's feet.

It was clear that the battle in the Naktong River area was the most bloody and terrible that there ever had been. For nearly one month, the communists could not cross the bridge to the other side. Both sides were, moreover, losing innumerable units in this battle. Everyday, countless soldiers were getting killed and yet the battle went on with both sides pouring their last desperate efforts and resources into it.

The rumour that the water of the Naktong River was dyed red with blood was being circulated and probably it was no rumour but a fact.

The clinic where Ihwa worked was receiving far more wounded soldiers than they could treat. All of these were from the Naktong River battleground. Some among them could barely mouth their name and serial number through bloodless lips before they fell unconscious right on the spot.

"Main Complaints : Abrasion from a shell, bleeding from the thigh. . . ." Ihwa scribbled down quickly, getting angry that precious time was getting lost while she was making these entries on the check-up slips.

(I wouldn't mind doing this with non-urgent patients, but. . . .) And, in fact, these preliminary check-ups were dropped altogether soon enough.

The treatment after the extraction of bullets or the amputation of part of the body was left to auxiliary staff like Ihwa who worked almost without rest. Even at night, operations and treatment continued under candlelight shielded by black curtains.

Both inside and outside the wall of this temporary clinic was a crucible of helllike sufferings. Ihwa spent nightmarish days with not even enough leisure to look up at the sky.

One morning, Ihwa went to the washroom to clean her hands before going into the auditorium to take her turn at eating. A medical student named Kim Myongshik was standing in front of one of the approximately two dozen faucets. He took a long time to wash his hands. He was still at it when Ihwa, who had gone in after him, finished washing her hands and dried them with her handkerchief. Ihwa saw that Kim Myongshik was lathering his hands with soap.

Ihwa smiled at him casually and turned to go to the auditorium. Just then, however, Kim Myongshik spoke to her, raising his two hands upto his nostrils as if to see them better as he went on rubbing them,

"Comrade Ihwa, why don't you take a day off, today, eh?"

Hearing him say this, Ihwa could not help being startled. Not only was she surprised that this person was suggesting leave at a desperately pressing time as this but also she was taken aback by his having talked to her in that conversational way. No one had ever spoken to her in that fashion ever since she came to this clinic.

"Today? Why?" asked Ihwa in a lowered voice.

"Well, don't you want to see if everything's all right at home? Besides, getting out of this place is likely to get more difficult from now on," said Kim Myongshik, again in a casual tone.

Turning the faucet on, Kim Myongshik bent over the wash basin. Ihwa waited for him to finish washing for a while, and then started toward the auditorium seeing that Kim Myongshik who was still bent over the wash basin was not likely to put an end to his ablutions so quickly.

Kim Myongshik was a tall thin young man. He had a longish face and rather sharp features. There was nothing about him that resembled Tonggeun, and yet, for some reason he reminded Ihwa of her brother. Was it perhaps his facial expression which was always relaxed and unconcerned? Like Tonggeun, this young man, too, seemed to be straining his emotions through a sieve of objectivity before he gave any expression to them.

When this person looked serious, one had the impression that he was not really being serious but was pretending to be so.

Throughout the meal, Ihwa thought about Kim Myongshik's advice. When she inevitably thought of Tong-hun hiding in the pit shelter, she made up her mind to go home.

Once she decided to pay her family a visit, she suddenly became anxious to know about so many things. How Ogyop must be overburdened! Has the house escaped bombing?

She had come away from home hoping to forget the bad memory of what had happened between Ji-un and herself. Yet, hers had been act of irresponsibility toward her family. Her heart ached with remorse when she thought about it. And what about Kang Soku? Isn't he making trouble for my family?

When she left the mess hall, Ihwa did not return to the

treatment room but went to see Prof. Choi who was from the Attached Hospital of the National University because she had seen some of the girls working at the clinic go to the professor for a permit to go out.

"I would like to have some free time today," said Ihwa. "I have never contacted my family since I came in here. I won't take long."

Ihwa saw that Prof. Choi was grimacing with his eyes fixed on the floor of his room. The professor remained silent for quite a while. Then he raised his face finally and said,

"Your request is very hard to grant at a time like this."

What he said sounded all the more oppressive and final on account of the polite tone the old professor adopted. But Ihwa could not understand the full meaning of his gravity. So she said again,

"Then... do you mean I can't go?"

Prof. Choi waited another long while before he answered,

"You'd better ask Comrade Master Sergeant Koh."

The professor looked at Ihwa through his glasse with dull sorrowful eyes .

Ihwa went to Master-Sergeant Koh who was a medical officer. She found him walking back and forth in his room. He was not even wearing a sanitary gown.

The face and attitude of this man were very tense as if he were under great pressure of some kind. Even before she opened her mouth to speak to him, therefore, Ihwa knew that her request would be turned down.

Still, he asked Ihwa why she was there.

"I would like to go home for a visit. It won't take long. I want to make sure that my family is safe from the bombing," said Ihwa.

Relative freedom had been allowed those female helpers who were there on a voluntary basis but Ihwa had not so far taken advantage of this privilege for her own needs or wishes. She could not understand why she was being denied the use of this privilege so totally now.

"You must...refrain from taking leave...for the time being. We are now in a very critical impasse,"said the Master-Sergeant, walking back and forth in the room more precipitously.

His eyes as he looked at Ihwa were full of confusion and worry in which the tiny request Ihwa brought to him could have no part.

Leaving the master-sergeant's room, Ihwa went to the treatment room. She regretted that she had not gone to see Tong-hun before things reached this point. Preoccupied by her own misery, she had not had room in her mind to think about her family.

But there was little time for regrets or selfÇblame. Wounded soldiers on the threshhold of death were rushing in without a break, making it impossible for anyone working at the clinic to indulge in personal ruminations, which seemed like nothing but a triviality under the circumstances. Thus she accepted as fate the fact that she would never be able to leave this place without a shock.

Evening came.

Ihwa was with seven or eight wounded men in a room crowded with beds that were all different sizes and heights. Above each bed were hanging bottles of Ringer's solution and plasma. Looking at her watch, Ihwa carefully supervised injections of all the patients. The small wrist-watch she had worn when she came now served as an indispensable medical tool. When she took her break, she had to lend it to another co-helper.

Kim Myongshik came into the room unexpectedly.

"You can take off, now. Go and get ready," said Kim Myongshik and Ihwa saw that he was not urging her to go just for fun although she had no way of telling whether or not he knew any definite reason why Ihwa should go home that night.

Maybe I could just take off my blood-soiled gown and walk out of the front gate with a casual nod to the guard, thought Ihwa deciding to trust Kim Myongshik's advice that she should pay her family a visit.

"Thank you for the advice. I think I'll go," she said to Kim Myongshik.

"You can get somebody else to take your turn. I wish I could help you out but. . . ." he said with his eyes on the large steriliz er he was holding in both hands on top of which were piled balls of absorbent cotton and a bandage. His gown was soiled with blood stains, also.

"It's alright," said Ihwa.

"It's not long before curfew now, so it may be difficult for you to come back tonight,"said Kim Myongshik, leaving the room.

Going to the window, Ihwa looked out toward the gateway across the yard. From the second-floor vantage point, Ihwa had a good view of the entire vicinity.

Some medical officers and orderlies were walking back after closing the ambulance door. Two more orderlies were helping a high-ranking officer with splints on his leg to walk out to where a jeep was waiting. After the officer was hoisted onto the seat, the jeep took off along with the ambulance.

(A transfer. . . .)thought Ihwa.

They were moving even the patients out of here.The vehicles, Ihwa judged, must have gone toward Seoul Station. Maybe a train which would carry these soldiers and officers to Pyong-yang or Wonsan was waiting at the Station. . . . The area around the gate looked unusually crowded and disturbed this evening. Many men either in sanitary gowns or army uniforms were moving in and out of the gateway.

Maybe some of the men that are going out of that gate are going home to say goodbye to their families because they are such devoted party members that they do not hesitate to leave their wives and children, thought Ihwa. Or, some of them could be going to the Station on some important duty.

It did look as if going home would not be a problem thanks to all the movements and confusion. She could even decide not to come back at all. She had not given her address or anything in this place, nor did anybody know her identity.

Yet the two patients whom Ihwa was watching over now were literally on the dividing line between life and death. Their hearts still beat but they had no consciousness and their pulse, too, stopped every now and then. The rest of the patients were also in quite a critical condition, having lost a great deal of blood. They were in no state to be transferred.

Ihwa decided that she could not leave these helpless men to anyone else's care. And besides, no one was free enough to take over somebody else's duty.

Walking back from the window, Ihwa examined each bed, feeling the patient's pulse. Soon she forgot about what was taking place outside. She consulted her watch and checked to see if the medicinal liquids were trickling into their veins at an adequate speed. From one of the patients, she pulled the injection needle out.

"Thank you, Comrade,"said the patient looking up at Ihwa with enfeebled eyes.

"Do you feel better?" said Ihwa feeling so moved by the man's utterance that she almost cried.

"Yes...much better. . . ."

But there was no perceivable reason why the man should feel so much better. All the same Ihwa was always so glad when a patient who had lost consciousness woke up that she thanked heaven.

Kim Myongshik who had come back with a bundle of something in his arms passed by after standing to the doorway watching Ihwa from the back for a few seconds.

The number of People's Army medical officers and medical assistants decreased by several men daily. Except that time when Ihwa watched the vehicles carry off patients from the gateway, however, all these transfers were being undertaken very quietly under the cover of night. In time, medical equipment and medicines, too, were cut so that the rate of death among the patients rose sharply. Even so, the clinic was packed with patients who kept coming in.

The buildings across the street fell one by one under the bombing. All day long, the smoke of gunpowder filled the air while black fumes and dust blocked out the sky.

Since the night when Ihwa noticed the transfer of patients, the co-lodgers of the room she slept in were reduced to one woman named Lee Keumsun. Maybe the others went home, or maybe they went north with the patients and People's Army medical staff, thought Ihwa. Lee Keumsun herself declared briefly that she did not know when asked by Ihwa if she knew what happened to them. The two women never discussed this matter again.

One morning, Ihwa noticed that the number of doctors and patients were visibly reduced. The tension and atmosphere of disaster inside and outside of the clinic was at breaking point creating a murderous desolation in the air.

As if this extreme tension was conveyed even to the patients struggling between life and death, one of them asked Ihwa in a faint panting voice as she stood by his bed,

"Tell me, Comrade, where in the south is our army now?"

The People's Army was doing entirely nothing about the daily increasing air-raids these days. Not only the high-flying bombers but also the fighters that flew so low that they nearly touched the house tops were left almost completely unchall-enged.

Only the sounds of rifles filled the streets like at the time when they first came into the capital.

Even the guards of the clinic tried to shoot a family member of a doctor working at the clinic. This person had come to the gate of the clinic and asked the guard persistently to let him see the doctor.

The eyes of the orderlies shone harshly and they watched each other's movements constantly. Even Kim Myongshik switched back to his former attitude of impersonality toward Ihwa. Ihwa told herself that this was no time to talk about going home or taking leave.

Another night came and along the corridor an endless line

of wounded soldiers were waiting to get into the treatment room. Although all day Ihwa kept changing the dressings on the wounds until her arms ached unbearably, her work was not over. And this was no wonder because even those patients who had been getting redressed every two days were now out in the line to have their dressings changed.

Wiping the sweat off her forehead with an elbow, Ihwa looked out at the corridor which was noisy with the sound of footsteps. Just then, an orderly called her from the open door,

"Comrade Wu Ihwa! Come out to the yard with your possessions."

Ihwa was changing the dressing on the shoulder of a sergeant who was as thin as a dried leaf. After she finished changing the dressing, she readjusted the triangular bandage around his neck. The next patient had a plaster cast on one arm from which a watery discharge was oozing out. As if he was undecided whether or not to show Ihwa his arm, this patient stood glancing at Ihwa's face uneasily.

"Come up here, please. Let's clean up the wound quickly," said Ihwa picking up the alcohol-soaked cotton ball.

Just at this moment, however, a voice roared out in the corridor, "About turn!"

"Forward move!"

The patient with the plaster cast on his arm threw one more glance at Ihwa. Then he went toward the line of men following the order given by voice.

Ihwa took off her gown and with the folded gown on one arm went out to the school yard. Wounded soldiers were standing in line but some were moving toward the gate in silence. Outside the gate, the sound of trucks taking off one after another continued.

Some of the medical staff who were also standing in line a little away from the rows of soldiers were holding their medicine cases in hand and several were wearing gaiters.

Ihwa remembered that she had left a cardigan and a blouse in the room where she slept but did not go back there to fetch them. Through the front door which was in the dark because of the 'light-out,' Ihwa saw a number of men being taken out on the stretcher.

Ihwa and other staff members were led out through the gate and then they were ordered to get aboard a truck. All this time, they were watched by a guard who held his gun at the ready.

Nobody spoke.

The truck with the staff members took off behind a numerous other trucks. Through the night air which had begun to cool down, the trucks drove in single file. And it was in the direction of the East Gate that these vehicles were speeding.

Some of the streets which Ihwa had known well looked different because of the bombing. She glanced into the distance toward Pildong where her house was but could see nothing but the grey shadow of the mountains. They got off in front of a small building which was Chongryangri Railway Station.

Finally, the train began to move with a thump. Through the darkness of the night, the train ran slowly picking up speed. It was midnight, now. All things between heaven and earth seemed to be hiding without so much as making one movement or noise. A greyish-blue moon was casting timid beams from the center of the night sky which was as black as if somebody had spilt ink all over it.

Ihwa rode the last car which was a freightcar enclosed by knee-high wooden panels.

About three dozen people were riding together in this car including the medical staff of the clinic and soldiers. Ihwa sat on the bare wooden floor of the car hugging her knees with both arms, and looked at Seoul which began to recede in the opposite direction from the running train. The city disappeared into darkness very slowly.

Ihwa felt that she would probably never see the city again. Yes, she felt almost sure that she wouldn't.

Just as she cut all ties with her life of only a few months ago, her ties with her parents, brothers and sister, and also Ji-un, she was now breaking her bond with the familiar sights of this city.

One of her newly-acquired pieces of knowledge was the fact that all things can be wiped out without a trace. The family in which she was born and grew up, her school which was the soil in which her spiritual life grew, and Ji-un who was her teacher in love were all gone from her now. Yes, all things disappeared from one.

Ihwa drew in her mind the faces of her parents and the other members of her family. But these faces receded farther and farther away just like the house roofs and electric poles along the roadside.

The train was moving at an incredibly low speed. It seemed that even the train was trying to muffle its breathing. The passengers on the train looked as if they were all paralyzed. Everybody sat still, with vacant eyes. Even the soldiers with rifles on their shoulders were fixing their empty eyes on far mountains as if they were not in complete possession of their minds.

The train halted now and then. If anybody had had a firm intention to escape and had kept himself alert, he could have succeeded without too much difficulty.

Ihwa, however, merely sat forlornly. The shadow of death was too close for her to extricate herself from its touch. She felt, in fact, as if her very skin and hair were already inseparably fastened to this black shadow of death.

Ihwa breathed in the cool night air. Although the air had the tangy taste of smoke mostly, one could at times breathe in fresh air, too, which was not contaminated with the odor of war. At these times, Ihwa felt a small but keen joy in being alive. And she felt that this life albeit drenched in sorrow surged to the very end of her limbs with some force. This feeling gave her an urge to run or do something of that sort to give vent to this powerful energy.

But, of course, she could not do any such thing because it would mean almost certain death under the circumstances.

Hoping to find stars in the sky, Ihwa looked up. She saw, however, only thick layers of cloud which looked as if they were innumerable strips of some thin black fabric torn up by coarse hands.

Ihwa kept on looking up still wishing to find some stars. Then she recalled something that was very similar to stars. It was the memory of Tong-hun's eyes which she now visualiz ed in her heart.

When Tong-hun smiled silently, his eyes shone with a clear luminescence just like stars. Even when others were laughing and talking noisily, Tong-hun merely smiled with his clear eyes without saying anything.

It had been a long time since she last saw Tong-hun's face with its clear eyes. Within the pit where he was hiding, those clear eyes might have been blurred by dust and lack of light so that they would by now look as dull as human hair coverd with spider webs. Ihwa felt her heart choke with a new sorrow.

A great sorrow-sorrow for things from which she had to part and things she had to forget-overwhelmed her with the explosion of a violent sob. Burying her face in both hands, she sobbed uncontrollably.

"Comrade! Comrade!"

Somebody was whispering to her had shaking her by the arm. This person's discreetly lowered tone woke Ihwa to reality and she raised her head from her hands.

The fierce, impersonal world lay before her eyes again. The soldier who was sitting perched on the wooden side of the freight car with his rifle on his shoulder was looking sternly at Ihwa. The train was picking up speed. With her face raised Ihwa let her quiet tears run down her cheeks.

A confusion like the one that had overtaken the city at the onset of the war was taking place among the citizens. While the radio broadcast was still raving about the exploits of the courageous People's Army, the latter had fled out of the capital.

Citizens could be sure that the end of this war was truly near. But no one could tell just how many innocent people would still have to lose their lives before the end actually arrived.

Large formations of bombers continued to drop bombs. The cannons were shooting from(it seemed) all the mountain slopes without a break. The bombing and shooting continued from day to night and from night to day turning so many areas into a sea of flames and smoke.

The rumor about UN troops landing in Inchon seemed well -grounded. This was an event that the citizens had been waiting for with so much anguish. Only when this long-awaited event took place it caused too many deaths. One may say that this was inevitable, but the shells and bombs made citizens scatter like ants in all directions sometimes jumping into a stream to escape being burnt by the flames but then being crushed to death by other people who jumped in after them.

The Namsan area in which Mr. Wu Taegap's house was located seemed to have been chosen as a main target for shellfire. The slopes of Namsan were punctured in so many places by the shells and the tiles covering the roofs of Mr. Wu Taegap's house were blown off.

Then the communist soldiers in the sarangchae pulled out. A number of small and large vehicles took off making loud engine noises after which the house looked almost empty. The People's Council office across the alley, too, was closed down. The windows of the office of the Women's League next to that of the People's Council were left open but its front door was blocked with barbed wire.

The first thing Ogyop did was to go to the shelter and bring Tong-hun home.

Tong-hun's hair was long and unkempt, his face was pale, and he staggered weakly. Although it was nearly evening, he blinked a lot as if the light were too strong. His knees were bent as if for good.

"We must go somewhere," said Ogyop. "Carry this bag of

rice, Tong-hun. And you'd better hold onto this, mother. The jewelry will recover its value again, you'll see."

"All right, daughter, so let's. . . ."

"You had better put on your hat, Tong-hun. Your hair is. . . ."

Just at this moment, however, a pillar broke with a screech and a sliding door flew up into the air and then landed on the yard. It was a bizarre sight which the remaining members of the family watched with gloomy hearts.

Both Yong-a's mother and the Old Man were gone and only the Old Woman was making herself busy making rice-balls.

"We will have to walk. We will be hungry on the way,"said the Old Woman.

The Old Woman had suggested that the family try going to her country house. Judging that there was no better alternative, Ogyop agreed. Although she was worried about Ihwa, she could not think of any other action.

"Go and tell father to step out, now," said Ogyop.

"All right," replied Tong-hun going inside without taking off his shoes.

Ogyop turned to go and see the Old Woman.

As soon as she turned, however, she emitted a low but sharp scream as if she had seen something terrifying. It was none other than the figure of Kang Soku standing in her way holding his whip in both hands.

Ever since Ihwa had disappeared, this man had harrassed Ogyop constantly.

"Where has Comrade Ihwa gone? Tell me, will you?"

This cruel-faced sergeant asked Ogyop again and again and at these times even Ogyop lost her presence of mind and experienced extreme fear. After some time passed, however, he dropped his rough manner with her.

He grew quieter and even more civilized. Yet the sensitive woman could not but feel the meaning of his persistent eyes on her whenever they had chance to be in sight of each other. Thus his existence began to drive her into an unbroken state of fear and uneasiness. In time, she was more afraid of Kang

Soku than the bombs.

That he did not take any further steps beyond staring at Ogyop with his cold reptilian eyes was probably thanks to the presence and authority of the captain who was his superior and who resided in the same house. It was easy to see, however, that Kang Soku who was much older than the captain with the black wart on his left cheek was developing an uncontrollable hate and rebelliousness toward his young superior. Often he could seen be staring after the captain playing with the whip in a menacing manner with both hands. But this was a secret which only Ogyop sensed.

He was standing now just outside the middle gate, like a pole, without a smile or word. Ogyop felt a chill run down her spine. The captain with the black wart was no longer in the house. There was now nobody who could protect Ogyop from this hateful man.

Kang Soku pulled a pistol from his side and then still holding it in his hand stepped into the inner courtyard. Ogyop knew that he did not mean to use it on her but all the same she could not keep herself from moving backward.

"Come with me. Let's leave together," said Kang Soku with an unnatural grimace on his face. At the corners of his mouth which seemed to be perennially jeering, a few wrinkles had formed as rigid and unnatural as if they had been glued on.

Panting from lack of breath, Ogyop shook her head, her lips bleached white with fear.

"You must come with me!" said Kang Soku.

Right at this moment, however, a noise which was different from that of gunfire came from outside the sarangchae. It was the sound of a sidecar coming to a stop.

The captain with the black wart looked in through the small side gate between the sarangchae and the house. The flames from the bombed area nearby made orange reflections on the visor of his hat.

"Master-Sergeant Kang! What are you doing here?" he shouted.

In spite of himself, Kang Soku winced at hearing the captain's voice and lowered the hand holding the pistol. His eyes instantly became white with hate and fury, however, and he refused to answer.

"Come over here. I want to talk to you," said the captain and then turning back walked away around the corner.

For a few seconds, Kang Soku did not move, as if he was following some thought. Then he brought the hand holding the pistol to the level of his chest and perused it, shuffling it on his palm as if to guess its weight. Then suddenly he put the pistol back into its holster at his side in a quick jerky movement. Then he stomped away toward the sarangchae following the order of his superior.

A suffocating panic enveloped the inner courtyard while an ominous silence spread through the half darkness of the evening hour during the interval between explosions. A number of planes were disappearing toward the edge of the sky like a flock of bats.

Not a sound came from the sarangchae. A heavy silence fell.

Then, bang! bang! Came two pistol shots.

It seemed that one of the two fell dead and the other whoever it was would be reappearing on this side. Footsteps were heard. The sound approached through the side gate.

"I've come to take you with me, Comrade. I am sorry I can't help the others. Tell them to get to safety as best they can. But you had better come away with me at once."

It was the captain. He said at once,

"The danger has come near. The English and American invaders won't leave you alone, comrade Ogyop," said the captain, then as if he could not suppress his impatience any longer he took Ogyop's arm with both hands and shook it.

Ogyop, however, shook her head in refusal. She wanted to offer him an explanation but the words did not come out her mouth.

"Don't you realize what horror will take place soon? If you are really that ignorant, I must take you away by force. . . ."

said the man grabbing hold of Ogyop bodily. The communist officer's eyes were bloodshot and his breathing was rapid and harsh.

"Little Sister!" called Tong-hun coming between the captain and Ogyop.

Mr. Wu Taegap, too, dashed toward the man. Since he sprang down directly from the taechong where he had been watching this scene, he was barefoot.

"No, please don't take her, Comrade Officer," said Mr. Wu Taegap in an entreating voice.

The captain, however, pulled out his pistol and aimed it at them pointing the muzzle from Tong-hun's chest to Mr. Wu Taegap's in turn. His face was transformed by the desperate urgency of a hunted man.

Suddenly, with a short scream, Ogyop sprang between his pistol and her brother. At the same instant, the captain halted himself with a jerk. His face and lips were filled with terror at what he might have done if he hed pulled the trigger, albeit unintentionally. His hand was trembling violently. Clutching the pistol anew, however, the captain shouted,

"I will shoot whoever interferes!"

Again, Tong-hun leapt toward him. Seeing this, the communist officer pushed Ogyop away from in front of him. Now Tong-hun and the man stood facing each other. The man with the gun was standing completely still without even breathing. Ogyop felt that he was about to shoot her brother.

"Just a second! Please, wait a second. I will go. I will go if you will put the gun down. Please don't hurt people," said Ogyop panting painfully. Then, looking Tong-hun in the eyes, she said,

"Go quickly with mother and father. Please, go at once. And don't worry about me. . . ." said Ogyop her two eyes saying more than her lips. Then she nodded her head delicately as if to say 'go'. Audibly, she said once more, "Please do as I tell you. Please!"

Her imploring eyes caused a sharp pain in Tong-hun's heart.

He knew what Ogyop's intention was.

"Little Sister . . . . "said Tong-hun he, too, conveying more things with his expression than with his voice.

Madam Shim went out first through the gate trembling and crying. The Old Woman followed her carrying a large bundle on her head.

The communist officer was still holding Ogyop tightly by the waist waing his pistol in this and that direction with his other hand.

Since the sidecar broke down, they had to walk. Although during the dark hours, they followed the open road, they entered a mountain path after dawn to avoid the strafing of the fighter planes.

Already, they were quite far from Seoul and from the bombing and flames, but the fighter planes that suddenly appeared low in the sky and the dead bodiés of stragglers that were strewn all along the road they were walking made them realiz e that the nightmare had not yet ended.

By this time, Ogyop had got so tired that she could not see ahead of her clearly. Her head likewise was half paralyzed. But the communist officer kept on walking never letting go of Ogyop's hand which he was clasping tightly in his.

Ogyop staggered or fell at times and then the communist captain allowed her to sit down and rest for a while. But he always urged her on after a brief while as if unable to withstand the tension of non-action.

Often, the captain looked back toward the capital which they had left behind. He seemed to be in fear of something in particular. When now and then a few communist soldiers over -took the two and asked him such questions as, 'Have you seen Unit so-and-so pass this way? We are from Squadron so-and-so of Battalion so-and-so...," the captain invariably replied that the unit the other mentioned had passed that way although they had not seen any unit of soldiers go in that direction ever since they first set out on this road. But the soldiers who heard the captain's answer hurriedly walked on ahead of them.

At one point, Ogyop realized that she was really too exhausted to move on. She was not hungry having eaten the meal which the captain made a civilian family whom he woke up from sleep prepare for them at the outset of their trip last night. Yet, she felt a terrible thirst. Even the air she breathed seemed salty and scorching.

Wiping the drops of perspiration that rose on her forehead with the back of one hand, she looked up at the crimson sun which had just started to throw out its rays. Feeling an acute dizziness, however, she fell onto the captain who was holding her by the hand.

Startled, the communist officer caught her in his arms. The girl in her pink blouse, short black skirt and pigtailed shiny hair was immobile, her face looking as white as paper and her eyes closed tight. The captain felt that the girl's hand he was holding, too, was getting colder as seconds passed.

Picking up Ogyop he went to the shade of a tree and laid her down on the soft grassy ground. Since he did not have a handkerchief or anything else he could use for the purpose, he dipped his own hands in the cool water that flowed down the valley and cooled Ogyop's forehead with his hands. He looked down at her in sorrow and dread.

Ogyop opened her eyes after some time. Sitting up, she said to the communist captain,

"I cannot walk so fast. If you wait for me, you will get caught. I think you had better walk on by yourself."

"I can't do that," said the captain sitting down beside Ogyop and looking down into the valley. He sat silently pulling grassblades with his hand for a while.

Ogyop kept her mouth shut, too. She had nothing more to say if he was determined not to let her go.

"My name is Lee Songdo," said the captain. "I was living in Hamheung when the war broke out. I am trusted by the party and my superior, too, recognizes my devotion to my work.

I will be able to stand by you and protect you. You have nothing to worry about."

"....."

"Nobody will be left alive in Seoul in the end because we already have plans to attack it again. We must do that in order to salvage the southern half of our country."

A look of pity appeared on Ogyop's face for a second, but still she kept her silence without raising her head.

"I will guarantee to everyone that you have been a very enthusiastic sympathizer with communism. But you, too, must be careful. You must never say anything about your family in Seoul which may sound not quite right among us," said the captain.

(This man is a machine, nothing but a machine....) thought Ogyop listening to his words. Does he think that I could really think and act like the members of the Women's League or the People's Army women soldiers? She remembered the two shots after he had disappeared into sarangchae where Kang Soku followed him.

(Yes, this man is non-human....)

"When our mission is accomplished," said Lee Songdo and then paused for a second looking down and biting his lip. One of his uniform sleeves was torn about a palm's length down from the shoulder. Maybe, he had caught it on a branch while walking through the darkness.

Half of his lowered head was in the shadow of a tree. His black wart which was now in the shadow was one element in this man's otherwise rigid, albeit handsome enough face. Maybe his Maker meant it as a playful joke. Ogyop turned her eyes away from his wart.

"When our mission is accomplished," he said again. "Then ... I will be able to make you happy, Comrade Ogyop. Marry me, please."

For a long while after he said this, Lee Songdo sat still without budging. Then he turned his head as if mustering up enough courage to look at Ogyop.

His boyish bashfulness moved Ogyop's heart but she said nothing.

Marry a communist military man? It was unimaginable. What she really needed to do was escape from this man. She needed to break out of his clutches as and travel back to Seoul.

"Even if I had to leave again as soon as we get to Hamheung, you could... I could. . . ."

He seemed to be looking for a good way to put what he was thinking into words. For a second, he seemed to give up on conveying his thought, and then, as if changing his mind, he tried again,

"What I mean is you can join the army if you like. We can be in the same department and. . . ." Again he lost the words.

He tried to go on explaining what he had in mind many more times over, but finally the other's persistent cruel silence put an end to his effort.

They started walking again. They climbed up the mountain slope and fought through the bushes. Yet they had to keep not too far away from the road which stretched beyond looking quite white among all the green. They had to keep their eyes on this road at all times as they walked and at times they had to run across a field in order not to make a detour over a mountain which was too far away from the road. The sun was high up in the sky.

The communist officer walked on mostly in silence, but now and then he talked to Ogyop in a gentle voice. He asked her if she was not thirsty or tried to cheer her up by telling her that he was sure to find a farm house a little way ahead.

Going closer to the roadside was too dangerous because of the planes that kept coming back there incessantly. Finding a house in the woods was very difficult.

Even when he was not talking to her, Ogyop could feel a youthful tenderness flowing out of his body and enveloping. Ogyop experienced this feeling with a sense of despair.

Still, she did not show any sign of sympathy outwardly. As if disappointed by Ogyop's lack of responsiveness, the communist officer walked on looking dejected and biting his lip. They took another rest on a mountain slope. In front of their eyes was a rather long stretch of flat land. It was clear that they would lose a great deal of time if they were to make a detour along mountain paths to get to the other side of the plain. The distance across the flat land to the mountain foot at its end was about two hundred meters. The man with the black wart seemed to be measuring that distance with his eyes.

If he were to move at my pace, he would surely be caught before he got to his destination, thought Ogyop. Since sunrise, countless stragglers had passed by them that day alone.

Ogyop wanted to tell him how he was being held back because of her and how dangerous it was, but she knew what his answer would be. He would say that he could not go on by himself. And so she kept her mouth shut.

She felt she had to get up as soon as her heart stopped beating so hard that it nearly burst. For him, she wished that her breathing would calm down soon.

Lavender-coloured flowers of wild chrysanthemum were seen here and there among the grass. Ogyop remembered how these flowers were abundant in the grassland near the pit shelter at the back of her house. Then she noticed some wild strawberries that were ripe and shiny like rubies half hidden by the wild chrysanthemums and grass.

Ogyop touched the berries with the tip of her fingers. Instantly, the ripe berries fell scattered among the grasses as if they were so many glass beads. She picked up these berries one by one from among the grass.

About half a dozen berries were gathered in her palm. Raising her head from looking at the berries, Ogyop saw that the captain had been staring at her. Without realizing what she was doing, Ogyop held out the hand with the berries toward him saying,

"These are edible. They must be sweet."

The communist captain at first did not seem to understand the meaning of Ogyop's words. Then he blushed all of a sudden. Bending toward her, he made a move as if to pick up a few berries from her palm. But suddenly, he grabbed the hand holding the berries in his and brought his cheek down against her caught hand.

This explosion of male passion startled Ogyop. Softly, she extracted her hand from his grasp and stood up before he could say anything.

The two young people were rescued from this situation of confusion and awkwardness by a noise from the bushes behind them. Undoubtedly, it was made by some soldiers who were travelling northward with a vague blind hope of finding their commander. Ogyop and the captain turned back toward the noise of the conversation these unseen stragglers were having. The voices stopped coming nearer before the speakers appeared out of the bush, however. Covered by the branches and the leaves, even their clothes were invisible. But their voices were clearly audible. It was apparent that the unknown stragglers were quarreling with each other.

"I don't want to go. Don't drag me on!"

"Are you out of your mind, you fool? There's no such thing as freedom here. They are all slaves who live down here. Haven't you learned that much at school?"

"The truth is I've found out that's not how it is. I am going back and I will look up my brother who's said to've come south when he was a kid."

A brief silence fell after this. Then the other voice said,

"Hey, don't do this to me. I'll give this watch to you if you don't go back. I've held onto it because I wanted to show it to someone back in Pyong-yang. But here, I will give it to you now. And this sub-machine gun, too. I will give this weapon of honor to you."

"Don't stop me. I've come this far because I didn't want to part from you. But I don't want to go back to that place again. I mean it."

The captain walked over to the bush from which the voices were coming and, pushing aside a branch, looked in. Two boy soldiers were standing there. They were wearing ragged uniforms and sneakers that were coming apart and which they had bound with pieces of rope. Startled by the sudden appearance of the captain before them, the two boys stared at him wide-eyed.

It was only to confirm which of the two boys was the traitor that Lee Songdo delayed the execution a second or two. As soon as this point was cleared up, he pulled out his pistol and shot the boy dead without one word more.

He did not pay any attention to the other boy but walked back to Ogyop. Ogyop saw that he was neither aroused nor perturbed. Rather, his eyes had become more serene and peaceful.

As soon as she registered this in her consciousness, Ogyop began to feel an insurmountable anger toward the man. Her eyes which were always so kind and calm now stared at him with fire in them.

The communist captain, however, did not seem to understand why Ogyop's face had turned so angry all of a sudden. With a look of incomprehension, therefore, he stared back at Ogyop.

Glistening tears began to form in Ogyop's eyes. If this had been Ihwa, she might have raised her head high and screamed at the top of her voice. She might have given immediate vent to her fury and hurled a battery of accusations at the man.

However, this was Ogyop, and she did not make any scene over this. Only, in a low voice, she said simply,

"Is killing people nothing to you?"

After saying this one sentence which was as much protest as she had in her power to muster up, Ogyop shed a flood of hot tears.

But why was she shedding all these tears? Did it mean that in the course of the difficult and perilous journey they had managed together since yesterday, she had developed an affection toward this alien man?

While continuously contemplating an escape from this man,

refusing his appeal for love which was a mixture of violence, loyalty, and bashfulness, had she then developed a dependence on one underlying streak of humanity which this man did not have?

All was over now, in any case. A chilly wind blew across Ogyop's heart and she felt that she could not stand being by this cruel man's side any longer. She began to run down the slope without any idea which way she was going. She was merely running toward the flat land where the ground which had been the bed of a river was white and open and where there were shingle and prickly grass. . . .

Lee Songdo who was running after her shouting something suddenly screamed.

"The plane! Drop down!"

But maybe it was Ogyop's imagination that made her think she had heard him say these words because in truth she could not have.

The plane which had soared up perpendicularly from behind the mountain ridge had dropped down to just above Ogyop's head and started shooting with its machinegun, bang, bang, bang, bang. . . .

Ogyop threw herself on the ground and started rolling.

The plane which seemed to have gone away come back in no time and swept the ground underneath with its machinegun fire.

The earth in front of Ogyop's face scattered and stones split in two. Ogyop buried her face deeper inside her bent arms.

Until a deadly silence descended and red dragonflies came down to rest on the hem of her skirt, Ogyop remained prostrate on the ground sobbing and sobbing into her arms.

Some more time passed. Ogyop pulled herself up. She felt calmer now. And she was not hurt anywhere. The flat land before her was all quiet.

Then her.eyes spotted human body a little way from her. It was Lee Songdo. He was lying on his stomach with his arms stretched out in the direction of Ogyop.

The train carrying Ihwa and the others from the clinic moved very slowly during the night. Since there were many spots where the railway needed to be repaired before the train could move on, moreover, the distance covered by it in the entire span of a night was indeed quite small in the light of the time taken.

Before daybreak, Ihwa and her party had to get off the train and hide in some public building such as the local elementary or middle school far from the railroad. While they were taking cover in this manner, the train either went forward to hide in some tunnel or went backward to some other place of safety.

Although there were many unwounded soldiers riding in the front cars, the transfer was a great problem every time because of the many severely wounded soldiers.

Even after they had finished transporting the wounded to shelter by means of stretchers or by lending them a hand, more problems ensued because they had to take many strict precautions such as not building fires to cook and so on. There were long waits before one could get a ball of rice, and cleaning the wounds or washing clothes, too, became very difficult.

Some of the soldiers who were suffering from 'especially painful wounds called out in whimpering voices all day long,

"Comrade Nurse! Please!"

"Please come and look, Comrade Nurse!"

All the medical staff including the military doctors and military nurses were exhausted with the fatigue of hard travelling on top of their great overload of work of the past many days and, whether because they could not spare themselves in helping their suffering patients or because they had no means of assuaging their suffering, they were ignoring the pain-filled screams that pounded on their eardrums all day long.

The only person except Ihwa who paid any attention to these suffering soldiers was Lee Keumsun.

As Ihwa judged, Lee Keumsun was a true communist. She seemed, therefore, to be pleased with the fact that the group was being moved to Pyong-yang. She only seemed discontented that they were going there in this piteous beggarly fashion on account of the 'heinous last ditch-effort of the American and English imperialists.'

"They won't last long. Take my word for it!" said Lee Keumsun every time planes flew across with an ugly roar.

Ihwa gave a massage to the arms or legs of the patients who were especially in pain. Also, she rubbed around the wound with a ball of absorbent cotton dipped in alcohol solvent. Sometimes, she rubbed just any spot on a man's body to make him feel better. This was done with those of the wounded whom the doctors judged to be hopeless. It was the best Ihwa could do for them. And, in fact, this practically useless attention often helped the patients calm down for some while although their screaming resumed soon enough.

"Thank you, Comrade," said one soldier to Ihwa who came to his side and massaged his arm for him. He had lost one arm from the shoulder down. Yet, it was the other unwounded arm in which he complained of a great pain. Ihwa gave a good massage to the arm.

"When you go back home this time, will you be seeing your family?" asked Ihwa with the intention of making the man forget, even for a while.

"I left home long ago." said the soldier. He was not much older than Tong-hun. "Even so, there must be somebody at homé, isn't there? Your mother, your sister, or. . . ."

"Yes, they would be living at home," said the wounded man in an uncertain voice.

"I see," said Ihwa with a smile, not knowing what else to say and realizing how difficult it was to carry on a conversation with him.

"Did you go to school?" She tried again.

"I received my education from the party."

"What sort of an education? I believe it would be quite different from the kind of education we received from our schools, wouldn't it?"

The soldier remained silent for a while, and then he began

to explain,

"Each one of us is a cell belonging to our party. Cells are very important. Very important," said the soldier underlining the word 'very' with his tone.

"If a cell has accomplished its mission, it can have no regrets even if it should die out. This is an honourable end for it. We are all born to live and die for our nation."

"I believe so. But...," Ihwa went on talking although it took her some effort to hide her feeling of alienation from this soldier. "I am sure your parents will be very glad to see you again."

"I don't know. I am not sure I know them very well. And I don't think they know me well," said the soldier with an expressionless face.

The sergeant who lay beside this soldier died before he was moved back to the train that night. Before he died this man recited some words of praise for their Leader and called out several 'manse(long live!)'s for him in a dwindling voice and then he stopped breathing.

As if he had no one near him, this man went on his way to the eternal home all by himself without calling the nurse or seeking the attentive eye or comforting hand of a friend.

Their last hours which Ihwa witnessed were all more or less like this. In a dry voice, they called out 'manse's without emotion and then received death, again, without any sign of emotion. They died the death of a fish. Then the unwounded soldiers took out the body and threw dirt on it.

There was one exceptional case, however. There was one young soldier who kept on calling out 'mother!'

"Mother! Oh, mother! Mother! Mother!" cried this boy who had one leg cut off from the knee down and had been hit by shells in many parts of his body. Except for his rather endearing face, blood-stained bandages were covering him almost entirely. The stump of a leg that looked like a log had started to heal back at the clinic, but now, the wound was putrefying and giving off a foul odor. There was no more supply of penicillin.

"Mother! Mother!" he called with tears welling out of the corners of his eyes.

"Does it hurt a lot?" said Ihwa, and the boy nodded his head. Then without taking his eyes from Ihwa's face, he whispered repeatedly, 'mother,' 'mother,' 'mother!'

"Wait a moment. I will go and fetch some medicine," said Ihwa and went to look for master-sergeant Koh who was a medical assistant and was in charge of distributing medicine. Ihwa found him kneeling down beside a wounded man in the room at the end of the corridor. He was giving the patient a shot.

"Won't you take a look at the soldier who lost his leg, please? Couldn't you give him a pain-killing injection, even some cocaine?"

Master-sergeant Koh looked up at Ihwa's imploring face, and then he sighed audibly.

"Two aspirins...," he said to the orderly standing beside him. The orderly opened the doctor's bag he was carrying and taking out two white tablets handed them to Ihwa. The wounded boy swallowed down the aspirin obediently. Then he entreated Ihwa not to leave his side yet.

"Please don't go, Comrade. Just a while longer. . . . I will die very soon."

Ihwa stayed holding his hand. The wounded boy called again and again, 'Mother!,' 'Mother!'.

Now and then, as if remembering it suddenly, he said,

"Comrade Nurse, please go to my other wounded comrades. They must be in need of you. But please come back to me just once more."

This boy had lost consciousness by the time the group was getting ready to move back to the train after sunset. He had a high fever and his pulse was irregular. Also he went into frequent convulsions which, it was apparent, would cease for good in about half an hour.

In order to file through the half-darkness toward the railroad, all the temporary occupants of the one-night lodging thronged out of the building. The two orderlies who came into the room where the wounded boy lay unconscious put the flashlight on him. Then they left this boy's bedside to carry another patient out.

Ihwa remained standing by the boy who was definitely still alive even if he would surely be dead in half an hour. Lee Keumsun peeped in from the corridor beckoning with her hand.

"Come with me. I have something to talk to you about," she said. When Ihwa went to the doorway, she was already walking ahead hurriedly toward an empty room. Ihwa saw two sets of army uniforms spread out on a table in the empty room. They looked relatively clean. There were even two leather belts which the medical officers fastened around their waists.

"What do you say? Don't you think it would be a good idea for us to change into these? They will keep us warmer against the chilly night air, too," said Lee Keumsun in a rather uncertain tone.

"I believe they would," said Ihwa, proceeding to put on the uniform jacket on top of her dress. Both the sleeves and the trousers were too long for her so that she had to roll the bottoms up many times and fix the trouser waist with the leather belt.

"Wait a minute. The belts will be too big for us," said Lee Keumsun and with a pair of scissors used for operations, made additional holes in the belts, "You are pretty even in those, Comrade Ihwa," said Lee Keumsun who added, tossing a somewhat ragged military hat to Ihwa, "Here, put this on, too." Lee Keumsun smiled as she pulled the visor of another hat down over her forehead. She was unusually friendly today which gave Ihwa a strange feeling. But she was glad to see the other's smiling face for a change, so she attempted a joke uncharacteristically,

"If you come upon a general's insignia, be sure to pick it

up for me. I want to wear it on my hat."

Lee Keumsun hurried out of the room. Now the building was almost deserted except for Ihwa and the young soldier in her care. Only a squeaky noise as if somebody were pulling at some heavy object came from one end of the long corridor. Ihwa went back to the room where the young soldier lay unconscious. She did not know what she should do with him but she knew that she could not just leave him there and go away.

When Ihwa came up to the open doorway with its flimsy wooden sliding door, she saw in the darkness of the room that the body of the wounded boy was being lifted by someone. As she looked closer, she discerned two men who were putting the body down on a stretcher. Then, they bolted out of the room with the loaded stretcher right in front of Ihwa's eyes. There was no time for Ihwa to identify the carriers, but one of them looked like Kim Myongshik. He was wearing on army uniform and hat so that it was all the more difficult for Ihwa to know who he was but she was almost sure that it was Kim Myongshik. Taking a roll of bandage which she had washed and dried during the day out of the teacher's desk, Ihwa hurried after her group.

The night air was cool on Ihwa's skin. During the intervals while the train stopped at different points in the deep valley between the mountains, one could hear the chirping of crickets coming from under the seats of the train.

The medical room was the car right behind the engine. This had originally been the restaurant car but now its windows were hung with black drapes so that lights could be kept on throughout the night for emergency patients. Yet the actual situation was that a few doctors sat around doing nothing because they now lacked the essential medicines to apply to serious wounds.

Only the orderlies were moving back and forth between this temporary clinic and the cars at the back, sometimes fetching things such as water kettles but other times carrying out dead bodies to be regularly disposed of in a pile at some convenient point.

Even in the pitch-black darkness of night, the planes came with horrible roars. The flare bombs were dropped and then an illumination which was bright blue and theatrically clear embraced mountains and plains for a stretch of time.

Sitting in one corner of the temporary clinic, Ihwa was rolling up a ball of bandage thinking how even such commonplace things as bandage were getting scarce. The medical staff that were occupying this train compartment were as taciturn as back in the old military clinic in Seoul. They did not even talk about such obvious topics as shortages of medicine. This meant that about two dozen people engaged in mutually-related works were riding the train thrown together in the same compartment without knowing anything about one another's thoughts.

Every time the door of the compartment opened, Ihwa looked up with the expectation that maybe it would be Lee Keumsun walking in this time. Ihwa kept wondering where her sole female colleague was. She tried to think that maybe it was because Lee Keumsun was now wearing army uniform (just as Ihwa was) that she had not been able to recognize her among the people who moved in and out of the travelling clinic. When Lee Keumsun did not appear before her eyes by near daybreak, however, Ihwa suspected that maybe the former was riding with some other group among the passengers. She now remembered that the train had started after a considerable delay and that even at the end of this prolonged lingering of the train at the starting point, she had not seen any sign of Lee Keumsun. Could it be that she did not get aboard this train in the first place last night, Ihwa asked herself.

The last conjecture Ihwa made was too startling to contemplate, but if it were the right guess, it was a thing to be welcomed, not a thing to moan about. All Ihwa needed to do was pray that she made her escape successfully.

A little before sunset, the group started preparing for another march toward a local elementary school, dividing the luggage and so on. Suddenly Master-Sergeant Koh came up to Ihwa and asked,

"Do you know where your female colleague is now?"

Ihwa shook her head saying,

"No, I don't."

"She has been executed," said Koh in a high-pitched voice so that everyone looked in their direction. "She tried to escape. There's no doubt that she was an enemy spy," added the man staring at Ihwa with hate. The thick rust-colored lips of the middle-aged man gave Ihwa a nauseating sense of uncleanliness.

"Look at that," said the master sergeant again pointing at something outside the train window.

What Ihwa saw there was a blood-stained leather belt. It was the same leather belt which Lee Keumsun had punctured with the operation scissors before tying it around her waist.

"I've brought it here as a warning to you comrades," the master-sergeant hollered in an even more shrill voice, casting a searching look around the compartment.

In silence, Ihwa picked up the luggage allocated to her and got off the train. Into the bottom of her heart, a streak of iced water flowed. She detested and abhorred Koh. Maybe she hated him more for having brought the blood-stained belt to the train to show the group than for his execution of the deserter. That night, the civilian medical staff were separated from the wounded soldiers in their care. They were moved to another train along with part of the medical personnel of the communist army. From this time on, their northbound travelling became markedly faster than before.

"There are many things we have to do in Pyong-yang. We must get there as quickly as possible," said a communist medical officer.

What this man meant perhaps was that doctors who have

lost the means for treating patients cannot do much good even if they should decide to stay with their wounded. Rather than this, they would do better if transferred to places where they could be useful.

Those who were not fully trained to serve the medical cause, moreover, stood a good chance of being channelled to non-medical branches of public work similar to what the members of the Woman's League had been doing.

But Ihwa had no wish to become a communist. Now that there were no urgent patients stretching their hands out to her for help and not even recycled bandages to roll up, Ihwa suddenly felt a sense of emptiness gnawing into her heart. The only thing she could think of doing under the circumstances was to try to escape the way Lee Keumsun had done.

Even if she should go back to Seoul, however, Ji-un would not come back for her. She felt nearly sure of that. And her family—.How many of them would be there alive she could not guess — would have no power to mitigate her sorrow and make her happy again. It was a thing of utter impossibility.

Even so, she would go back. The more she thought about this, the more it seemed to be the only feasible thing to do under the circumstances. Even if she herself could not be happy, she would be able to bring a little solace to her family.

Now that she thought back on it all, she could not help the thought that she had been a fool in the first place. Yes, she definitely had been a fool. Still, it could not be denied that she had been able to forget her own pain to a considerable extent by devoting herself to helping those who had been cruelly wounded. She had no regrets, therefore.

It was easy enough to make a decision—a pretty vague one at that—to escape, but it was a different matter to determine the method by which to carry out the plan. The train, in the meantime, kept on running steadily northward.

Now and then, however, this train, too, stopped at different points, spending quite a time at each of these junctures. Whenever these stops occurred, Master Sergeant Koh increased his vigilance over the medical staff, glaring this way and that to make sure that nobody was making a false move. Ihwa came to the conclusion that except when working with his operation instruments, this man was absolutely no different from any other communist officer. The train moved again after heavy noises of iron chains clanging came from the direction of the engine. Every car of the train was filled with soldiers who were carrying deadly weapons. While the group was with the wounded soldiers, being whole in the body alone seemed to be a powerful strength. In fact, one was so strong that he or she could afford to help others. But now, now they were all prisoners, Ihwa and her working colleagues. They were completely powerless and unfree. The infringement on freedom they were suffering from now was different from the kind of restriction they had to accept in order to perform their work as medical staff more efficiently. The lack of freedom Ihwa and other members of the medical staff were experiencing now was of a more spiritual and existential nature. And for this reason it was more intolerable. She had to get out of this terrible bondage.

With an extra-careful eye, Ihwa examined all the members of the medical staff. They were all impassive and sullen on the surface. Yet Ihwa hoped to see some evidence of their inner vulnerability in their rare unguarded moments. If only she could get assistance from someone in the group, then perhaps she might successfully escape. . . . But, of course, this, too, was an unreliable wishful thought.

A few medical students were having an interesting conversation with some soldiers. Mostly, they were talking about the student life at the University of Moscow. Ihwa decided that these student colleagues of hers would not prove any use for her purpose although judging from Lee Keumsun, one could never tell what really was in a person's innermost mind. The elderly Prof. Choi had sad-looking eyes. Yet they were more resigned than sympathetic. Asking him to take any drastic action for her seemed impracticable in any case. The rest of the staff had an uncertain attitude. Also, they acted as if they were being overtaken by panic from time to time. Having ascertained that none of the fellow travellers staring at him, someone among them turned toward the window, his face nearly touching the window pane. In fear and despair, he started figuring out how far and how fast he was being carried away from his home.

Her colleagues looked either too cowardly or too cautious. If Ihwa told them what was on her mind, they might faint from sheer consternation.

Ihwa could understand why they were like this. Life was a precious thing and to be a little too discreet in order to protect this precious thing was nothing to be wondered at.

As a last resort, Ihwa sought out Kim Myongshik with her eyes and examined him. Sitting a few seats away from Ihwa, he was deep in sleep with his hat covering his entire face and his legs propped up on a bundle of luggage. Ihwa decided that it would take some time to complete her examination of this man as a prospective assistant in her escape.

Just as she was about to turn away with a low sigh, however, Kim Myongshik woke up and, lifting his hat from his face, looked at Ihwa. When their eyes met, Kim Myongshik smiled and then he dropped his hat back on his face. From every sign, this man looked as if he had not a worry in the world. He seemed as relaxed as an ordinary traveller enjoying his ride.

Giving up hope of finding help among her colleagues, therefore, Ihwa closed her eyes in order to get some sleep herself.

(A chance for escape might come up even tomorrow. . . .) thought Ihwa deciding that it would be best for her to put in some sleep now.

Still, her eyes went back to the window to watch the black fields, the glistening river, and the shadows of distant mountains rushing backwards.

Suddenly, a crashing noise as if the train were bumping into some heavy object came from the forward part of the train.

At nearly the same time, all the cars of the train came to a stop after a violent shake-up. None of the passengers seemed to know what had taken place. Yet it was not wise to show too much concern or curiosity about the event because it was not the rule around there. Nobody manifested either interest or worry directly there.

Gradually, however, everybody came to know of the cause of the abrupt halt. The locomotive had gone off the track. There were no casualties. But the passengers had to be held up for at least several hours.

When, finally, the train was pulled back into motion, it was almost daybreak and a misty lightness began to descend. The train was about to go through a station. In passing, Ihwa glimpsed a signboard that said : Chol-won.

Ah, so that's where we are, thought Ihwa looking out of the window at the surrounding mountains. Once, a long time ago, she had come to this place in order to get on a train bound for the Diamond Mountains. It was an event that took place before the division of the country. Ihwa remembered that the terrain was rocky and wild from this point on.

The train was still running in the morning. It seemed that whoever was directing this move decided that there could no more lingering even it meant a pretty high probability of the train being bombed.

Ihwa was restless. Yet, there seemed to be nothing she could do under the circumstances. She merely repeated inwardly : I don't want to go, I don't want to go. Half resigned and sullen, she went up to Master Sergeant Koh and asked his permission to wash her face. A small compartment at the end of the train which might have served as a observation-car was now being used as a combination water closet, repair shop and medicine room with at least some supply of basic first-aid materials such as absorbent cotton or tincture of iodine. It was here that one could get water for drinking and minimal washing. Ihwa started for this compartment, walking through the narrow aisles of several passenger cars.

Reaching her destination, Ihwa ran into Kim Myongshik administering some tablets to a high-ranking officer in front of the screen that partitioned the compartment into two sections. Ihwa got an aluminium-cupful of water and taking it to the window washed herself by spilling a little water out of the cup onto her palm with which she wetted her face. The distant roofs of the town which they had just left behind loomed up dimly in the light-blue morning mist.

As soon as the officer left, Kim Myongshik came up to Ihwa and took a seat beside her making a thumping noise as he satdown.

"Nice view, isn't it?" he said reclining against the back of the seat with both palms cradling his head from underneath.

In order not to show her irritation at his total lack of sensitivity toward her inner conflict, Ihwa clenched her teeth.

But suddenly, Kim Myongshik whispered after throwing a quick glance over the screen at the other side of the compartment,

"What if one took action now."

Ihwa's heart sank with a thump. Coming to her senses at once, however, she nodded to Kim Myongshik in assent.

"All right, then. Come here after the train starts moving next time we stop at a station. But you must not leave your seat before the train takes off, Okay?" said Kim Myongshik and then went out of the compartment without waiting for Ihwa's answer.

Ihwa lingered, taking air from the open window and calming herself. When she returned to the car where her colleagues were, she did not find Kim Myongshik there. Maybe he is chatting with someone in another car, thought Ihwa.

During the next stop at a station, the rice-balls were distributed. There was also the routine of loading a new supply of coal which detained the train for a while longer.

Master Sergeant Koh got off the train and walked back and forth along the platform. A strange quietness enveloped the entire scene. Even the sight of the men who were feverishly carrying some loads near the locomotive and various noises that occurred because of this frenzied activity seemed like something happening at a far distance, something in a picture. Maybe I am too tense to be sensible, thought Ihwa. Somehow, she was losing touch with reality. Four airplanes were flying high in the sky making four shining white dots against the backdrop of greyish blue.

With a sudden sense of despair, Ihwa felt an insane urge to jump off the train and run, run, run. . . . Yet, she remembered Kim Myongshik's advice and put a harsh restraint on her impulse.

Kim Myongshik was back in his seat eating his lump of rice.

When the train started again, Ihwa went to the end car carrying water jugs and empty cups which she picked up from the floor. Usually, these things were left lying anywhere until the next meal but collecting them now and taking them to the end car where they belonged was nothing to draw special attention. Master-Sergeant Koh himself seemed to find it quite in order.

A short while later, Kim Myongshik followed Ihwa into the end car. He was not carrying anything but had his hands stuck gingerly in his trouser waist. His shoulders were up. Maybe he is cold, thought Ihwa vaguely looking at his unsmiling face.

As soon as he entered the room, Kim Myongshik went to the screen and cocking his head looked over it into the other side of the compartment. Then he walked back from the screen and took down a brown leather briefcase from the shelf underneath the ceiling.

The train began to slow down. It ran more and more slowly and then a darkness swallowed everything. They were in a tunnel.

"OK, now!" ordered Kim Myongshik shortly, pushing the door at the rear of the compartment open.

They jumped in silence. Ihwa fell on her hands against the rail, her legs jerked backwards. The rails were vibrating fiercely.

"Are you hurt?" asked Kim Myongshik's voice in the darkness.

"No, I don't think so," Ihwa answered but without conviction. Pulling herself up she took a couple of steps. It did not feel as if she were injured in any place. Some distance from them was the white entrance of the tunnel opening its mouth wide and the inside of the tunnel was filled with strong vibrations made by the train. The coal smoke choked their throats.

Kim Myongshik took Ihwa by one arm and together they began to walk toward the white entrance of the tunnel.

Before they made a bolt into the light of the sun, Kim Myongshik looked back. The train had just finished pulling out of the tunnel and another white hole remained where it had disappeared.

"This way! Let's take that road!" said Kim Myongshik picking his way between the rice fields ahead of Ihwa who hastened after him.

Even after they stepped onto the road, the two of them walked for some more time without a word. When a thicket came into sight by the road, however, they decided to take a rest.

"There's blood on your chin. It's a nasty scratch," said Kim Myongshik looking Ihwa in the face for the first time since they had jumped.

Ihwa brought her finger to her chin to feel the injury.

"Wait, wait! I don't think your hand is clean enough. It will cause trouble if germs spread in there. You know that we are surrounded by cadavers," said Kim Myongshik.

Ihwa examined her hands, turning up the palms. Both her hands were blood-stained from scratches and covered with dirt.

Looking this way and that, Kim Myongshik found a spring with clear water.

"Bring your chin over here," he said spreading a handkerchief which he took out of one pocket. From inside the handkerchief came a piece of gauze folded and apparently dipped in chloroform judging from the yellow stain and strong smell.

As if he were in the treatment room, Kim Myongshik cleaned Ihwa's chin. "That hurts! But what made you think of bringing such things. . . ."

"Well, I knew you'd run into this kind of a mishap."

The sun was high up in the midday sky. There was a roar of planes.

"There they go again. We must go too. But we must not pick up too much speed at first because we will have to walk a long long way. All right? And, if we get caught and interrogated on the way. . . ."

Without finishing the sentence, he turned one of his gaitered legs sideways and took off his black shoe. It was a strange-looking pointed shoe. Ihwa watched with apprehensive eyes. From inside the shoe, Kim Myongshik took out two sheets of paper which had been folded over many times.

"We must tell them that we are going to Seoul to convey this to headquarters. Put this away carefully in your upper pocket."

Taking the paper from Kim Myongshik, Ihwa asked in a puzzled voice,

"But where is this headquarters?"

"Let's just say it's in the Attached Hospital of the National University. I have a feeling they have some such set-up there related to medical affairs."

Ihwa burst out laughing. She opened the folded paper and took a look. The writing she found on it was a mixture of abstruse sentences interlaced with strange symbols at the end of which there were impressions of several different seals of unidentifiable character. The contents of the two sheets seemed similar.

"What on earth does this mean?"

"I don't know myself," said Kim Myongshik with a smile.

"Although I must confess that it was no other person than myself that wrote them." Then as an afterthought, he added,

"I had a model. In any case, there's nothing wrong in our

not knowing what this signifies because I can bet that there are few people who would understand it. I am confident that any inspector who takes a look at this thing would think that this must be a document of the utmost gravity and let us pass."

"What an utterly incredible. . . ." Ihwa muttered in shocked admiration.

"We need not even know on whose orders we are taking this to Seoul. And you, Ihwa, you 'd better leave most of the answers to me. You can tell them that you were ordered to accompany me just in case anything should happen to me but actually don't know anything about this matter. And that's fact, too, isn't it?"

"If they ask me where I started from?"

"Tell them you belonged to an itinerant medical team and that you were given the order at a temporary place of lodging of which you do not know the name. This way, you can be truthful at least in parts which is a help when you're pulling this kind of a stunt," said Kim Myongshik in a jovial joking tone pushing one of the folded sheets of paper back into his shoe.

They resumed walking along the road.

"What time is it by your watch?" asked Kim Myongshik.

"Five minutes to ten."

"It's only nine o'clock by my watch. I set this on the day I entered the clinic and I have never since checked whether it keeps the right time."

"It's the same with mine."

Since low-flying planes began to appear, they had to go into the woods and proceed on their southbound peregrination by picking their way between the trees. This slowed them down considerably.

The rice fields were heavy with crops, however, and there were occasional piles of harvested rice plants. Yet no one could be seen working in the fields. Maybe these people, too, became active only after sunset like owls

Grasshoppers flew out of the rice fields, sometimes flitting across in front of Ihwa's eyes. For the insects, this was probably just another fertile year.

When a fairly large station building came into sight at a distance, Kim Myongshik said, with worry on his face for the first time,

"What if they received a wireless message about us. . . ."

Kim Myongshik's voice, too, sounded worried. Slowing down his walking pace, he looked around to see if there was some way of passing by without going near the station. The railway and the road were lying a little higher than the rest of the terrain.

If they were to avoid the road, they had only to cross the field which meant making a detour. The field, however, was in full view ofthe railway station and on the mountain slope at the end,of the field were signs of the site having been an encampment not long ago. It was quite possible that there still was a cannon or two and a few soldiers hiding nearby. The only other alternative was crossing the river for which there had to be a boat.

(Make the long detour around the upper reaches of the river?) If they did this, however, they would not be able to supply a convincing explanation if they should get caught.

"Shall we try the direct way?" said Kim Myongshik without turning his eyes. He appeared to be asking himself rather than consulting Ihwa.

"I have a pass in addition to that paper I showed you. I don't know how valid it will prove to be. But I am going to put it to some use if I can. As for you, Ihwa, just remember to say you don't know anything, that you were ordered to accompany me."

It looked as if Kim Myongshik had made up his mind to take the direct route.

"I will do that," said Ihwa.

Together they walked down the white road toward the station. The town was spread out on the other side of the station, half of it shaded by the mountain.

A few armed soldiers standing in front of the station came

clearly into sight. Ihwa felt her heart beat uncontrollably.

Suddenly, several bombers appeared at the southern edge of the sky. Ihwa and Kim Myongshik jumped down the embankment and fell on their faces.

The dull sinister roaring of the bombers approached, gnawing into one's very inside, and then, bombs began to fall looking like strings of black beads.

The noise of the airplanes passed above the two young people's heads. Next moment, there was deafening explosion followed by many others in succession.

Ihwa raised her head and looked around. The railway station was burning, enveloped smoke and flames.

Kim Myongshik grabbed Ihwa's one hand, and together they began to run.

The first great obstacle the two young runaways met was thus removed thanks to the confusion created by the smoke and flames of exploding bombs. Even after Ihwa and Kim Myongshik had put quite a distance between them and the railway station, they could see that black smoke was still rising up into the sky.

They walked on all day long. The civilians in the houses they sought on the way to ask for some water or food gave them what they wanted but seemed to wish them gone as quickly as possible.

Everybody else was fleeing northward, why then are these two travelling toward the south? They seemed to be wondering. Yet, nobody asked them in so many words.

In a way, it was fortunate that their benefactors were so tight-mouthed. That way, they stood less chance of detection. And besides, Kim Myongshik played the part of a communist officer quite well. Whenever they left a village behind, Ihwa burst out laughing and said with a mixture of admiration and shock,

"How could you lie like that, Myongshik!"

Kim Myongshik would then smile good naturedly without saying anything.

"How did you know I had the intention of escaping?" asked Ihwa.

"I knew all right," said Kim Myongshik and then added, "It's very easy to guess that kind of a thing with you. Once somebody looks at your face, he is sure to know what's on your mind. I was actually afraid for you on that accout."

"And I'd thought that I was covering it up quite successfully," said Ihwa with a somewhat puzzled face.

They ran into more and more stragglers as they went on. They were powerless common soldiers, however, and therefore Ihwa and Kim Myongshik had little cause to fear them. And they, on their part, did not seem to find the two young south-bound travellers particularly suspicious.

As a rule, these stragglers who were dragging their feet and had restless uneasy faces asked with surprise in their tone,

"What's the matter? Why are you coming back?"

Then Kim Myongshik replied in an exceedingly dignified voice,

"I am carrying a message from higher quarters. But you had better hurry on, comrades."

The stragglers left them after turning sorrow-filled eyes on the two people.

It gave Ihwa and Myongshik delight to tell these stragglers that other soldiers had just passed by so that if they hurried they could catch up with them. Hearing this, the stragglers' eyes shone and their faces became revitalized. From this one could tell that what oppressed these soldiers more than the fatigue and fear was the thought that they had fallen out of their group with nobody to depend on.

"Do you think I might meet up with my unit if I followed you, comrades?"

This was what one master-sergeant Ihwa and Kim Myongshik met on the way had asked.

When crossing a wind-swept rocky field, Ihwa felt desolation take possession of her soul. Why do people have to either chase, or be chased by, other people in bloodshed? Ihwa asked herself. The faces of her family came to her mind's eye in these moments.

Ihwa feared that her house in Seoul had been destroyed by a bomb. If, as Ihwa hoped, her family were still alive despite this likely disaster, they would be sure to be worrying themselves sick for her.

Her father who had thought that the communists were friends of people like himself and because of this ridiculous misconception suffered painfully....and her mother... her mother who was like a little girl and was utterly incompetent....Tonggeun who had disappeared like the wind and poor Tong-hun whom they had locked up in a pit ....And then her sister Ogyop who bore all the burden on her frail back....

Everything was so sad and absurd. Drawing her family's pictures in her mind gave Ihwa such sorrow that she began to pant.

And where is he? How is Ji-un getting along these days?

Since she did not wish to have any more pain and restless sorrow, Ihwa decided hurriedly that Ji-un was dead and finished.

Around sunset, Ihwa and Kim Myongshik ran into a communist officer in the middle of a road. Although he did not look tired out, his face was pale. He asked the two in a sharp tone where they were headed for.

"For Seoul. With secret documents," said Kim Myongshik briefly but fixing his eyes fast on those of the officer.

Unlike most of the stragglers, this officer had weapons on him. Both Ihwa and Kim Myongshik could see his pistol reflecting the blood-colored sunset in its leather holster at his waist.

"Hm..." grunted the communist officer twisting his lips as if in a jeer.

He will ask to see our I. D. cards, glare at our temples, and then, his hand will go to the pistol at his side and....Ihwa anticipated these steps with grim determination.

Many times during their journey here, they had hidden

behind a copse or some such thing when they saw anything suspicious ahead of them. Ihwa was sorry that they had not done the same thing this time when they first spotted this man in the distance.

"Hm, you say secret documents?"

Just as Ihwa had thought, the officer glared at Kim Myongshik and then gave another glare at Ihwa after muttering these words with apparent displeasure.

Thoroughly resigned, Ihwa stood waiting with an impassive face.

Then, suddenly, Kim Myongshik began to talk in his loud jovial voice,

"So how are things in Seoul? Do you think we can get there without too much difficulty? The thing is we are in a terrible hurry, you see."

The communist officer merely peeled his lips slightly outward without making any verbal reply. For some reason, with his strange facial expression, this man began to look like a drunkard.

"If you hurry up a little, you will be able to fall in with a couple of corporals and some privates. I met them over there around that bend. Do hurry up and travel with them," said Kim Myongshik again as if unaware of any danger threatening him and Ihwa.

"Hm...," grunted the man again, and this time it sounded more like a response to what Kim Myongshik said.

Then the officer stepped down into a gravelly field off the road and began to walk toward a far field where tall reeds were tossing their heads in the evening sun.

"No, not that way. You must take this road. You must walk straight from here," shouted Kim Myongshik.

The communist officer did not turn back. He walked straight toward the reeds.

"Excuse me, what time is it now?" shouted Kim Myongshik again.

"Five o'clock," shouted back the communist officer and

continued to walk on the gravel.

Kim Myongshik made a sign with his eye to Ihwa. They made utmost haste to flee from that place. Although they did not run for fear of arousing suspicion, they walked so fast that they nearly choked from lack of breath.

When they turned round after some distance, the communist officer who had reached the field of reeds was on the point of falling down on the ground on his side.

"What's the matter with him? Did he shoot himself" said Kim Myongshik.

Ihwa nodded her head meaning to say that was her guess, too. And then she said audibly,

"I think he knew we were lying. Don't you think so?"

"I don't know . . . . One thing I know is he's this way in the head," said Kim Myongshik making a circle with his finger above his head meaning that the man must be crazy. Then as if remembering, he looked at his watch and set the hands.

"My watch was wrong, after all," he mumbled.

"What made you ask him about the time? I mean how could you have the nerve to . . . ." said Ihwa.

"Well, let's just say I tried a psychoanalytical gimmick. I took a course in psychoanalysis, you know. Except that I dropped out in the middle. The course was given by Prof. Choi, you know that grandpa who went with the train."

Night was getting dark. The two began to look around for a house to lodge in the village where they had just arrived.

"There's a lighted house over there. Looks warm inside, doesn't it?" said Ihwa pointing in that direction. Not that she really thought that a lamp light was a guarantee of warmth inside the house.

"Shall we walk over and ask them to put us up?"said Kim Myongshik and together they walked up to what turned out to be a moderate-size country house and asked to see the master.

"Do excuse us. We will turn off the light right away. Right away. We were just looking for something. Do excuse us," said the owner of the house hurriedly lowering the wick of the lamp, apparently thinking that the two uniformed people had come to his door to reprimand him for having the light on after the "lights-out." It was a deep voice laden with languor and hate.

"Ah, yes, please hurry and screen off the light. And fix us some supper. We are headed for Seoul on an important mission," said Kim Myongshik.

The old master of the house stared at Kim Myongshik and Ihwa in bewilderment. He looked as if he wanted to say something. But he did not and ended up by stepping down to the kitchen to tell his wife who had been standing there like a log to fix up something for the nocturnal visitors.

The house did not look as if just the old couple were inhabiting it. But there was no sign of younger residents anywhere.

Ihwa felt uncomfortable about intruding on the old couple in that way, so she whispered to Kim Myongshik,

"Shouldn't we offer something in payment?"

Kim Myongshik shook his head decisively, however.

Both Kim Myongshik and Ihwa gulped down the cold rice cooked with various coarse grains as if it were the most delicious thing they had ever tasted. The old wife pushed the water bowls to them with a worried face.

The floor which was covered with a reed mat was warm to the touch. Feeling a great fatigue that seemed to be dissolving her, Ihwa leaned back against the wall. Her eyelids came down of their own accord. Outside it was getting chillier and Ihwa could not think of walking any more tonight.

With the intention of asking the old wife to let Ihwa sleep by her side for the night, Kim Myongshik stepped out of the room and started looking around for the mistress of the house Then, suddenly, he turned back and hurried into the house.

"Let's get out of here quick. Hurry. The house next door is full of real communist soldiers."whispered Kim Myongshik to Ihwa.

Out on the road, they ran for about an hour without another thought in their head. They never dreamed of sleeping in a warm room after this incident.

When they arrived at another village, Kim Myongshik surreptitiously inspected the houses in which people were asleep and then chose a decrepit storage house at end of the small village as their temporary lodging. There was a thick pile of hay that gave off a clean fragrant smell and the planks of its walls kept the chilly air off.

With some decent space between them, Ihwa and Kim Myongshik buried themselves in the pile of hay.

"Where is your home, Ihwa?" asked Kim Myonghik.

"It's in Pildong. My house is the closest to the foot of Namsan. And where's your house, Myongshik?"

"It's near Seoul Railway Station. There's only my mother living there," said Kim Myongshik. And then as if to himself, he muttered, "I wonder if she's safe. . . ."

Ihwa remembered that she had not had a chance to thank him up to this moment.

"It would have been so much easier if you had left by yourself. What made you take me along?" she said.

"Well. . . . You saw yourself how the stragglers, too, travelled in twos and threes rather than by himself. It's safer that way,"said Kim Myongshik. But Ihwa knew that it was because he had a warm heart that he had let her tag along.

"I would like to thank you. Alone, I didn't know what to do. Truly I thank you."

"Don't mention it at all. Besides, we don't know yet if we will succeed in this thing."

"The rest is merely luck."

"I hope heaven will help us for a bit longer anyway. . . ." said Kim Myongshik.

It seemed that Ihwa had fallen asleep with her back buried in the hay and her knees cradled in her arms. Then she woke up.

Chill had filled the room. And also the presence of Kim

Myongshik, who was lying so close by, kept her from getting into a deeper sleep despite the great fatigue she felt.

Without making any move, Ihwa examined him with her eyes. He was lying sideways in his place in the hay propping his head on one arm. It seemed that he, too, was awake. Ihwa could see that his arms and head were moving, if only slightly.

All of a sudden, Ihwa thought : if this had been Ji-un lying there! Her pulse became rapid and a flush covered her face.

Once more, sorrow and bitterness overwhelmed her. But at the same time she felt a strangely sweet feeling spreading through all parts of her body.

(Ah, Ji-un,) she called inwardly, biting the back of her hand.

By now, Ihwa felt a strong aversion even to recollecting what had taken place that afternoon a lifetime ago.

If only Ji-un were here, if only. . . . Ihwa trembled, overcome by an uncontrollable desire.

Kim Myongshik seemed to sink into a deep sleep near daybreak. Listening to his steady breathing, Ihwa, too, dozed off.

When sunshine filled the countryside, the two young people sprang up out of the hay. Outside, everything was bathed in sunlight, the rice field and the vegetable patches and the children who stood by the road. Ihwa and Kim Myongshik bolted out of the storage house onto the road.

The strafing started when the two travellers had covered only a short distance from the village. It was an unusually violent attack. And it lasted a long time with only short breaks in between. Far and near, bombs kept falling incessantly, also.

The sight of all this shooting and bombing made a truly strange spectacle under the orange-bright sun.

"This is only the beginning of the day and they are already hard at their job.This is going to be a day to remember, I think. . . ." muttered Kim Myongshik.

Just as he had predicted, the air-raid that day was uncommonly severe and Ihwa had to drop down on the rice field time and again. And almost every time, she thought she was going to die. Because of all this shooting and bombing, the distance Ihwa and Kim Myongshik could cover that day was very short.

Tom raised himself up from the telescope. Then without bothering to dust off the dirt from his trouser knees, he walked up toward his colleagues. His chestnut brown beard was so thick that one was likely to mistake it for his hair when glimpsing it quickly from certain angles.

This marine corps where tough, powerful men with a reputation for legendary prowess were gathered abounded with characters who prided themselves on the luxuriant growth of hair on their lower countenance.

One man had a russet beard which looked like the round brush with which Korean housewives scrub their iron pots. Another man grew whiskers which were yellow in color and framed his face from the chin right up to the ears. Another man wore a splendid Kaiser mustache while still another had a stub of a mustache that reminded one of Charlie Chaplin. In all, these men made quite a colorful sight.

Thomas Craighton, who was reputed to be a heavy drinker, was very strong and gentle.

"Why do you look so sad, Lieutenant Yun? Are you too happy to be back in your home town?" hollered Tom as he passed the tent at the entrance of which a few liaison officers were standing.

Tom and Ji-un were quite close but Ji-un did not feel up to answering his last question for some reason. His face which was tanned copper was, just as Thomas Craighton had pointed out, filled with sadness.

Ji-un walked over to the telescope abandoned by Tom and looked through it down the mountain slope.

The Han River which they had crossed in a boat shone silver in the distance. Part of the Yonhi College campus came into view through the telescope lens and the makeshift paper taegeukki (national flag of the Republic of Korea) stuck at the front gates of houses, too, drew his attention.

The pine leaves sparkled under the morning sun. At the far end of the many hills that rose one after another, a dim expanse that was supposed to be Seoul stretched vaguely.

"What do you see, Lieutenant Yun?" asked Tom behind Ji-un's back. He was holding an aluminium cup from which he sipped coffee with apparent relish.

"As soon as this coffee break is over, we will begin another attack. And this time, we must put an end to it, really!"

The sound of cannon fire which had been continuing from the previous night had ceased for a while.

"Aim carefully, I tell you," said Ji-un lifting his eye from the telescope and staring down at the ground at his feet.

"Of course, I will. But weren't you the one who told us the target of our attack? What's wrong?"

It was true that Ji-un had interpreted the report of two college students escaping from Seoul who had said that communist soldiers were concentrated on the slope of Namsan. This seemed quite plausible even from what he could remember of the time when he was leading a fugitive's life in the capital. This, too, he had told Tom and other colleagues of his.

After a preliminary check-up by wireless and the dropping of signal bombs, the attack began.

Through the telescope alone, it was possible to confirm the shapes of anti-aircraft guns, heavy machine guns, and trenches. Now one could also see a greater number of communist soldiers moving about among the pine trees than in the early morning. From the foot of the mountain, smoke rose all day.

"I know what you mean. But I am worried because there are houses and people close by."

"We are aiming precisely. But it seems to me that you are worried because your girl friend or some such person is living close by the mountain, am I right?"

"That's right. My fiancee's house is in that vicinity."

"What? That's a disaster!" said Tom throwing his hands up in the air.

"Her house is a little distance to the left of our target but-. . . ."

"Don't worry, then. Maybe the house will get some sparks but I am sure your sweetheart is long gone from it."

"Well, even so, there are many other houses besides hers-. . . ."

Gulping down the remaining coffee in the aluminium cup, Tom sauntered over to the ridgeline. Finally, shooting started again. And Ji-un could see the back of Tom posted behind the mortar, his blue kerchief flying in the wind.

The privates who had nothing to do walked back and forth with their bayoneted rifles on their shoulders. Only those around Tom were as busy as firewheels. Mostly, these soldiers were in their sweat-drenched T-shirts.

After this heavy bombardment of shells would come the 'ipsong(entering into the castle),'which meant that Ji-un would be able to tread the earth of Seoul again.

Although he tried hard to keep calm, Ji-un could not overcome his agitation. Two other colleagues of his also looked tense and aroused unlike in any other battle they had fought so far. One of these two young men, a literature major at college, was a man of few words. Yet, today, he did not seem to be able to keep his mouth shut.

Ji-un was so restless that he could not stay in one place but kept moving from one place to another.

"What's the matter with you, Lieutenant Yun?"

"Is anything the matter, Lieutenant Yun?"

People asked him, puzzled by his unusual restlessness. Then he merely answered absently, 'I am all right,' or 'nothing's the matter.' But his face became more and more distraught as the hours went by.

Is Ihwa safe? Not dead, hurt, or taken away? Thinking of her in this concrete way drove him nearly insane. Also a dark presentiment that all was not well with her nagged him persistently.

Shame, anger and sorrow. . . .

When he was leaving Seoul, Ji-un was burning like coal with a mixture of these feelings. Maybe it was the intensity of his agony that made death wince from his approach.

He succeeded in breaking through the death line and became a liaison officer. He fought a number of desperate battles before he could come back up to the proximity of Seoul. The experience of survival through the dangers of bombs and bullets had a salutary effect on his mental state.

He would tell Ihwa frankly and sincerely how ashamed he was of what he had done. His mind was made up. But.... would she be there, alive?

(Ihwa, please be there in safety!)

It was about two o'clock in the afternoon when the marine corps arrived in the city. By this time, Namsan was under the commander of the National Army reinforced by the troops that came in from the Wangshibri direction. Church bells were ringing joyously and the citizens were pouring out into the streets singing 'manse's.

The city was immediately full of people walking or running. Some of them, grownups and children who were returning from their places of refuge, looked so worn out that it was a wonder they could still stay on their feet. Survivors of the war were rising out of the smoke and rubble of broken streets.

Obtaining one hour's leave, Ji-un drove the jeep to Pildong.

It was just as he had feared. The entire area had been wiped out. With difficulty, he found the site of Ihwa's house which looked as if it had been burnt down several days ago. The foundation stones were peeping out of the ruins and here and there there were marks of somebody having dug into the earth.

At other house sites, Ji-un saw people bent down looking for something among the ruins. One woman was just squatting on the whitish-grey ash that had been her house.

"Do you know where the family who used to live here have gone?" he asked several people. But each of them merely shook their head without saying anything.

Ji-un drove the jeep to Pak Sanggyu's house. When he

arrived at the clinic, Pak Sanggyu was on the point of leaving the building.

"Oh, is it you, Mr. Ji-un? What a surprise" exclaimed Sanggyu excitedly shaking Ji-un by his arm.

Ji-un, too, told Pak Sanggyu how glad he was to see him again. He also apologized to him for the worry he had given him by not returning to the clinic that time, and explained how he had to go back to his unit right away. Then, he asked Pak Sanggyu if he had any news of Ihwa.

"I, too, am worried for miss Ihwa. I went over there to her house a while back and found out what happened. I couldn't even find any of her family. Although I believe they will come back eventually. . . ."

"But what about Ihwa? Did she not stay with them?" asked Ji-un breathlessly.

As if distressed by Ji-un's questioning, Pak Sanggyu stood biting his lips for a few seconds. Seeing this, Ji-un turned purple in the face. Finally, Pak Sanggyu seemed to make up his mind.

"Not long after you left, Miss Wu joined the medical forces in a clinic for wounded soldiers. I don't know how she came to take this action but my guess is that she was very painfully affected by your disappearance. Maybe the interference of the communist officer lodging in her outer house may have been one reason, too. I heard about this from miss Ogyop. Anyway, she entered the clinic for the wounded and then was not heard of-again, it seemed. So, I went to this clinic where miss Ihwa was supposed to have gone —it was the day when the heavy bombing started—and found out that there had been a mass transfer. I was told that the entire medical team was ordered at gunpoint to get aboard trucks and then the train going north. It seems that brother of Dr. Lee had told his family on his last visit to his house that he would be sent home on the occasion of the communists' pull-out and therefore not to worry. But he never came back, Dr. Lee said."

When he finished, Pak Sanggyu looked down as if he could

not bear to look at Ji -un whose face was becoming increasingly more sinister by the second.

"Dr. Lee's family are still hoping that his brother will somehow escape and come back," said Pak Sanggyu again.

". . . ."

"Anyway, come in for a while, won't you? Just a few minutes?"

But Ji-un held out his hand for a handshake saying,

"Thank you, but I must leave. I think I will go back to Pildong once more and drop by that clinic you mentioned. . . ."

Although he thought that it would be completely useless, Pak Sanggyu gave him directions.

"I may even come again tomorrow. And someday I want to show you my gratitude in a formal manner. But, for now. . . ."

Pak Sanggyu did not wish to aggravate the damage Ji-un must have suffered by detaining him. Therefore, he merely nodded his head without trying to delay Ji-un any more.

Getting into the jeep, Ji-un drove away. Left alone, Pak Sanggyu stood on the spot for some time.

Ji-un could not keep his promise to go back Pak Sanggyu's house. Two days after his visit to Sanggyu's house the marine corps was ordered to march north.

They went through Tongduchon and then Yonchon. Sitting in the back of the army truck, Ji-un looked down at the wide flow of water. It was the Imjin River. Under the autumn sun, the river flowed in platinum gold, slowly and confidently. . . .

There was another person who had sought the burnt-out site of Mr. Wu Taegap's former mansion after Ji-un had been there for the second time. This person was Ogyop.

Her pink blouse was torn and her skirt was smeared with dirt. Her pigtails were fastened with grass blades.

It was in this pitiable state that Ogyop had come back. She returned to her house dragging her feet through the rubble and ashes. The day was beginning to darken and the people who had been rummaging over the site of their one-time house went away one by one. The woman who used to live right nextdoor to Ogyop was on the point of taking out a battered aluminium tub laden with worthless objects with the help of her child, each holding one end of the tub when Ogyop arrived. Seeing the latter, however, the woman looked away hurriedly.

"How are you, ajumoni (common appellative for women usually older than oneself)?" Are your children all safe?" Ogyop accosted her.

The woman who had tried to pass by without greeting Ogyop turned hate-filled eyes on her, saying,

"Can't you see how I am? It's because the sonofabitches left those piles of oil cans in your courtyard that the whole neighborhood burnt down like this!"

The woman scuttled away after looking Ogyop over from head to toe with the utmost disgust.

Ogyop squatted down on the ashes like the woman whom Ji-un had seen in a similer posture earlier.

(Maybe I should have gone straight to Sungogri where Halmom(old woman)'s house is...,) thought Ogyop.

She had, however, not been able to give up the hope that maybe her house was unscathed and one or other of her family would be back in the house. That was why she had come here first. Besides, to Sungogri where the Old Woman's house was, there still remained a distance of a full day's steady walk. Now that she was here, she felt as if she could not bring herself to walk one more step.

The sun was perched above the western mountain peak. She had to leave even if she could cover only a fraction of the distance she had to go.

(But I want to rest five more minutes, five more minutes,) she kept saying to herself without making a move to get up.

Suddenly, there was a sound of footsteps and a crowd app-roaching.

Ogyop turned toward the noise. Half a brick wall was left

standing on the far side of what used to be Yong-a's house and it was in and out of the space inside this half-remaining wall that a group of National Army soldiers were stomping their booted feet. As Ogyop watched, two soldiers who seemed to have just come out of that place were walking in her direction dragging a woman who was about to fall down.

The faces of the soldiers were round-it was not merely the effect of their round helmets-and they looked tall and strong on the whole. They were clad in well-starched green fatigues and shiny new boots. Their ruddy complextion was strange to eyes that were used to the emaciated looks of the soldiers from the north.

The woman kept on tripping not only because of the rubble underneath her feet but also because the hem of her long skirt was caught in the debris ofthe ruins.

The group stopped before they reached Ogyop. Then the soldiers blinded the woman's eyes with a strip of cloth.

The soldiers walked back about ten paces. Then they aimed their rifles at the woman.

Ogyop's face went white on seeing this. Hurriedly she left the place.

The woman she saw with the soldiers was Yong-a's mother.

The woman who cooked for the enemy soldiers, the woman who had lost her husband to enemy guns, was thus executed by the National Army on the very site of her pro-communist activity.

Ogyop who arrived at the Old Woman's house in Sungogri found there Madam Shim who was constantly crying and Tong-hun who was suffering from severe intestinal trouble. Mr. Wu Taegap, however, was not in sight.

"Where's father?"

Upon this question of Ogyop, Madam Shim burst out weeping and beat the floor with her palm.

Tong-hun, who was stretched sideways on the floor throwing out his emaciated pale arms with their blue ridges of veins in every direction, said in a weak panting voice.

"We were caught by the tailor that day before we could walk out of our alley. He was with two men from the Youth League. They were carrying guns. Pointing these guns at whoever passed, these murderers drove all males inside their building. When they saw father, they seemed to lose all control. Their already bloodshot eyes turned bloodier and they captured father along with me, telling mother to go on ahead. A while later, they led away their captives, separating them into two groups, old men with old men and boys with boys. I managed to escape on the way thanks to a bomb that happened to explode just then, but father was. . . ."

Madam Shim raised her weeping voice anew.

Making an almost imperceptible grimace, Tong-hun closed his mouth.

"Have you heard from sister?"

"Not a word. Not a word. And Tonggeun, too. . . . He must have died somewhere. . . ."

"Calm down, mother," consoled Ogyop.

After a brief rest, Ogyop went to the kitchen to talk to the Old Woman.

"My son Unbo was accused of helping the communists. He fled to Chongju or Chungju, I don't know which." said the Old Woman, teary-eyed herself .

"Don't be disheartened. You will see him again if he stays alive."

"I believe so, yes…," mumbled the Old Woman drying her tears with the tip of her koreum (tie on jacket) and stirring the contents of the pot boiling over the fire with a spoon.

"Is this gruel for Tong-hun?" asked Ogyop.

"Yes, he can't swallow anything else."

Ogyop took the spoon from the Old Woman and tasted the gruel sticking to it. Then she said to the Old Woman,

"Take the pot off the fire for a minute. I will finish the cooking."

Going to the well, she washed her hands and feet. Then she changed into fresh clothes and took a short rest. After this, she began to perform her old role of family caretaker.

Going out to the vegetable garden, Ogyop picked fresh vegetables and brought them in. Then she went to the jang-dokkan(a place where each family keeps jars with soy sauce and soybean paste) and checked each jar.

Like in the old days, Ogyop took over the cooking, seasoning each dish carefully so that it would be tasty on the tongue. In a way, the Old Woman who was used to life in Seoul was more ill at ease than Ogyop in this country house even if it was her own. The old woman complained about the lack of cooking materials and seasoning all the time and proved herself good only cooking the rice. But Ogyop was different. In her hands, the commonplace vegetables turned into delicious dishes and the soybean paste which seemed bitter and salty became sweet and tasty.

From the very next day after Ogyop's arrival, Tong-hun began to have more appetite. He ate up the vegetable soup, millet gruel and boiled potatoes Ogyop cooked and served in increasing portions. Madam Shim, too, seemed to recover some of her spirits. With a white kerchief tied around her head, she of ten sat out in the maru(wooden-floored space between rooms).

As soon as the Old Man who had accompanied his son on his exile returned next day, Ogyop went with him to Seoul.

After asking around among people about the places where massacres had taken place, (they were Namsan, Sajik Park, the mountain at the back of Songbukdong, etc.), she searched each of these spots if that she might be able to find her father's corpse in one of them.

Contrary to hearsay, there were not so many bodies on the slope of the Namsan. Because of the heavy mortar fire, this spot had probably not been suitable as a massacre site. Ogyop searched this area carefully, however, and then moved on to Sajik Park.

There were already people gathered there. What awaited Ogyop in this place was the most cruel picture of hell imaginable. There were hundreds of cadavers which had been laid out in rows by someone.

The earth which had been dug out of the pit was wet underneath one's feet and there were many footprints on this pile of wet earth.

People were threading, wide-eyed between the rows, of which there were fairly many. A woman with her child on back was scuttling hastily, nearly bumping into the person ahead of her.

Long heart-rending screams rose here and there where the unhappy family of the dead found the object of their search. Some bodies were being carried out on stretchers already.

Ogyop inspected every row carefully, hoping in her heart that she would not find her father's body in this place either at the end of a thorough search.

No matter how harsh a society North Korea, where her father might have been taken, was nothing could be worse than being found as a dead body in one of these places.

Every time she looked at a corpse, her heart thumped for fear that this one might prove to be that of her father.

Ogyop's feet neared the end of the rows where trees and grass were intact from the ravages of the war. Stench from the cadavers already filled the air and seemed to contaminate even the trees and blades of grass.

One man was leaning vacant-eyed against a tree. Two little children were standing side by side looking in the direction of the rows of bodies. They seemed to be waiting for their mother to finish her inspection of the bodies. A new scream rose somewhere among the rows.

Ogyop's feet paused before one body. The torso of the body which was bent at a right angle was as characterless as any other body in these places and looked just like a lump of odd-shaped wood or metal. As for the clothes, they were so thickly smeared with dirt that it was impossible to identify them at a glance. It could have been because there was much bleeding that so much dirt was stuck onto this body.

The head of this corpse was turned sideways and the face was half hidden by a bit of clothing on the body right next to it. In order for Ogyop to examine this face clearly, the bit of clothing needed to be removed and the head straightened. This was a routine other examiners were performing, too.

But it was unnecessary.

The large amber button on the front of the top piece of clothing with its crust of dried dirt was something Ogyop had seen so many times. Even the pattern of the half translucent grey streaks embedded in the orange-brown stone was very familiar to her eye. It belonged to her father. The body was that of Mr. Wu Taegap.

The wind was rising. The clothing that had covered half the face of this body flapped and in that instant Ogyop saw an array of golden teeth. They were the same golden teeth that used to shine so conspicuously in Mr. Wu Taegap's mouth. Only two in the front had been natural white and all the rest were gold.

Ogyop's lips turned white. She fell into the arms of the Old Man who was standing by her side.

Kim Myongshik and Ihwa were intent on going closer and closer to Seoul. Although the bombing and machine-gun fire bound their feet for a time almost every hour, still, thanks to these attacks they could proceed without fear of running into communist soldiers.

Ihwa and Myongshik were doubly relieved because these frequent attacks not only guaranteed their unhindered progress southward but also attested to the fact that Seoul was now almost taken over by the National Army.

"If we travel on in this way, we may be caught as suspects by the Allied or National Army. Let's make ready to change our appearance," said Kim Myongshik laughing and wiping the sweat from his forehead with a dirty handkerchief.

"That's right. But don't you think it's too early yet? We are still in the vicinity of Yonchon, I think. . . ."

"Maybe you're right. Let's wait a bit and see."

"But how should we change our appearance? I can perhaps take off this hat and this jacket, but. . . ."

"Are you worried about me? Well, it looks like I can't improve my looks all that much. I could take off my gaiters and jacket but what then. . . . It won't make much difference in my case since I will only be a communist without his jacket if one so wishes to see me. But the greater problem is this thing hidden in my shoe," said Kim Myongshik, chuckling.

"We would feel relieved if we threw these papers away right here, but who knows, maybe the communists are concentrated around Euijongbu or thereabouts with the intention of having a last fight with the National Army and in that case we will need these papers. So let's wait for a while longer." he added.

They went round a bend in the mountains and suddenly, they saw a large river flowing unhurriedly but powerfully in full view.

It was good to look at the handsome river after their gruelling march through mountains and rocky fields.

Close to the foot of the mountain on the other side, the river was reflecting the mildly rugged shape of the mountain. On this side of the river, there was a stretch of earth covered with smooth, round pebbles. Reeds were standing in groups at certain intervals on this stretch of land.

"Is Yonchon the name of that river?"

"No, that is the Imjin River," replied Kim Myongshik.

Ihwa felt a sudden urge to dip her hands and feet in the clear water of the river. It was such a beautiful sparkling river!

"Let's walk along that river. It's parallel to this road, any way. Please!" entreated Ihwa.

"It's a tempting thought but. . . ."

Kim Myongshik's tone was hesitant as he answered Ihwa and looked in the direction of the river with discreet eyes.

"The reed fields are sparse which makes it difficult for us to hide in case we need to," said Kim Myongshik again.

"You are right," Ihwa agreed obediently.

Even while she walked along the road, however, Ihwa

glanced at the river every now and then. Seeing this, Kim Myongshik seemed to feel remorse about having been too insensitive to Ihwa's ardent wish.

"Shall we, then, just dip our hands in the water and take a short rest? We could use a wash in any case. . . . " said Kim Myongshik in a softened voice.

Delighted, Ihwa ran at once toward the river.

Ihwa could hear the sound of the river as its current flowed on making big ripples. What she saw and felt there was something which was similar to music, poetry and painting, something which was lovable and superior to mundane things.

From close by, the water looked deeper and darker than from afar. But maybe it was just because the water of this river was so transparently clear!

Walking down to the riverside, Kim Myongshik began to wash his face. But Ihwa kept on standing one spot merely facing the river.

She was overwhelmed by an elevated beauty which was beyond the reach of human affairs.

Was it not to love these profound things and to love each other that human beings were originally created?

The face of Ji-un flitted on the surface of the water.

But just then, from behind the opposite mountain peak, an airplane soared up. The small body of the plane descended perpendicularly after it had flown up high enough to expose the black cross pattern of its belly.

Still standing erect Ihwa looked up at the plane. Her attitude at this moment was like that of a girl who had forgotten how to hide or one who abhors such an action.

A noise of explosion and strafing drowned the sound of the water for a time. And the short-bodied plane flew away.

Kim Myongshik rose from among the reed sand looked for Ihwa. She was lying on her face among the pebbles, one step from another thicket of reeds. She was not moving. Countless bullets had penetrated her back.

(Ah. . . .) Kim Myongshik moaned kneeling beside the body.

There was no need to confirm with his medical knowledge. Ihwa was dead.

Taking Ihwa's hand in his, Kim Myongshik sat there for a long while. Then another explosion was heard from somewhere nearby. Lifting up Ihwa's body, he carried it into the reeds. Laying it down on the ground among the reeds, he cried covering his face with his hands.

Time passed. The last sunshine of the day descended on the Imjin River. The water of the river shone in iridescent, changing patterns. Surrounded by the profound silence of the area, the river was singing its song. The sky turned red and the river, too, changed into its last finery of the day which was a shining orange.

Ihwa's consciousness returned for a brief moment. It was thirty blurred seconds of breathing.

One of her hands was in the shallow water of the river. Tiny ripples were incessantly whispering nearby.

A small yellow flower was shining in the evening sun.

(Ah! The dandelion is in bloom,) Ihwa said in her brief, fading consciousness.

She tried to touch the flower. Then her consciousness was extinguished, this time for good.

There was no reason why the dandelion should have bloomed in the autumn. What she saw was only a gold medal that had once decorated the jacket front of some soldier. Anyway, it was a yellow medal.

Kim Myongshik left the riverside by himself.

[illegible]
that had been overturned, the heads or limbs of the dead passengers were sticking out. Some bodies were lying face down. Apparently those had been shot [illegible]

Even without the bridge, the river [illegible] guarded. Shots were [illegible] down the riverside, from which Ji-un could [illegible] people were trying to swim across. Many who had [illegible] and the river with the [illegible] on hearing those gunshots.

Ji-un looked down at [illegible] white sleeve of the gown [illegible] twinging pain in that arm even when it [illegible] he was faint with hunger.

Even so he wanted to [illegible] to go back to town where [illegible] strutting about. [illegible] of the river, Ji-un moved away [illegible] pace.

At dawn of the [illegible] diers, Mr. Wu Taegap [illegible] communist officers and [illegible] clothes. They [illegible] member of the [illegible] eptitious glances into the house from [illegible] Taegap was doing what he could with his total lack of experience to convince the men that he [illegible] camp but rather to their side, being deprived of property and money. He was no capitalist but was [illegible] But none of this had any effect on the men.

"You'd better save your speech for later," one of them shouted. Instantly Mr. Wu Taegap's face turned [illegible] Clumsily struggling to suppress his anger, he spat [illegible] ground. Just then, Madam Shin broke [illegible]

"What's this, do you want to go and be [illegible] with him?" said one of the gang glaring at her. Madam Shin's [illegible]

[illegible] believe me."

[illegible] was obliged to take off her silk chima and wear [illegible] cotton which Ogyop made the Old Woman [illegible]

[illegible] happening to us? What on earth is happening to [illegible] as she put on the Old Woman's black cotton [illegible]

[illegible] her an answer this time.

[illegible] arm with his right arm, Ji-un walked along [illegible] even tempo unperturbed by the gunshots that [illegible]

[illegible] fired by the anti-aircraft guns were exp[illegible] the entire expanse with sounds and [illegible]. Since one could see not even a shadow [illegible], it was beyond comprehension why the [illegible] so busy. Ji-un walked on glimpsing [illegible] unexploded shell spiralling down onto the [illegible]

[illegible] soldier could be seen in the street. The [illegible] defenceless. The incessant [illegible] shots [illegible], therefore, were utterly [illegible] and then Ji-un ran into dead [illegible] Some of them were soldiers [illegible] civilians. [illegible]

[illegible]